j

THE
TARTAN
SHROUD

Also by Ken Dalton

The Bloody Birthright

The Big Show Stopper

Death is a Cabernet

THE
TARTAN
SHROUD

Ken Dalton

Different
Drummer
Press

For more information concerning *The Tartan Shroud*, email the author at ken@kendalton.com

ISBN 978-0-578-11325-8
1. Humorous—Mystery—Fiction. 2. Pinky—Delmont (Fictional character)—Fiction. 3. Bear—Zabarte (Fictional character)—Fiction. 4. Pitlochry, Scotland—Fiction.. 5. Blair Castle, Scotland—Fiction. I. Title.

ACKNOWLEDGEMENTS

This novel came together with the help and assistance of the following;

From the friendly woman who made us feel like old friends in Edinburgh—to the couple in the tiny town who invited us into their home to show us pictures of their visit with the queen—to the old guy in the pub, the people of Scotland made our visits to their country an absolute joy.

To my artistic son, Hugh, who reads the first draft of the novel and then creates the provocative covers that make each Pinky and Bear Mystery a work of art.

To Wendy Maxham, Mary Hallock, and the mystery member of my editing staff for another exceptional picky, picky job of editing.

To Dr. Ye, and all the staff, nurses and Pharmacists, that dwell in the magical land of room 170, also known as the Kaiser Infusion Center, for giving me my second year of remission.

To the long suffering members of my writer's group:

Editor-in-Chief Mary Madsen Hallock
Jon Gunner Howe
Norm Benson
Thea Howe
And the divine Sarah Andrews

Finally, to my wife Arlene, for remaining my lover and best friend as we work through the second year of my remission.

This book is dedicated to Willie MacFarland who took my letter requesting assistance and created a life long friendship. I also dedicate this book to my friend, editor, and fellow writer, Mary Hallock who is moving to Washington. Mary has the uncanny ability to tell me my latest chapter needs a rewrite and not make me upset. Mary, you are the driving force behind my writer's group. Pinky, Bear, and Flo will miss your wise counsel!

ONE

Pinky Delmont-Genoa, Nevada

My favorite ex-wife, Willow Stone turned her head on the pillow and whispered in my ear, "Pinky, do you recall when you fed me that line, 'The cost of true love knows no bounds?'"

My mind, a touch clouded from Willow's lingering perfume, did not sound the usual alarm—to warn me that I was treading on dangerous ground. Willow and I had spent two glorious years in wedded bliss, and as a result, we knew how to make each other supremely happy, or, on the other side of the coin, how to inflict near-mortal wounds. After a pause, to indicate to her that I was searching my memory, I responded, "No my love, I do not remember. And what do you mean I fed you a line? I am not in the habit of feeding lines to—"

"I'll refresh your memory. You conned me into bringing you two bottles of an extremely expensive wine while you already owned many cases of the identical label. A cabernet, I might add, that languishes, unopened, in your wine cellar. That, my ex-husband, would be accepted in any court of law, as feeding your ex-wife a line."

"My dear, try as I might, I do not recollect that exact occurrence, but for the moment, I will accept the possibility, even though it could be minuscule,

1

that you could be correct. But what is your point?"

"My point is that the cost of true love has no bounds and after our little romp last night it is time for you to reciprocate."

Damn, what scheme was this woman working on? "My dear, assuming I have the need to reciprocate, what do you have in mind? A weekend at my lakeside condo? A gold bauble? A rare jewel? A dinner at—"

"None of the above."

Willow tossed the sheet back, slipped her exemplary legs over the edge of the bed, and stretched in the morning sun. Brilliant rays of light shown upon her red hair, alabaster skin, and perfect curves. As my eyes feasted on the most beautiful woman I had ever known, I considered her other attributes—a genius intelligence matched by a driving ambition to be the best District Attorney in Nevada, if not the ten western states. Willow was not a female to be trifled with. So whenever she directly challenged me, I was cautious. "My dear, I must admit you have me at a disadvantage. If not one of my generous suggestions then—"

"A month of your time."

"Have you lost your mind?"

"No. I'm just calling in all my chips."

She turned, faced me, and the sight of her nakedness caused my heart to flutter. "Pinky, I desperately need your help and I would be lying if I told you you'd be back in your office in a couple of weeks."

Willow sat down and wrapped her arms around me. The touch of her warm, soft skin against mine took my mind off the law, my practice, my bank account. "A month you say?"

She kissed me. But it was not just a kiss. When her lips brushed mine, waves of pure passion flowed through my body.

I said, "Would we be together for the whole month?"

She moved even closer and said, "Yes. Together. A month for sure. Perhaps as long as five weeks."

"Where," I murmured, "are we going to spend our month to five weeks of bliss?"

"Scotland."

My mind shot across a map of the United States, and the stormy North Atlantic, to the land of kilts and whiskey. The notion jolted me out of my reverie. "Scotland? A month to five weeks in Scotland? My dear, if you had said Lake Tahoe, or Carmel, I would have considered your request. I can not travel to Scotland, away from my practice for that length of time—a few days, perhaps a week, but nowhere near a month."

Willow leaned into me and pressed me back into the pillow. "Pinky, I thought we both agreed that the cost of true love knows no bounds."

"But I can not—"

"No buts. The two of us are going to Scotland."

I attempted to edged away from her overpowering presence. "My dear, over the years we have developed a unique relationship. However—"

"I understand our relationship better than you do. Six months ago your secretary caught me off-guard when she asked me if I had ever truly loved you."

"And your answer?"

"I told her that ours was a complex relationship

3

that proved smart women can do dumb things. I guess, in a way, I've always loved the Pinky Delmont I know is hidden under that cynical, money grubbing persona you display to the rest of the world."

"So much in love that we became husband and wife."

Willow blinked. "That is true."

"And then you summarily divorced me."

"You know the reason for the divorce was much more than a lost love."

I snapped, "Enough about my inadequacies."

"Don't get testy with me."

"Sorry. Give me one good reason why I should go to Scotland for a month."

Willow hesitated, then said, "Ten years ago, my Scottish cousin, Fergus Murray, the Tayside Western Area Crime Officer, had a case involving a young girl's disappearance. After a cursory investigation by one of his Detectives the case was written off because the Detective concluded the girl had run away from home."

"My dear, the police make mistakes every day. You have not provided me with anything close to—"

"The remains of that girl's body were just unearthed—on a golf course—by a construction worker while my cousin stood less than fifty feet away."

Her story was interesting but there was no way that I could possibly stay away from Carson City that long. Perhaps a week, but never a month. "My dear, I still do not see—"

"Pinky, shut up and let me finish the whole story. My cousin is on the short list for promotion to be Tayside's Chief Superintendent of the Criminal

4

Investigation Department. According to Fergus, achieving that title would be the equivalent of me being named the United States Attorney General. He's very concerned that his error in judgment could cost him his chance for the promotion."

"Willow, I remain in the dark concerning the need for me to be absent from my law practice for an inordinate period of time!"

"Okay. The punch line to the story is Fergus called me because he had read an article concerning a defense attorney who practiced law in Carson City, the same city where I am the District Attorney. His first question to me was did I know J. Pincus Delmont?"

How was this possible? No one had interviewed me for an article. "I find this all very hard to comprehend. What is the name of the magazine that published the article?"

"According to Fergus he spotted the article on-line. Pinky, he was impressed that you got your last three clients released from jail because you discovered the real murderer. I told my cousin that I knew you and he begged me to use what influence I had to convince you to go to Scotland to help him investigate the girl's murder. He feels—"

"I suppose it would be possible to get away that long if I had a young attorney who—"

Willow said, "Stop right there. I have the perfect man for you."

"Who?"

"Yesterday, a young man stopped by my office seeking a position. I informed him that my organization didn't have any openings at the moment, but he would be perfect for you. He's pompous, verbose, and in a charming, boyish way, good looking."

"I fail to understand how a verbose, pompous individual fits into my practice."

"Wake up and smell the coffee. His name is C. Thomas Hennessy."

"Hennessy? The same name as the French Cognac?"

"One and the same. As far as I know he's not related, but one never knows. Now, I can give you the phone number on his application form. Then you can call him and tell him to come to your office for an interview. Does that remove your final reservation?"

"I can not be sure until I talk to the lad. Regardless, between an additional attorney, and Bear, my confidence has increased that Carson City could do without J. Pincus Delmont for a month."

"I hate to throw another monkey wrench into you life, but Bear's part of the Scottish package. The author of that magazine article stated he wasn't sure who was truly responsible for all your success—you, or your investigator, Bear Zabarte."

"That's it! Scotland is off! Call your cousin back and inform him I will not assist him in his time of need! There is no way that Bear Zabarte, an ignorant bartender, was instrumental in the ultimate solutions of—"

Willow jumped up and cried, "Oh my God, it's nearly nine and I have a court appearance at ten." She ran into the bathroom, opened the shower door and turned on the water. "Pinky, for one moment, try to control your overpowering ego and consider my needs—those beautiful years we had—the last few hours—can I count on you to come with me to

Scotland?"

I pondered my options and slowly determined that moments of time with Willow, in any part of the world, were priceless. "Yes, my dear. You can count on me. However, if during my interview with that Hennessy fellow I determine that this boy-wonder of yours does not meet my high standards—"

Willow called through the steamy shower. "Can't hear you. Now, I'm going to be in court most of the day so you'll have to call Bear and make sure he'll go."

"No need to get his commitment. The man is my investigator and as such, he does what I tell him to do and he goes where I tell him to go."

Willow's voice, still filtered by the flowing water in the shower, said, "I didn't hear that last bit. Just shout yes—that you'll call Bear."

"Yes," I shouted. "I will contact my investigator."

"Okay. I heard the yes part, and Pinky, don't worry about fixing breakfast for me, I'll grab a cup of something at the courthouse."

TWO

You know, when you're a little kid and your Grandma gives you the straight scoop, you'd better listen 'cause she's old, pretty nice, and you know she'll kick the crap out of you if you don't.

Okay, so the last time Grandma Zabarte told me something important, I wasn't a kid, hell no, in fact, Grandma called me her big bear. Anyway, that last time she was in the hospital, no more than a couple of days before she died. She hugged me with her bony arms, and said, "Boy, don't forget, a true Basque knows better than to take anything for free. Free things make you weak and we Basque have survived for thousands of years by being strong."

The old gal wasn't right all the time, but I can guarantee you'd make more money betting on Grandma Zabarte's words than you could playing three-card poker at The Nugget in Carson City.

So what did Grandma Zabarte's last words have to do with me standing at a bus stop in Boston, on the tail end of a hurricane, with rain pouring down the back of my neck? Hell, I'd never been in any part of a hurricane before. In Carson City, we get the usual crappy weather in the winter, and once in a while some rain in the summer, but Northern Nevada's never seen anything like a hurricane. As I

8

watched the gutters overflow, and the manhole covers lift off the pavement, I knew I'd screwed up big and once again, my old Grandma had told me the straight scoop!

So what did I take for free? An All-Expense Paid Dream Trip to a Boston Red Sox Baseball Game at Fenway Park, that's what! And Grandma might kick my ass from here to Sunday for taken a freebie, but shit, I won the trip fair and square.

How'd that happen? Once in a while I'd throw down a six-pack of brews watching the Sox on TV. Two months ago the brand of beer I buy to watch the TV games ran a bullshit contest. All I had to do was send in a little corner of the cardboard six-pack container and they'd pull out one winner. That part was easy. I had a garbage can full of six-pack containers so I mailed in a couple, no, it was a couple of dozen entries. Shit, you could've knocked me over with a feather when the phone rang and a dude told me I had won the trip to see the Red Sox in person.

What did I win? Free roundtrip airfare for me and Flo from Reno to Boston. A free hotel room for a couple of nights. Three hundred bucks for grub and beer, and the best part, a white limo to drive us to and from Fenway Park, the home of the Green Monster—Ted Williams—and the 2004 World Series Championship baseball team, the Boston Red Sox.

When Flo heard me whooping it up in the living room she peeked her head around the corner and said, "Hold it down in there. I was playing Free Cell on my iPad and your yelling caused my finger to move the wrong card."

"Forget that. I just won us a free trip to Boston, and we get box seats behind home plate for a Red

Sox game at Fenway Park."

"Humph. Have a good time."

"What do you mean have a good time? The trip is for two people. We're going together."

Flo walked into the living room. "Have you lost your mind? Ettamae is just getting acclimated at school. She can't afford to miss a day for a legitimate reason much less a stupid ball game in Boston."

"Oh! Maybe you can ask Willow to—"

"Don't even go there. That child needs stability. I know her Grandpa is rehabilitating in that senior home a mile away but that's no substitute for the nuclear family and in this circumstance, that's us."

"What do you mean, we're an atomic family?"

"I didn't say atomic, I said, nuclear. There's a difference."

"Now I get it. You don't want to go with me to Boston."

"Not considering our present family situation."

"Flo, that's what I was talking about when you wanted to keep the Kid. There's nothing wrong with her, but—"

"And her name's Ettamae, not Kid. She and I will remain in Carson City while you gallivant across the country attempting to regain your childhood."

"Huh?"

Flo gets like that once in a while. In fact, there are lots of times when she's downright hard to get along with. And now, with Ettamae around, she's . . . anyway, now you know why I'm standing all alone, in the rain, at some place called Copley Square, waiting for the number eight bus.

So what happened to my fancy white limo? Well, the driver told me he was leaving Fenway at the start of the second rain delay. He was sure that the hurricane wind and rain would force the umpires to call the game at the end of the seventh inning and we could go back to the hotel. But I told him that I was going to stick around. Hell, I'd never been to Fenway, the coolest baseball park in America, and I wasn't going to leave until they threw me out of the joint. About two hours later, the rain slowed down and the umps restarted the game in the eighth inning. By the time the game was finally over, I was soaking wet and had no clue where my hotel was. A couple of friendly Sox fans helped me find the closest subway. They told me to get off at the Copley Square station and catch the number eight bus to my hotel. I did what they told me to do and now you know why I'm standing in a downpour of warm rain, soaking wet, watching for the number eight bus.

I was starting to look for a cab when my cell buzzed.

"Bear, where are you?"

Shit, it was Pinky. Ever since he got back from California he's been a bigger pain-in-the-ass than usual. He's got this new secretary, I forget her name, the broad that took over for Lu. Don't get me wrong, the new babe's not dumb or anything, but she ain't no Lu.

"Boss, I'm in Boston, the wind is blowing so hard a cat just flew by, and the rain's coming down by the bucketful. Talk louder."

"Boston? What are you doing there?"

"It's a great story. I won this free trip to see a Red Sox game and—"

"My good man, I pay you an exorbitant sum each and every month to be at my beck and call. Do

11

you understand what that means?"

The shrimpy bastard sure knows how to grind a man down. "Yup."

"I do not think you do. At my beck and call means you are to return to Carson City immediately. Willow and I leave for Scotland tomorrow morning."

"Did you say Scotland? What the hell's happening? Are you and Willow going on a vacation?"

"Where the present District Attorney of Carson City and I spend our time is none of your business."

"Last time I checked you didn't have anything for me to do in Carson City. Did you come up with something that you need me to investigate while you're gone?"

"What is it about the words, 'return at once', that you do not understand? And once you arrive back home you are to pick up your passport, pack your bag, and jump on the next plane to Scotland."

"Scotland? But, Boss—"

The line went dead just as the number eight bus arrived. I got on, paid my buck and a half, and before I got to a seat my cell buzzed again.

"Boss, I'm glad you called back. We must have—"

"Bear, it's Willow. Do you have a minute?"

Jesus, I thought, there must be something really big going on back home. The last time Willow called me on my cell was a couple of years ago when Pinky flew back from Italy. "According to the driver of the number eight bus I've got five minutes. That's how long it will take to get me back to my hotel. What's up?"

"When you arrive at your hotel, go to the front

desk and get me a fax number. I need to send you two photos and a few documents."

"Willow, I'm in Boston and—"

"I know where you are. I talked with Pinky before I called. We need you back in Carson City as soon as you can get here."

"Like I said, what's up?"

"Call me from the hotel with the fax number. After you've had the chance to look everything over, call me back."

"I don't know why I'm doing this, but okay."

A summertime rain in Boston is really weird. Back home, in Carson City, when we get summer rains off the mountains, the air turns cold and you could freeze your ass off in a couple of minutes. But the temperature sign across the street from my hotel told me it was 75 degrees. Under my plastic Red Sox poncho I was sweating like a pig so right there, in the lobby of the fancy hotel, I pulled the poncho over my head and shook like an old dog trying to dump as much rainwater off me as I could. Then I asked the dude behind the front desk for a fax number and called Willow.

Five minutes later the dude behind the counter handed me a stack of faxed papers. I walked to the hotel bar, laid down the pile and ordered a cool one. I downed the brew, ordered a second, sat back, and started on the papers.

The top one was a picture of what looked like a human skeleton, wrapped in something and lying in mud. I spotted a shovel on the ground next to the skeleton and checking the size of the rib cage and shoulder against the shovel told me that the bones were small, like a teen, or a really big kid.

I'd seen lots of skeletons before, but this picture hit me real hard. Those bones, I guessed, were about the same size and age as Ettamae, the kid who'd changed me and Flo's life. I remembered talking with Ettamae about school while she ate breakfast the morning I left for Boston. That's when I figured that the skeleton in the picture might be a kid who'd never eat breakfast with her family again.

The next paper was a close up shot of the remains and I spotted a tiny stream of water running from the ribs, down the backbone and onto the pelvis like a little mountain creek. I brushed away some water from my eyes, probably left over from the rain, pulled out my cell and keyed in Willow's number.

She said, "Hi. Any questions?"

I tried to say something but the words got caught in my throat, the same thing that happened to me when we lowered Grandma Zabarte's box in the ground at the cemetery outside of Elko. I took a swig of beer. "Willow, have these pictures got something to do with Pinky telling me I'm going to Scotland?"

"Yes."

"Okay. Now back to the pictures. It looks to me like the skeleton's just a kid."

"Good pick up, but there is more to this problem then the skeleton's age."

"What's that?"

"Bear, according to my cousin, it's probable that she's a girl who disappeared about ten years ago. Now that her remains have been found we know that she was murdered and—"

"Willow, except for that one time when you tried to throw me in the slam for murder, we get along

14

pretty good and you've always been straight with me so cut to the chase. What the hell do you want from me?"

"Call Pinky and tell him you'll go to Scotland."

"What about Flo? I'm not going to Scotland without Flo. Right now she's all pissed off at me about—"

"Don't worry her, I'll take care of Flo."

"Good luck." I didn't see how Willow could do that, but if she could, this trip was sounding better by the second. Scotland is where they make all that great whiskey. And I heard they brew up some really good beer. I started to see that this deal could turn out to be like a paid vacation for me and Flo. "Before I say yes, I've heard they talk funny in Scotland. They don't talk French, or anything like French do they?"

"They speak English, the same language we use here. Now, concentrate and tell me that you'll go to Scotland."

Shit! Between Flo, the Kid, and now Willow, I had three females biting at my butt. "Okay, as soon as we hang up I'll catch the first plane back, but Pinky'll have to pick up the extra bucks the airlines will charge me for changing my flight."

"I'll make sure he takes care of that extra expense. Bear, thanks."

THREE

Pinky Delmont-Carson City, Nevada

Allowing the proper amount of solemnity to enter my voice, I said, "Thomas, while I am away from my office, you are in my employ to assist Kim when she schedules court dates. You are to do nothing more, nothing less."

"But, Pinky, working here is the perfect opportunity to advance my legal standing in the community."

"Damn it, you have no legal standing to advance. Two weeks ago you passed the Nevada Bar and then spent a day attempting to gain employment with the District Attorney. Frankly, you have less legal experience than my previous secretary, Lu."

"Pinky, the scuttlebutt around town is that your boss keeled over and died when you were a brand new attorney, and you presented the closing argument to the jury and your client was acquitted. Is that story true?"

"Yes, my boy, that tale is factual, but we are discussing a different situation."

"Not really. I'm not saying you're going to croak, or anything like that, but I could handle all your court cases while you're in Scotland."

"My boy, I would allow that to happen, as Bear would say, when pigs fly. Now, return to your—"

There was a light knock on my office door. I said, "Enter."

Kim, my new secretary, and potential majordomo of the J. Pincus Delmont legal empire, walked in. In her mid-forties and slightly attractive in a matronly way, Kim and I were still involved in the 'new employee' dance. Frankly, she had been with me for two months and three days, and I was beginning to comprehend that this female might not possess the 'second in command' mental attitude that I required from all my secretaries. Without question, she was not as mentally tough as my previous secretary, but hopefully Kim would learn to take the reins without picking up the power-hungry negative traits exhibited by Lu.

Kim mumbled, "Pinky?"

If I accomplished nothing more with this woman before I fired her, I would infuse a backbone into this female. "Kim, speak up—stand erect—hold your head high—stick your chest out—act like a man."

"But Pinky, I'm—"

"Yes, yes, I know. Now, what caused you to interrupt my conversation with Thomas?"

"I received a call from the court clerk."

Slowly, ever so slowly, my anger began to rise. "And?"

"He expressed concern with your request for a five-week continuance."

"And what was his concern?"

"Uh . . . The five weeks I think."

"Kim, I have explained this more than once. There will be moments when I am forced to be elsewhere. This trip to Scotland is but one example. When this type of situation occurs, I count on you to keep my calendar current. For example, concerning the trial you just mentioned, you need to guide the court clerk into accepting the continuance. Have I made myself clear?"

"I, I think so, but what happens if—"

"My dear, no ifs. Resolving scheduling conflicts is a major aspect of your job. Now, do you have anything else?"

"Uh . . . I guess not. Oh yes, call Willow."

"Fine. Now, if you will both excuse me." While I dialed Willow's number the minions exited my office.

After two rings I heard the lovely voice of my favorite ex-wife say, "Pinky, I just talked with Bear, and—"

"I told you I would contact him and I did. What possessed you to call him?"

I detected an exasperated sigh from Willow's end of the conversation. "That's what I was trying to tell you. He's returning on the first plane heading West out of Logan Airport. I also called Fergus. He's happy we are going to assist him but he wants to be sure we understand the need for complete secrecy. As I mentioned before, Fergus is up for the post of the Head of the Tayside Police Criminal Investigation Department. That may not sound important to you, but in Fergus' world of Scottish law enforcement, it's almost the equivalent of becoming a Nobel Laureate."

"Perhaps, but I still do not comprehend how Bear and I can remain under the radar while we wander about a foreign land pursuing a murderer who buried a young girl's body on a golf course."

"Fergus will take care of that. One more item. Did you know that Flo and Bear have been taking care of a young girl since they returned from Sonoma County?"

"No, because I purposefully remain in the dark concerning what that woman does beyond hacking into a computer at my direction. And what do Bear and that woman have to do with solving the murder of a—"

"If you would stop talking and listen, I will tell you. Fergus is married and he and his wife have two boys, both around the same age as Ettamae. That would—"

"Who, or what is an Ettamae?"

"Pinky, I am well aware that your brain resides inside a tiny kingdom known only to you, but I am positive you met Ettamae when you were in Healdsburg. An eleven or twelve year-old, girl. Very bright and advanced for her age. Red hair. Tall with—"

"I do recall a young female with an explosion of flame-colored hair during a breakfast at the Red Rose B & B. Might this be the individual we are discussing?"

"Yes, and you will also purchase round-trip airfare for Ettamae."

"I fail to comprehend why you feel that urchin should be included in the flight to Scotland."

"Pinky, kids like to play together, and go to school together, that's why."

"Willow, I grew up as an only child and as far as I can determine, my solitary experience did me no harm."

"That observation is yours, and yours alone. Now, listen to me, no Ettamae, no Flo. No Flo, no Bear. No Bear, no Pinky and Bear team. One more

19

airfare won't break you. Remember earlier this morning, you promised me that you —"

An impression of Willow, standing au naturel in the morning sun, short circuited my common sense. "All right, the child goes."

"Now that we are on the same page, I'm on my way to your office. I have a video from Fergus to show you."

"But I am—" Before I could say more the phone line went dead. I looked up and my new legal assistant had re-entered my office while I was talking with Willow. "Thomas, never enter my inner sanctum without my personal invitation."

"But Pinky, we never finished our discussion."

"What discussion?"

"Our discussion concerning the legend that you, J. Pincus Delmont, an attorney just out of school, stepped in when his superior died and was responsible for the acquittal of a man on trial for first degree murder?"

I sat up and smiled. "The legend is true. But much water has run under the bridge since that day."

"I heard that you are on more than twenty straight acquittals."

I responded, "Twenty-four!"

He said, "Wow!"

"Thomas, what does the C in C. Thomas Hennessy, stand for?"

"I'd rather not say."

"My boy, I did not ask what you would rather do, I asked about the letter C."

"Caesar. But call me Thomas. Most people make fun of Caesar. What does the J stand for in J. Pincus

Delmont?"

"None of your business. Now clear out of my office and make yourself useful. Assist Kim in her rescheduling endeavors. As soon as Willow arrives, send her in."

A moment later Willow walked into my office with a laptop computer under her arm.

"Pinky, sit back and watch."

After she clicked a few buttons, a man's face appeared on the screen. I assumed it was Willow's cousin, Fergus. His jaw line looked as if it had been chiseled out of solid granite. His skin was ruddy with freckles across his nose and cheeks and he looked to be in his mid-forties with a sheaf of sandy hair. Willow tapped her keyboard and the face began to speak.

"Willow, coincidence is a curious thing. A week ago I was playing golf with a group of friends at the Pitlochry course. It was a nippy winter morn. Before I hit my final pitch toward the tenth green I noticed a man on a small dozer moving some dirt near the stone bridge about thirty yards left of my target. During a heavy rain storm last month, the burn had overflowed and caused some damage so the golf club had hired a contractor to repair the foundation of the rock bridge that crossed the burn. In the middle of my backswing, the man on the earthmover let out a scream that would have curdled the blood of a banshee."

The face on the laptop screen disappeared and we were now staring at a video of a skeleton partially covered by dirt. Fergus' voice continued over the picture. "I ran over to the newly turned earth, knelt down, saw a torn plastic sheet and the fibrous remains of a wool tartan. Inside the ripped tartan lay bones. In my professional opinion as the Western Area Crime Officer, the size of the skeleton indicated that the body was small, perhaps not fully grown. I called headquarters in Perth and told them to send a homicide team to the golf course. The next day, after an extensive search of missing persons in the Perthshire area, I came across the report of a missing female that matched the general size of the skeleton. The lasses name was Mary Patterson. Her father, James Patterson, had filed the original report ten years earlier. According to her father, Mary was twelve when she disappeared. The golf professional at the Pitlochry course is reviewing his records to see who did similar work on that stone bridge ten years earlier, the same time-frame when the Patterson lass disappeared. Cousin, although a decade has passed, we could have a prime suspect to pursue.

As soon as you arrive I will drive you to the Pitlochry golf course where the body was discovered. I will take both of you along and introduce you as my kin from America, to avoid making the golf course visit look like official police business. I hope you don't think poorly of me, operating behind the scenes on this case, but I have worked for more than twenty years to be considered for the Tayside Criminal Investigative Department promotion and I do not want to toss away this opportunity because of an improperly closed missing person case. I look forward to seeing you soon."

FOUR

Bear Zabarte-Carson City, Nevada

I yelled, "What do you mean, we can't go?"

Flo stopped packing her bag and said, "I didn't say I can't go. I said you and Ettamae can't go until you get a passport."

"Pinky won't like this."

"I know it's hard for you to cope with this, but Pinky Delmont doesn't have control over the issuance of United States passports."

"Really? Who does?"

Flo shook her head, like she was trying to clear out a nest of spiders from her ears. "The U. S. Government, that's who. When Ettamae gets home from school we'll go to the post office to fill out the paperwork and get your pictures taken."

"Hold on, what's a passport look like?"

"Like a little book, about three by five, and it has a photo of you on the inside page. Why?"

"A couple of years ago, before we met, I had a girlfriend. She wanted to go to Hawaii so I got a passport. It's funny, nobody ever asked to see it."

"Bear, you don't need a passport to go to Hawaii. That's part of the United States."

"Really? We've got some time before the Kid comes home so while I'm waiting I'm going to see if the Sox are on TV."

"If you touch that TV remote I'll pull that damned screen off the wall and throw it in the trash. You have to find your passport and finish packing, but before you do that, you need to go to Pinky's office. We need some expense money before we leave."

"How much?"

Flo stopped talking and scrunched her eyebrows together. "How long did Willow say it would take?"

"About a month. But she—"

"The three of us for a month—four weeks more or less—times twenty-five hundred a week—if I watch every penny we could scrape by on ten thousand."

"Are you nuts? Pinky will kill me first. Besides, Willow told me we'd be staying at her cousin's place—eating there too—so I'll ask Kim for a couple thousand. If we need more I can always get it."

"But we'll never make it on—"

I flashed Flo my killer stare, something a guy's got to do now and then so his woman remembers who's boss. She hit me back with her best pissed-off pout. I said, "Like I told you, I'm heading to the office to pick up a couple thousand. Call me when the Kid gets home. I'll meet you at the downtown Post Office to do the paper work crap for her passport."

Before Flo had time to explode I bailed and drove my pickup to Pinky's office. Kim was sitting at her desk and next to her was a young dude all decked out in a fancy suit. He stood up and the little fart barely cleared my belly button.

The dude flashed me a politician's smile and stuck out his little hand in my direction. "My name is C. Thomas Hennessy. I am the newest legal addition

24

to the firm of J. Pincus Delmont." He turned and pushed me toward Pinky's office. "Come with me my good man. I'm here to lift the guilt from your shoulders. Come into my office and tell me why you need a lawyer."

Kim said, "Tom, save your breath. This is Bear Zabarte. He's Pinky's investigator."

The little dude looked me up and down. "That's good to know. I'm sure I'll be needing your investigative services very soon. Now, if you'll excuse me, I have work to do." He opened the door to Pinky's office and went inside.

Kim said, "Pinky won't like that. He told you to stay out of his office."

"What he doesn't know won't hurt him."

Kim put her finger against her lips, like she and I were secret book club buddies. "What do you need, Bear?"

"A couple of thousand for expenses for me, Flo, and the Kid."

"Ah, Pinky left an envelope for you."

I opened it up and pulled out a check with the attached note.

Bear
Enclosed is an expense check for fifteen hundred dollars. Before you lapse into your usual histrionics concerning the amount, note that you have three, one-way airline tickets waiting to be picked up at the Reno Airport. You and your group will be sleeping and eating at the Fergus estate outside of Pitlochry, Scotland. You will have no reason to drive a vehicle because Fergus will take us where we need to go.
As I reviewed the last three sentences, I was inclined

to tear up the fifteen hundred dollar check and write a new one for seven hundred and fifty dollars. However, in the spirit of continuing our stellar employer/employee relationship, I happily give you the fifteen hundred expense advance with the caveat that you are required to provide me with a detailed record of each and every expense against the advance.
Pinky

"Kim, Flo will go ballistic when she figures out that Pinky has only given me fifteen hundred. Shit, I don't think this is going to cover all our expenses."

"I'm sorry, but Pinky has installed some new office procedures. As of yesterday, there will be no more cash advances for expenses. All advances will be by check and Pinky's signature is required on all checks."

"That's bullshit! How in the hell am I supposed to get—"

The door to Pinky's office popped open and the short suit jumped out. "I think I have a solution. If you need more expense money, just call Kim. She'll contact me and I'll see that your needs are fulfilled."

"Is that legal?"

The suit said, "Of course it's legal. You have entered into an area where my legal expertise is top-notch."

I glanced at Kim. Her eyes caught mine then dropped suddenly like she became super interested in her computer keyboard. "Okay. Kim, if I need more money, I'll call you. What you do after my call is your problem."

My cell buzzed.

"Bear, Ettamae just told me that she has a passport. She and her parents were going to make a trip to Europe and then they were killed in that car accident. Did you get the expense advance?"

"Yup." I'll tell her it's only fifteen hundred after we get to Scotland. "Finish packing, Babe. We're off to the land of booze and beer."

FIVE

Pinky Delmont, Pitlochry, Scotland

After what seemed like a never ending night of flying, we were met at the Glasgow airport by Willow's cousin, Fergus Murray, along with a blustery wind, and a chilly rain. During the eighty mile drive to the Murray farm outside Pitlochry the precipitation managed to degrade into a bone-chilling sleet—a poor harbinger for what I had hoped to be a glorious holiday in sunny Scotland.

Fergus drove us to a newer building no more than a hundred feet from the main farmhouse. He said, "You have your choice of two apartments. After the other couple arrives, they will stay in the adjacent apartment."

Willow said, "Why have you built two apartments?"

"One for each son, so they will have a place to live while they work on the farm."

I said, "But what if they do not want to become farmers?"

Fergus stared at me as if no one had ever broached that question before. "We'll see you at eight in the morning for breakfast." He pointed at a door on the side of the farmhouse. "The kitchen is through that door. Get some sleep, we'll have a long day tomorrow."

The following morning, after a restless night due to jet lag, the raging storm, and my questioning as to why I had succumbed to my ex-wife's entreatment, I was not my usual friendly self as Willow and I gathered around the Murray family breakfast table.

The family, Fergus, Fiona and two strapping boys, linked hands, and our host concluded his morning blessing with, "And we thank the good Lord for the safe arrival of my American cousin and her . . . a . . . friend. Amen."

Pondering Fergus' designation of me as Willow's friend, but properly endowed with Divine favor, I took a sip of coffee and said, "My good man, what do you have planned for us today?"

"We'll drive to the Pitlochry golf course to view the scene of the . . . Oh, I received an email from a woman named Flo and she informed me that they would arrive later today. I responded to her that I would send a constable to pick them up at the airport and he will take them to the Pitlochry golf course where we will meet. Willow, I was unaware that there was three in their party. The only place large enough for three on the farm is the old Croft cottage. I've been upgrading the structure—to rent out for holidays—but I fear it's not completed."

Ah-ha! Bear's witch would join me in my misery. A smile crept across my lips. "Do not fret about the poor accommodations. I keep Bear and his woman on a short leash, and due to my diligence, they have become very resourceful at making do."

Fergus said, "Can you explain 'short leash' to me?"

Willow said, "That's Pinky's code for cheap."

Fergus nodded. "While we're at it, I find it very difficult to address a grown adult as Pinky. You see, in Scotland all males named Robert are called Robbie, in deference to the great Scottish poet, Robert Burns. But there is no Scottish poet named Pincus, so Pinky is out of the question. In the future I will address you by your last name, Delmont. I mean you no disrespect and I trust none is taken."

Fergus was like that. From the moment we met, I determined that he said what was on his mind with no attempt at filtration. "My good man, if calling me Delmont shortens my stay away from my law practice, so be it. Now, can we get on with the investigation?"

"Aye."

An hour later the three of us were riding along the fairways of the Pitlochry golf course in a maintenance cart. The frigid wind peppered my face and tiny jets of frozen air shot through folds in my wool muffler. I tightened the scarf around my neck and tried to forget that if not for my scheming ex-wife, I would be home adding to my bank account by extricating a client from the tentacles of a zealous law enforcement organization.

"'Tis a nippy wind this late in the spring," said Fergus as he stuffed his hands into his pockets.

I poked my dripping nose out of the heavy woolen scarf, a piece of clothing Fergus had loaned me, and said, "When we have a nippy little wind like this in Carson City, we called it the coldest day of the winter."

He laughed. "Aye, Delmont, but a true Scotsman doesn't feel the cold."

To truly comprehend the madness of his

statement, you needed to understand the demented mind of my ex-wife's cousin. As he drove us to the golf course, Fergus informed us that he had been born and raised outside of Pitlochry. On special occasions, he and some fellow policemen would take three-day winter treks, through fields of heather and white snow, eyebrows covered with ice, surviving on a pocket-full of oats for food and whiskey for drink.

Do you require more to further expound the insanity of the Scots? During my first breakfast, next to my sunny-side-up eggs, Fiona served me a large slice of fried Haggis. My stomach had been acting up since I ingested my food. Through the freezing wind, I called, "Fergus, what exactly is Haggis?"

"At the end of each day, the Pitlochry butcher takes all the left over spleens, livers, and whatever, adds some oats and grinds the mixture up. Then he stuffs the concoction into an empty sheep's stomach. That's what Fiona fixed for you this morning. Do you fancy Haggis?"

I hesitated for a moment to allow my stomach the opportunity to settle down. "I am not sure that is how I would describe my feelings toward Haggis."

"So you'll want Fiona to fry some each morning?"

"I think not, and I will inform her when I am ready resume."

"Aye."

From my limited view, Scotland seemed to be built around the deprivation of all pleasure and ingesting disguised offal.

However, there was one exception to my limited perspective of living in Scotland. Last night, Fergus welcomed us with a round of his finest whiskey.

Without question, his skills as a homicide detective might be lacking, but his choice of whisky was excellent.

Dreaming of a warming glass of whiskey, I said, "I suppose I should thank you for borrowing this motorized maintenance cart so we could ride out to the site, but I cannot stop my teeth from chattering."

"You're welcome, Delmont."

Willow rummaged through her jacket and pulled out two small packets. "Pinky, I have a couple of chemical hand warmers. They should help keep your fingers from turning blue."

I forced a smile through chattering teeth and remembered that the sooner I found Fergus' murderer, the sooner I could return to Carson City. "Thank you, my dear."

I glanced at Fergus sitting behind the wheel of the maintenance cart. He was around my age, but the ravages of the sun and rain had toughened his ruddy face into a combination of hard leather and deep-set canyons. His red hair was streaked with gray and had an unruly appearance, a portrait of a loosely tied bale of thatch. To tell the truth, my ex-wife's cousin resembled one of the hairy, wild looking Scottish cattle I had seen on his farm, minus the long horns.

Fergus pressed the accelerator and said, "How'd you and my cousin meet?"

At least his question gave me something to think about besides my never-ending discomfort. "We met in court. She was a young Deputy District Attorney and I was the defense attorney."

"So she was your adversary. Go on man, what happened next?"

"The first time I laid my eyes on Willow, she was standing by the court clerk's desk. Fergus, I pride myself on being the best prepared and focused attorney in Northern Nevada, but at that moment my mind went blank and I could do nothing but stare at her until the Judge entered the room. When Willow returned to the prosecutor's desk, I smiled and she smiled back."

He smiled and asked, "And?"

"Our relationship was one of those crazy love-at-first-sight things you see in the movies. After the trial was over we met for lunch, then dinner, and within the week I proposed."

"Fergus," called Willow from the back seat. "Are we nearly there?"

"Over the next hill. Delmont was just telling me how you two met."

"Cousin, if I were you, I'd believe about twenty percent of his story."

Fergus stopped the cart next to a small stone bridge. A hundred feet away was a large golf green and between the bridge and the green was a ten-by-ten foot square cordoned off with yellow police tape.

As I walked toward the tape line, the howling wind reached behind a black cloud, grabbed some icy crystals, and flung them down the back of my neck. And according to Fergus, this was springtime!

Fergus lifted the tape and said, "This is where the body was unearthed."

The Arctic mist slowly turned to a shower and then accelerated to a steady downpour. Fergus said, "I fear we've experienced a little turn in the weather. Perhaps we should return to the clubhouse and talk with the club pro."

After wandering about the golf course, a journey that felt as interminable as Peary's protracted trek to the frozen north pole, we returned to the clubhouse and entered a room that resembled a men's club. Dark leather couches and chairs lined the walls and empty card tables filled the center of the space. The room was empty of humanity, except for a bartender who seemed intent on rubbing off the reflection on a shot glass. Obviously, the golfers of Pitlochry were dry and warm, proving to me that they were a smarter lot than we were.

Fergus smiled grimly at the lonely bartender and ordered three whiskies. He handed one to Willow, one to me, and took a good-sized gulp from his own glass. "Murder is a horrible crime, but when a child is involved, it's even more difficult to accept."

The warm alcohol trickled down my throat and the internal and external heaters began to work their way through my wet clothing. Fergus waved to the bartender for three more and turned toward me. "Delmont, you're not a Highlander, but you must have a wee bit of Scottish blood flowing through your veins. Most men I know wouldn't put their law practice on hold and travel to Scotland to help out their ex-wife's cousin."

I raised my glass. "On that subject, I am open to any form of compensation that your organization makes available. Everyday I am absent from my practice sets me back a small fortune."

Willow said, "Pinky, you can't—"

The door popped open and a tall, broad-shouldered man walked into the room. His face was round, ruddy, and plastered from ear to ear with an expression of angry petulance.

Fergus said, "Colin, good to see you again. I hope you don't mind us barging in like this. I'd like you to meet my American cousin, Willow Stone, and her friend, J. Pincus Delmont."

Our introduction did nothing to abate Colin's testiness. He slammed a thick file onto the bar and growled. "Fergus, we've been over this ground before. In the future, contact my assistant. He will be more than happy to—"

Fergus' shifted his weight to the balls of his feet. "Colin, I'm conducting a murder investigation. A few days ago the remains of a young lass were discovered buried on your golf course. During the course of my investigation I might go over the identical information once, twice, or a hundred times. Keep complaining and I'll escort you to my car and we'll continue this discussion at my office in Perth."

Fergus' harsh words seemed to get through because Colin's irritated expression melted a bit, but not enough to manufacture a true smile on the golf pro's face.

Fergus continued, "A true Highlander would show his guests a little hospitality. My cousin and her friend have come a long way and will be in Scotland for a few weeks."

Colin shook my hand and gave Willow a perfunctory nod. "Mr. Delmont, should I assume that you are an overzealous police inspector, like your kin, Fergus?"

"I'm not a relative of Fergus, and no, I am an attorney."

"My God, that's twice as bad as a policeman. And the lady?"

Willow said, "I am Fergus' cousin, but I fear I'm

also an attorney."

Colin smiled, "Aye, but much prettier then your wee friend."

Wee friend? The combination of the whisky warming me from within and the now oppressive room temperature seemed to muddle my brain. Before I could respond to his affront concerning my height, the man turned away and showered all of his attention on Willow. After gazing at her beauty a touch longer than I thought appropriate, he said, "Fergus, I'll have my man pour us all a wee dram of my best single malt."

The bartender filled four tumblers to the brim. Willow said, "Excuse me, but I think I've had enough of the hard stuff. Could I trade my wee dram for a glass of white wine?"

Colin scowled, "Miss Stone, in the old days, drinking wine was thought to be so sinful that people did it in secret. You're in Scotland now. Most Highlanders start out their day with a 'skalach'. That's Gaelic for a wee dram."

Willow shook her head. "I understand, but I'd rather—"

"Colin's correct," Fergus interrupted. "Your great-grandfather Murray was known throughout the Highlands as a man with great knowledge concerning medicine. He believed that wine was dangerous. He thought it could cause a trembling of the hands, loss of appetite, and other dreaded diseases. It's just a wee dram. We Scots call this the water of life. You're cold and soaked to the skin. Drink up. The whisky will warm both your body and soul."

Colin opened the file folder he'd set on the bar.

"Fergus, here's the invoice from the company that did the work near the grave ten years ago."

Fergus glanced at the sheet, then folded the paper, and slipped it into his jacket pocket. "Miller and Urquhart Construction. I know the firm. They are based in Edinburgh." Then he pulled out a notebook and said, "Colin, how long have you been the professional at this club?"

I took a final swig and emptied my glass. Before I could say no, the bartender refilled it.

Colin frowned, "You have the invoice. Why is my employment history important?"

I began to feel very warm and the discussion between Fergus and Colin started to fade into the background.

Fergus said, "I'm conducting a murder investigation. Everything, and everyone is relevant, and that could include interviewing every employee that worked here before the remains were discovered."

Colin stamped his foot and demanded, "Are you accusing an employee of the golf course of murder? My God, Fergus, we've known each other for at least thirty years!"

As Colin's voice echoed around my head, I suddenly realized my feeling of detachment could be due to the multiple wee drams of whiskey!

Fergus said, "Calm down, Colin. All a murderer requires is the means, the opportunity and a motive. It's an obvious fact that everyone who worked here for ten years had the means, the opportunity and—"

Colin spat out, "Stop right there and write this down in your little notebook! I didn't murder anyone and I didn't bury a body by the tenth green. Does that make you happy now?"

I should have kept my mouth shut, but it seemed to me that Willow's cousin was just trying to do his job. I said, "I don't think you should be upset with Fergus. It is a policeman's job to ask questions."

Colin clenched his fists, and as small beads of sweat rolled down his red cheeks, the man, nearly twice my size, lunged toward me.

To my relief, Fergus stepped between us. "Delmont's right. I'm just doing my job. I'm asking you the same questions I'll ask everyone."

Colin backed away. "Fergus, you have the invoice. I gave you a statement. There will be no further discussions between us without my solicitor being present."

Then Colin moved so close to me that I detected a curious combination of whisky and peppermint on his breath. He took away my empty glass and handed me a full one. "Delmont, I know you're a guest of Fergus Murray, but after you finish that glass, please take your whiskey drinking down the road."

Before I could respond, the door opened. Bear, Flo, and a child, dripping wet, staggered in. Bear spotted me and yelled, "Boss, did you know these crazy dudes drive on the wrong side of the road?"

SIX

Ring-ring.

A ringing was detected by my brain. The sound seemed to emanate from the bottom of a deep well.

Ring-ring. Ring-ring. Ring—

Willow's voice cut into my reverie. "Pinky, it's Bear. He wants to talk to you."

I sat up and discovered I was on the couch in the sitting room and I had no recollection of how I had ended up here.

Willow said, "Are you okay?"

I was not, but I nodded. "I am fine."

"Do you want me to tell Bear that you'll call him back?"

"Listen to me. I am fine!"

"Don't snap at me." She tossed me the phone and left me sitting alone.

"Hello."

"Boss, this Croft joint we're staying in is great. Two bedrooms, a kitchen, living room, and a super wood stove that could heat up North Dakota. Flo and the Kid are real happy, except for the freezing bathroom part. Did you ever see the bathroom here? Well, the wall opposite the can is a giant rock and there are real icicles hanging down from the moss. Do you have the same kind of rock wall in your

39

bathroom? Is that how they build all bathrooms in Scotland?"

"Bear, I just woke up from a much needed nap."

"Oh! So how's the case going so far. Got any ideas who murdered that little girl?"

"No. Now hang up and quit bothering me."

"Right. Oh, before I hang up, Flo and the Kid send their love. Actually Flo didn't exactly say love, but you get the drift. Let me know when you'll need me and Flo."

"First thing tomorrow morning when we drive to Edinburgh. Good bye."

I laid back and tried to recall why I had decided against the Croft cottage. Fergus took us by after we looked at the apartment.

The abode had a small wood stove as the only source of heat. Back home, or at my condo at Lake Tahoe, during the winter a wood stove would have been sufficient. However, coping with the frigid springtime in Scotland, I would have spent all my time in the cottage wrapped in my warmest clothing. But the deal breaker was the bathroom with its wall of ice. I stuck my head in the door, flipped on the light, and a single glance informed me that the cottage was out. Willow was enamored with the idea of staying because of the unusual qualities, but I convinced her that my two strikes against the abode trumped her love of quaintness. Fergus immediately took us back to the new apartment he had built close to his home.

The phone rang again.

"Delmont, how are you feeling?"

Other than the fact that my mouth felt like it was packed with steel wool, I was breathing. "I'm fine."

"A couple of hours ago I took the other Americans to the old Croft house, the cottage you and Willow looked at but decided against."

"Fergus, the cottage was quaint, but not up to my standards. That is why I opted for the apartment."

"Now, will you feel up for our trip to Edinburgh tomorrow?"

"I might be if I knew why we were going there. What's in Edinburgh?"

"Miller and Urquhart Construction. I've set up an appointment with the owner of the firm. I thought you and your investigator should tag along."

"Will you be on official police business?"

"Not really. Edinburgh's outside my jurisdiction, so it's an unofficial trip."

"Thanks." I glanced at the window and it was dark outside. "What about Willow?"

"She told Fiona she'll be spending the day with the Principle at the children's school."

I'd forgotten all about that. During the flight to Scotland, Willow informed me that the only reason that she was here was to introduce me to Fergus and get out of the way.

I said, "Yes, I understand she is going to be in charge of cross-cultural education."

"You and your investigator will meet me in my kitchen at eight-thirty. With the drive, we should arrive at Urquhart's office a little after ten."

"Fergus, my investigator's given name is Bernat and we call him Bear."

"I understand that, Delmont, but we Scots are very formal. What is his last name?"

41

"Zabarte."

"Ha! It will be Zabarte from now on."

I stood, stretched, and the ugly memory of our visit to the murder site drifted back. "Any news concerning the identity of the remains?"

"Yes. I found a missing persons report that matches the sex and size of the skeleton. She was reported missing a few days before the construction work was completed. I believe that is all the information I want to discuss over the phone. We can continue this conversation on the drive to Edinburgh."

"Fergus, don't hang up on me. Did the missing girl have a name?"

He paused. "Aye, she had a name."

Perhaps all Scots were as circumspect, but to not give me the victim's name was ridiculous. Fergus' attitude was outlandish—enough to make me wonder what the man was hiding. I said, "Is there a legal reason that you can't tell me her name now?"

Another pause. "No. Her name was Mary Patterson."

I shuddered as the girl's name humanized that pathetic pile of bones.

Fergus said, "Her father, James Patterson, filed the original report ten years ago, and the Mis-Per file remains open today."

"How old was Mary when she disappeared?"

"A month short of twelve. Delmont, you need to understand there are many young lasses that run away around that age in Scotland. Most of them live in small towns. They watch the telly and long for the glamorous life of the big city."

"Fergus, you could be wrong about Mary

Patterson. She might turn up on the west bank in Paris married to a good-looking French sculptor."

"Aye, perhaps you're right. Delmont, I will see you and Mr. Zabarte in the morning."

The line went dead, and by the tone of his voice, Fergus did not believe that Mary Patterson was alive and well in Paris.

When I hung up, Willow said, "Are you hungry?"

"What time is it?"

"Nearly eight."

"I drank too much whisky today."

She headed toward the stove and filled a bowl with what looked like a thick soup. "That's OK."

I sat down and buttered a slice of coarse, oat bread. "Am I crazy or did that golf pro go over the top this afternoon?"

Willow set a steaming bowl down in front of me. "We did find a body on his golf course, but Fergus gave me the inside scoop on the man while you were snoozing. A few years ago, Colin Balfour played on the European tour and many of the locals were sure he'd be the next Nick Faldo. However, golf is a funny game and it seemed that his ego got in the way of low scores."

"I know nothing about the silly game of golf so I do not understand how a man's ego could destroy his chance for success."

"According to Fergus, every time he'd miss a crucial putt, the miss happened because a kid coughed, even though the closest child was two hundred yards from the green."

"I see. One more item concerning Colin. The man was insufferable. I thought golf pros were supposed to be personable."

"Most are, but we're now in the Highlands where men are men and golf pros are allowed to be grouchy bastards. By the way, in the future, I'd say no more than two whiskeys before lunch would be a prudent goal. On the way back to the farm, Fergus told me that Highlander's believe if a person could find out the exact proportion of whisky that ought to be drunk every day, and keep to that, one could live forever and all doctors and graveyards would go out of business."

I swallowed a spoonful of soup and snapped, "I would appreciate it if you did not make light of my condition."

"I apologize. Now finish your soup. According to Fiona, a bowl of hot lamb and barley soup will cure most of life's ills."

With each spoonful of the potage both my head and stomach were making great strides toward normalcy. "My dear, extend my gratitude to Fiona for her sound medical advice."

SEVEN

Bear Zabarte-Pitlochry, Scotland

I popped the cap of a Scottish Cream beer and looked around the living room of the old joint Fergus called the Croft cottage.

An hour ago, when Fergus pushed the three of us through the front door, he told me, "I think you'll be comfortable here. As you can see, the main room consists of a kitchen, a dining area, the wood stove, and a living area with a small telly. On the far wall there's a doorway that takes you to two bedrooms and a bathroom. Before I leave, I need to warn you of two minor problems. First, the north wall of the bathroom was dug into the hillside and we had to cease excavation once we hit solid rock. The second is an electrical wiring problem with the main bathroom circuit so the electric heater does not function. I fear you will find that room rather chilly."

Willow's cousin hit the nail on the head about that bathroom. The room was colder than a well digger's ass. Hell, you could see your breath there day and night. Trust me, the first time I sat on the john, the ice-covered rock wall was only a few feet from my bare knees so I put away the newspaper and finished my business before I froze to death.

Without saying a word, Flo grabbed the beer out of my hand.

"Hey, give that back. Belhaven Scottish Cream is my new favorite beer."

She said, "After you tell me what the trip to Edinburgh is all about. There'd better be room in that car for me. I'm not spending my days in Scotland sitting in this cottage sewing buttons on your shirts."

Shit! I forgot to tell Fergus that Flo was going with me and Pinky. "Don't worry, I'm sure—"

Flo said, "If Pinky, or that Fergus character want to clear up this case then they're going to take us as a pair or not at all. Now, finish your beer. We've got to unpack."

After Flo stuck all her bottles of perfume and stuff on the dresser, me, Flo, and the Kid walked over to the main house where we met Fergus' wife, Fiona, and their two boys. The Kid jumped right in and before we left the boys had invited her to go fishing at their secret spot on the creek tomorrow after school— a fishing hole, according to Fergus, known only to Highlander's with the last name of Murray.

The next morning we all got up, ran through the bathroom, and Flo warmed us up with a kick-ass breakfast of bacon and eggs. The Kid jumped up from the table, gave me and Flo a kiss, grabbed her jacket and sprinted out the door to meet up with the Murray boys so they could walk together to the school bus.

Flo watched the Kid through the window. "Ettamae fits in with those boys like they're her long lost brothers. Bringing her with us was the right thing."

"But what about her grandpa?"

"When he's finished with his rehab, I'm sure Pinky will pay for an airplane ticket so he can join us."

"You must be thinking about another Pinky Delmont. The bastard I work for wouldn't do that for his own grandfather."

"Don't worry. I'll work it out. Look, Fergus is backing out of his garage."

While we waited at the front door, I tried to come up with a cool way to convince Fergus that Flo should tag along.

The driver's window rolled down and Fergus said, "Mr. Zabarte, get in or we are going to be late."

I opened the back door and pushed Flo in. "Fergus, Flo's coming with us."

The crinkly lines at the top of Fergus' nose said no. "Mr. Zabarte, I do not know a delicate way to broach this subject, so I'll just say my piece. I do not take lightly to two unmarried adults living under the same roof."

Flo pushed me aside. "Look, buster. I dropped everything I was doing back home to come to this god-forsaken place to help you out, so I'll just say my piece. You accept us as a couple or not at all. And come to think of it, Pinky and Willow are not married. How does your screwed up value system deal with that?"

Fergus frowned, glanced at his watch, and said, "Close the door. We're going to be late."

I'll be damned. Flo stared Fergus down and he blinked. Wow! We jumped in the backseat. I said, "Hi, Pinky. How's the joint with you and Willow working out?"

"Not up to my usual standards, but under the

circumstances, acceptable. Now shut up and let me look at the scenery."

"Gotcha. Fergus, how far is Edinburgh from your farm?"

"About seventy miles. We will drive south to Perth and then take the M90 into Edinburgh."

Both dudes in the front seat acted like they were pissed-off at something 'cause they didn't say a word until the traffic backed up. I said, "Think there's an accident ahead?"

Fergus said, "Nay. Traffic always backs up at the bridge that crosses the Firth of Forth."

I said, "The what of what?"

Flo said, "The Firth of Forth is the estuary or firth of Scotland's River Forth—where the river flows into the North Sea."

Fergus said, "Madam, I am surprised to discover you are so versed on Scotland. Have you visited Edinburgh before?"

"I have, but never in an investigative role. How about you?"

"Many times, but never in an official role. I'm attached to the Tayside Police Force. The city of Edinburgh lies outside my jurisdiction."

Pinky jumped in. "I'm glad you mentioned jurisdictional boundaries. I'm confused. The body was found in Pitlochry, so why didn't the Pitlochry police handle the murder investigation?"

"Town's too small. It's part of the Western Division, one of a multitude of wee communities that make up Tayside. In the event of a major incident, such as this murder inquiry, the case would be turned over to the Western Area Crime Officer."

Flo said, "How big is the Tayside force?"

Fergus might be pissed off at me and Flo but she seemed to know the questions to ask to get on his good side.

Fergus said, "We are the fourth largest in Scotland. My Chief Superintendent is headquartered in Dundee. My office is in Perth."

I said, "And you're the top dude investigating the murder of the young girl found on the Pitlochry golf course, right?"

A tiny smile cracked the hard mask of Fergus' face. "In Scotland I go by the title of Western Area Crime Officer, but I can understand if you want to call me the top dude involved in the Mary Patterson murder."

We passed under a road sign that told me we were in the right lane for Edinburgh and Pinky said, "I suppose a city the size of Edinburgh has its own police force."

Fergus nodded. "Aye, they do. In fact, the moment my vehicle crossed the River Forth, we left my jurisdictional boundaries."

Flo said, "Did you have to call Edinburgh's Chief Superintendent and tell him you're coming?"

Fergus' mask went hard again and his neck turned bright red. Shit, this time Flo must have put her foot in it.

Even dumb old Pinky picked up that Fergus was pissed again and he tried to change the subject. "I suppose you and Fiona occasionally drive to Edinburgh for fun. What do you do in the city? Go to the theater? Concerts?"

"To tell the truth, Delmont, I'm just a country boy. I'd rather take Fiona and the boys salmon fishing on the Tummel."

As we headed into town the roads got narrower with cars parked on both sides. It didn't take me long to figure out that driving in Scotland was a whole lot easier than riding on the wrong side of the road. Fergus was an okay driver, but I kept ducking every time a parked car flashed by my window.

While he drove, Fergus got quieter than the stone wall in our bathroom. Finally, he cleared his throat, pulled out a paper from his coat pocket, and handed it over his shoulder to me. "Zabarte, I thought you'd be interested in looking over the original Mis-Per report on Mary Patterson."

I grabbed the sheet and looked at an old, beat-up piece of paper that had been filled out in pencil. Other than the name, Mary Patterson, I couldn't read any of it.

I handed the form to Flo and said, "Wow, even Carson City has a computer system that—"

Fergus barked, "Mr. Zabarte, we are a poor but proud land. Many of the advances you have in America simply don't exist in my country."

Pinky reached back, snatched the paper out of Flo's hands, and said, "Are you telling me that you don't have a common database for something as simple as a missing person report?"

"Missing persons, murder, rape, you name it. Delmont, we don't have a central database for any criminal activity in this country. That's why I've come to Edinburgh."

Pinky said, "I can't imagine running anything, something even as small as my one-man law practice, without a computer."

Flo snorted, "As if you have a clue concerning any aspect of the world outside of a courtroom!"

Fergus said, "Pardon my interruption, but we need to change the subject and discuss Miller and Urquhart before we arrive. The North Sea oil discovery made Scotland a major center for an explosion of work opportunities. Some of our quiet little villages suddenly took on the aura of a boomtown, similar to your California gold mining areas a hundred and fifty years ago. And once we blended in groups of roustabouts, roughnecks, and whatever into the gentle, peace-loving Scottish population, mayhem increased."

Flo said, "Gentle peace-loving Scots? Come on, Fergus, you people have been killing each other for centuries. You can't fool me, I saw <u>Braveheart</u>."

He snickered, "Aye, starring that faux Scot, Mel Gibson. As I was saying, since the North Sea oil strike there's been a huge demand for workers in Northern Scotland and that brings us to the firm of Miller and Urquhart, Ltd. They have been in the business of supplying contract workers for more than a hundred and fifty years, and as you'll see, they maintain impeccable records in their archives."

Flo said, "I don't understand. Why didn't you just pick up a phone, call Miller and Urquhart, and ask who worked the Pitlochry job ten years ago?"

Fergus snapped, "My dear woman, that's what I have been attempting to explain to you."

We drove in silence for a moment and then Fergus resumed in a softer voice. "I'm sorry I jumped at you, but I'm tired of Americans coming here and telling us that everything we do in Scotland is out-of-date. Many of the old firms, like Miller and Urquhart, do business in an old fashioned, pre-computer way. Although they maintain impeccable records, finding what we are looking for will require human interaction with a person who knows what he or she is doing, along with a bit of luck. You'll see for yourself in a few minutes."

Flo said, "Could you define what you mean by 'a pre-computer way'?"

"I will try but first, you need to consider Scotland's relative age compared to America. We Scots know all about the modern ways, but we don't have the money or the time to go back and input thousands of years of records into a computer. Last year, in Tayside, we started to input every new investigation into a data base. Now all we have to do is pull out all the old records and input the last two thousand years."

Flo leaned forward. "As I said, I don't see how—
"

Fergus said, "Quick, on your right, that's Holyroodhouse, The Queen's official residence in Scotland."

I looked out the window and for a second forgot about the murder of Mary Patterson. My first real castle! I wondered what Pop would think? I said, "Fergus, what are those round things near the roof?"

Fergus laughed. "Turrets, and when the Queen is in residence the peaks of those turrets will sport a special flag."

I said, "Come on. Does a real Queen live there?"

"Aye, she does when she's in Scotland on official business. You know, she's the Queen of the United Kingdom and the United Kingdom includes England, Wales, Northern Ireland, and Scotland. Ah, here we are, the headquarters of Miller and Urquhart."

He pulled into an empty parking spot, and when

we reached the front door, Fergus pulled open a giant oak slab of wood that was about twelve feet tall and three inches thick. Fergus announced our arrival to a cute broad who sat behind the counter. The young babe had creamy skin, freckles, red hair, and really, really nice boobs.

Flo gave me an elbow in the ribs and said, "Get your mind off her chest and back on the Mary Patterson investigation."

Before I could elbow her back, the cute redhead took us through a big door, not much smaller than the one out front.

We walked into an office and I sort of blinked at my first sight of the dude sitting behind a desk. The sign on his desk told me he was James Urquhart, and my eyes told me he was old. I don't mean getting old—I don't mean sort of old—I mean this dude had to be at least a hundred and ten. Without a doubt, he had to be the oldest guy I had ever seen who was still sucking air.

Thin strings of white hair looked like they had been glued to his bald head. The skin on his face had about as much color as a defrosted frozen turkey. His head wobbled on hunched shoulders. Really, the dude looked like he was two quick heartbeats from ending up on the wrong side of the grass.

The old guy stuck his hand toward Fergus, and said softly, "Officer Murray, it's been a long time since your last visit."

Urquhart's bushy white eyebrows bounced up and down while he checked out the rest of us. Finally his gaze stopped at Flo. "And these people . . . ?"

Pinky was first. "J. Pincus Delmont from America."

He nodded but his peepers never left Flo's boobs, proving that even a white-haired coot was never too old. He waved one of his bony fingers that we should sit down. "Ah yes. It's about time we get over that revolutionary thing and learn how to deal with you Americans."

"And I'm Bear and this is Flo."

The old dude nodded. Finally, he pulled his eyes off Flo and back to Fergus. "Now what can I do for you?"

Fergus handed Urquhart the Pitlochry Golf Club invoice. "Your firm did some work at the Pitlochry Golf Club approximately ten years ago. This is a copy of your final invoice. I would appreciate it if you would have someone search through your records and give me the name or names of the men who did the work."

Urquhart's beady, black eyes scanned back and forth between Fergus, the paper, and Flo's chest. Finally, he picked up the phone and a bony finger pushed one button. "Denzler, come in."

The door opened and a round, white-haired woman entered. She looked old enough to be Urquhart's older sister. He sat up. Suddenly, his voice got real strong. "Denzler, these people need to find the name of a man who worked on a job in the Highlands some years ago. Take them to the archives."

The old broad nodded, took the paper from his hand, and walked slowly out of the room.

"Now is there anything else I can help you with?"

Fergus rose from his chair. "No. Thank you, sir. I'm sure Mrs. Denzler will find the name I'm looking for."

Me, Flo, and Pinky followed Fergus out of the office where Mrs. Denzler was waiting. She said in a small voice, "Falla may."

I whispered to Flo, "What'd she say?"

"Clear the wax out of your ears. She said follow me."

The four of us trailed after the old broad down a long dark hall and through a doorway. The room was darker then the inside of a black dog, and damp, sort of like one of those dungeons in that Queen's castle we passed on the way here. Denzler grunted and a single, yellowed light bulb came on. As my eyeballs adjusted, I saw that we were in a big room, maybe a hundred by a hundred feet, and it was filled with rows, and rows, and rows of wooden file cabinets. As far as I could tell all the cabinets were painted the same gray. That's when it hit me what Fergus was saying about the pre-computer way of doing business.

Mrs. Denzler stared at the invoice for a minute and shook her head slowly. "This wa tak a bit. Sta' 'ere."

Fergus looked at Flo and whispered, "As I told you in the car, the information age hasn't quite reached the firm of Miller and Urquhart."

We stood under the single yellow bulb while the old broad shuffled off into the dark. Just about the time she was going to disappear, she turned left behind a wall of file cabinets. Because she was so short, as she cruised down the wall, her head would disappear, but once in a while, we'd see the top of her white hair pop up. Once she found what she was looking for, I'd watch her hand reach up, pull a dangling string, and a weak bulb would light up the area.

Flo whispered, "Fergus, I'll go along with your statement about the information age, but banks of fluorescent lights have been around for a long time."

"Shhh."

I stood there and tried to follow Denzler as she cruised through the dark, but mostly I heard her work her way around the room.

Click, a light would go out.

Shuffle—shuffle—shuffle.

Click, a light would go on.

A drawer would open, then another, then the drawers would close with a loud bang.

Click, a light would go out.

Shuffle—shuffle—shuffle.

She wandered around that way for about fifteen minutes and then we heard her tiny voice say, "Aye, air 'tis."

She killed the last light and shuffled back to us, opened the door, and we all tumbled into the hall.

"The workman's nam's Gordon Tanna'ill. 'cordin to this," she waved one of the papers, "dnina work for us anymar. We sent 'is final chick to The Stronvaar 'otel in Aberdeen."

Fergus smiled and asked, "Could you make us a copy of that please?"

She nodded, set the sheet down on the counter, walked to the opposite wall, plugged the copy machine cord into the wall socket, and hummed a little tune as she waited for the copier to warm up.

While we waited for the broad to make the copy, I glanced down at the sheet she had left on the counter. Reading as best I could upside-down, I saw

56

a bunch of dates and jobs for a dude called Gordon Tannahill. I elbowed Flo. She eyeballed the sheet and waved it at Denzler. "Hold on. We'll need two copies of this."

The old broad stopped in her tracks, like that was the first time another woman had ever talked to her. She glanced at me, then at Flo's hand holding the paper, but didn't make a move. Her eyes darted to Fergus. After a moment, Fergus nodded and Denzler grabbed the paper from Flo and made two copies.

Fergus took both copies and said, "Mrs. Denzler, please express my appreciation to Mr. Urquhart for his assistance and thank you for all your help."

I sort of ran for the door to clear out of that spooky place. Once we strapped ourselves into Fergus' car, Flo laughed. "That was fun, like watching an old 1940's English movie, but I still think a simple phone call could have achieved the same results."

Fergus flashed Flo what I think was his nasty look. "As I tried to tell you, we do things differently in Scotland. I'd say we had a very productive day. We have the suspect's name, Gordon Tannahill, and his last known address, The Stronvaar Hotel in Aberdeen."

He pulled out a pocket calendar, glanced back and forth between a couple of pages, and frowned. "I have to attend a conference on improving Police-Community relations tomorrow. If you're still interested, we could run up to Aberdeen the following day."

Flo said, "Why wait until the day after tomorrow? What if Tannahill decides to skip?"

"Madam, what is your Christian name?"

"Florence."

"Excellent. I am pleased to have discovered an American who does not hide behind the cloak of a nickname. During your stay in Scotland, may I address you as Florence?"

Flo smiled. "You may call me Florence or Flo. What ever turns you on."

For the first time since we met, I noticed a tiny smile crinkle Fergus' mouth before he said, "Now, back to our investigation. Mary Patterson's body was buried next to the tenth hole ten years ago. Florence, if a man named Gordon Tannahill turns out to be the killer of Mary Patterson, do you think he would be ignorant enough to sit in the lobby of the Stronvaar Hotel for the last decade waiting for me to arrest him? I think not. The day following my conference will be soon enough."

EIGHT

Pinky Delmont-Pitlochry, Scotland

After a brief drive around Edinburgh, a route Fergus designated his 'tourist loop', he dropped me off at the apartment around four-thirty. Willow had not arrived so I laid down on the couch to take a well deserved power nap when the phone rang. I picked it up, guessing that Willow was calling me.

"Pinky, C. Thomas Hennessy here."

"Hennessy? You have interrupted a moment where I was collecting my thoughts after a particularly trying day of investigation. I trust your call will prove more important."

"I apologize because I neglected to consider the time difference."

Through the miracle of one of Scotland's genius exports, Alexander Graham Bell, Hennessy sounded as if he were standing by my side. "No problem, my boy, it's late afternoon here. I trust the weather in Carson City is better than it is in Pitlochry. Yesterday, while standing on a golf course with Willow and her cousin Fergus, a wild and frigid storm caught us unawares. Then this morning I spent—hold on a minute. Why are you calling? I gave you specific instructions not to interrupt me except in a case of extreme emergency. What has happened?"

"When I arrived at the office this morning, there was a large man waiting in the parking lot."

"A large man? You will have to do better than that. What was his name?"

"He did not offer me a name. He told me he needed to talk to you at once—it was a matter of life or death. I told him you were unavailable. Then—I know this will sound a bit insane, but I'm trying to tell you everything as it happened—the man, right there in the parking lot, grabbed both my arms, lifted me up, and shook me as if I were a rag doll. After he set me down, the brute demanded to know where you were. Frankly, his aggressive behavior upset me, but I am pleased that my common sense reminded me to not react in a combative way."

C. Thomas Hennessy a combatant? This was becoming funnier by the minute. "Go on, my boy."

"After he completed his physical threat, the brute pulled me toward him, I brushed against his chest and the man had a weapon concealed under his coat."

My stomach tightened. "A weapon?"

"Pinky, that was when I knew that we were in trouble."

"We were in trouble?"

"Actually, you are the one he is looking for, but as your single representative in Carson City, I felt I must include myself in the threat."

"Go on, what happened then?"

"He gave me twenty-four hours to tell him where you are hiding or else."

"Or else what?"

"I did not ask for a more definitive answer, nor did he offer one. However, the man was very fit—

capable of physical harm with his bare hands—and then there was the concealed weapon. Now you know why I called. What should I do?"

Could Hennessy be talking about the hit man from Vegas? No. He was large, but no one would consider that thug fit. "Describe the man who accosted you."

"Over six feet tall. Very muscular with broad shoulders. Females might consider him handsome, but his lips curled in a way that gave him a permanent, sardonic expression."

Oh my God, Hennessy had just painted a portrait of Ice Conner, the rogue cop who last year escaped from Bear's incarceration outside of Laughlin, Nevada. "Did you call the police?"

"No, because he told me if I called them he would find out, and then he would be forced to pull out my fingernails, one by one, and then kill me to put me out of my misery."

I was positive that Conner was persona non grata with Carson City law enforcement, but he could still have an informant or two inside the force. "Hennessy, from your description, I believe I know who you met in the parking lot and if I am right, do not, I repeat, do not call the police. I will discuss this phone call with my associates and call you back in a few hours with further instructions."

His sigh of relief was audible over the five-thousand-mile phone connection. "Pinky, I am a young man taking the first steps along what I presume will be a long, and successful legal career so I will withhold making a final decision until I receive your phone call. However, if I am not one hundred percent satisfied with your potential solution, my next step will be to pack my meager belongings into my vehicle and drive east until I reach the Atlantic Ocean."

The phone went dead and my knees buckled. As I slumped into a chair Willow opened the front door and walked in.

"Hi. How was your trip to Edinburgh?"

I took a deep breath. "Forget Edinburgh. We have a serious problem on our hands."

I informed her of the call from Hennessy. The color of Willow's face faded from her normal creamy-white to a ghostly hue.

She said, "Bear was right. That night, on the desert outside of Laughlin, he tried to convince me that Ice was dangerous. Get Bear on the phone. I'm sure the three of us can come up with some kind of a solution to this problem."

NINE

Bear Zabarte-Pitlochry, Scotland

I was freezing my ass off, sitting on the ice cold bathroom floor, trying to figure out the damned bathroom heater, when I gave up and drained the last of my beer. To tell the truth, I didn't know a thing about electrical wiring but I had to try to do something before a really important part of me froze off. After I popped the cap off my third bottle of Scottish Cream, I heard a loud noise, like a tree or a car crashed into the front door of the cottage.

Flo hissed, "Bear, get out here and be quiet. You need to see this."

I ran out of mother nature's ice box and across the living room as quietly as I could. Flo was standing by the window and she motioned to me to hurry over. She pulled the curtain back a bit and I peeked out. Standing on our front steps was a short, stocky dude, dressed in brown pants and a heavy green coat. He had white hair that sort of lifted a brown cap off his head. In his right hand, he held a big wooden stick, bigger than a baseball bat and while I watched, he smashed the door again with the fat end of the club.

Flo whispered to me. "Who is it?"

"Got me, but I'm going to find out." I opened the door a crack and stuck my number twelve behind it, sort of like I had a doorstop attached to my leg. "Hi. What's up?"

The man grabbed the cap off his head, lowered his club, and didn't say a word. The left side of his face looked okay but the right side was all messed up—not bleeding or anything—sort of like five years ago he'd been in an ax fight without an axe. The lower half of his right ear was gone and a large scar went up from his half-ear to his forehead, then down through his right eye socket, and ended at the corner of his mouth. The wonky thing was that his left eye looked directly at me but his right eye cruised around, first looking up and then down, like the damn thing had a mind of it's own.

"Mornin'. My name's 'Enry Bramble." His blue-gray left eye was locked on me. He cocked his head slightly, looked over my shoulder and spotted Flo. For a second I thought about slamming the door in his face before he could bash me over the head with his club, but I decided he was just another old dude with a screwed-up face. "Glad to meet you, Bramble. What do you want?"

He rubbed his chin, and said, "You dinna know me, sir?"

I had to force myself to stop staring at his wandering eye while I tried to figure out his thick accent. "I'm sorry, Bramble, if you just asked me if I know you, the answer is no. I don't have a clue who you are. Should I?"

"Aye. Dinna you see me at the gulf course the day you were there?"

What the hell was he talking about? I made sure my foot still blocked the door and checked out this old dude. Once I got beyond his face and the club in his hand, he seemed harmless enough. "Sorry, Bramble. We've never met before this morning. Do you live around here?"

"Aye. You see I walk the gulf course every day searchin' for lost balls. I saw you the day you walked into the clubhouse with your woman."

Flo pushed her way past me. "Mr. Bramble, let's get one thing straight. I'm not his woman, what ever that means."

I said. "I'm sorry, Bramble, I didn't see you there. What can we do for you this morning?"

His body shivered in the frosty air and he said, "A cuppa would be brilliant."

I hesitated. Between the massive scar, his wild right eye, and the heavy club, I wasn't sure if Flo wanted him in the cottage, but didn't know what else to do. "Come in, Bramble. Would you like me to pop the top on a Scottish cream?"

Flo snorted, "Bear, you're the only man crazy enough to drink beer on a freezing day. I'll put the kettle on."

"Thank you, ma'am."

He walked in, headed straight toward the wood stove and warmed his hands. "'Fraid I'm not as young as I use to be."

The water in the teapot, sitting on the top of the wood stove, got hot real fast so Flo had two cups of tea sitting on the table in a minute. She said, "Do you care for milk or sugar, Mr. Bramble?"

"Aye."

He sat down and dropped his cap and club on the table. I pushed the pitcher with cream and the bowl of sugar to his side of the table. While the dude poured cream and two giant spoonfuls of sugar into his cup, I sat down across from him. He wrapped his stubby fingers around the cup, and held it tight for a minute, like his hands were still cold. As he and Flo took their first sip of tea, I tried to figure what he was all about. We're a good mile off the main highway. I didn't hear a car drive up. The dude didn't just drop from the sky, and he seemed to be here for a reason.

Flo said, "Care for more tea, Mr. Bramble?"

"Nay, and you can call me 'Enry."

I reached across the table. He gripped my hand. "My name is Bear and she's Flo." His hand was one big callus. This was a dude who had worked hard all his life, like digging ditches with a shovel, that kind of hard work.

He said, "I know who you are. You're a kin to Fergus."

"Actually, it's the boss' wife, Willow, who is Fergus' cousin. But how do you know all this? We only got here a few days ago."

"Every day, after I walk the course searching for lost gulf balls, I stop by the police station for a cuppa. Sergeant McKinlay told me all about you Americans and how you were coming to help Fergus solve the murder."

Jesus, if this old dude knows what we're here for then everyone knows. "Do you spend a lot of time at the police station?"

"Aye. They make a fine cuppa."

Flo said, "Henry, what sort of work do you do?"

"I used to be a Forester, but 'ad a wicked accident. Now I'm a Beadle at the local Church."

I said, "Beetle? What the hell does being a bug have to do with work?"

Flo said, "Pipe down and let the man speak. What are your job duties at the church, Henry?"

"I stop by the parish each day to do what needs to be done. 'Tis an important job, ma'am. I'm a parish officer. I 'elp to keep order during the service. Once in a while, I'll drive the minister to a funeral."

The dude seemed harmless enough and I still had to try to fix that damned heater. I jumped up. "Henry, thanks for stopping by this morning. Down right neighborly of you. Come by again. Anytime you're in the area."

He grabbed the skinny end of his club, crashed it onto the table. The tea cups, cream pitcher, and sugar bowl all jumped around but nothing fell off the table. "We 'ave not finished our talk yet."

Flo chirped out a squeak as I grabbed Henry's arm that held the club. "Put that damn thing down or I'll pick you up, club and all, and chuck your sorry ass out the front door."

Henry's wild eye tried to focus on my hand. "Let go of my walking stick."

"Not until you agree to stop smashing our kitchen table."

"Aye. I agree."

I let go of his arm. He laid the club he called his walking stick on the floor and started to rub the scar that ran down the right side of his head.

I said, "Okay, now what is it you want to talk about?"

"'Tis about the wee lass the police found at the gulf course."

I sat back and took a long look at the dude sitting across the table. "What about her, Henry?"

He sat in the chair and his fingers worked up

and down the scar tissue like it was bread dough. "First, when 'er bones were uncovered, the police dinna leave 'er alone in the rain. Good on them. Second, you need to know that all the town people appreciate the kindness you've done crossing the Atlantic to find 'er killer."

As the old dude talked I spotted a tear fall out of his crushed eye socket and tumble down his right cheek.

Flo said, "I can understand how you feel, Henry. We have a young daughter."

"Aye, your kin, Ettamae. Right now she's in school with the Murray boys."

Flo frowned. "Henry, I don't know how you know where Ettamae is, but a man of your age should know it's not polite to spy on . . . hold on, did you know the young girl whose body was found on the golf course?"

"Aye, 'er name was Mary Patterson. She was reported missin' by 'er da, James Patterson, 'bout ten years ago." He tapped his finger on the table for emphasis, "And that's what I'm 'ere to talk about."

I set my beer down. This old coot knew a whole lot more than he should about little girls, both dead and alive. Maybe he killed Mary, wrapped her body in that fancy Scottish blanket, and . . . nah, that would be too easy. But just in case I guessed right, I stepped on his club with my shoe and said, "Go ahead, Henry, what do you want to tell us about Mary?"

His hand nervously went back to rubbing his right ear as he whispered, "I dinna think Mary's the only one."

Flo's mouth dropped open. "I don't think I

understood you. Would you repeat that?"

He said, "Mary's not the only lass from 'ere who was murdered !"

I said, "You're kidding."

He brushed a tear from his cheek. "No! Mary's just one of three lasses that 'ave been murdered. The police ignore me 'cause they think I'm a crazy old man while the devil 'imself walks the streets of Pitlochry searching for 'is next victim."

TEN

Bear Zabarte-Pitlochry, Scotland

Henry's words hit me like a ton of bricks. The old coot with the wonky eye claimed there were three murders in Pitlochry—like there was a Scottish serial killer running loose.

The phone rang.

I glanced at Flo and her lips were quivering, like she was thinking about catching a fly.

Henry's right eye bounced around.

On the third ring, I grabbed the receiver. "Hello."

"Bear, this is Fiona. When I walked past the cottage just now, I noticed a bike parked by your front door. Do you have company?"

"Yup. An old dude named Henry Bramble. Do you know him?"

"Everyone in Pitlochry knows Henry. What's he doing so far from home?"

"I don't know. Where does he live?"

"A touch north of Pitlochry in a wee cottage near the Clunie Footbridge."

"I thought Pitlochry was six miles from your farm."

"Aye, it is."

I put my hand over the phone and said, "Henry, did you ride a bike here this morning?"

"Aye."

"It's colder than a witches tit out there. If I tried that I'd freeze."

"Aye."

Fiona said, "Bear, I have a doctor's appointment in Pitlochry in a few minutes. I can put Henry's bike in the boot and give him a ride back to town. I hate to rush your visit but I have to leave soon, otherwise I'll be late."

"Thanks. I'll let Henry know you'll be by as soon as I hang up."

"No problem. Everyone in the area does what they can to help the poor man. I'll be there in a jiffy."

Help the poor man? "Hold on, Fiona. What do you mean, help him?"

"He's harmless enough, but ever since the accident he's been a wee bit off in the head."

"So you're telling me that all his stories about the murdered girls are just BS?"

"Bear, I'm just a simple farm girl in Scotland so I'm not up on the latest American slang, but if BS means a fabrication, then you are on the right track."

"Thanks. I'll tell Henry you'll pick him up." I hung up the phone. "Henry, what makes you think Mary's death is part of a series of murders?"

"'Bout twelve years ago, a lass named Margaret Struan disappeared and she was never 'eard from again. One year later, Kerry Claydon vanished. Then the next year, Mary—"

"Did the police ever find Margaret's or Kerry's body?"

"Nay, but 'tis important you understand that the three lasses were twelve and thirteen, all 'bout the same age, when they—"

There was a light rap on the front door, the door opened and Fiona poked her head in. "Sorry Henry, but if you're riding back to town with me, we'll have to leave right now or I'll be late."

He reached out, gave my hand a heavy squeeze and headed out the front door toward Fiona's car.

As he dumped his bike into the trunk, the old dude turned and said, "You and Flo listened to my whole story and I thank you for tha'. Now find the killer and I'll petition the Queen to grant you membership into the Order of the Thistle. Bear, tha' would make you a Knight of the Thistle, and Flo would be a Lady of the same order."

Flo said, "What's he going on about?"

"Don't have a clue."

Just before Henry got in Fiona's car, he turned, waved his walking stick in the air, and said, "*Nemo me impune lacessit.*"

Flo yelled, "Fiona, do you understand what Henry just said?"

"Aye. It's Latin and roughly translates to, 'No one attacks me without punishment.'"

"Babe, I still don't get it. What's the old dude trying to tell us?"

Henry rolled his window down and yelled, "We canna' fear what the devil will do to us when we corner 'im."

Flo shrugged her shoulders. "Got me."

As Fiona's car pulled away, I yelled, "Thanks, Henry! I'm sure we'll do whatever the hell it is you just told us to do."

I stood in the cold air and thought about what Henry had said. Three teen age Pitlochry girls disappear without a trace. It could be a coincidence, but I should run this story by Fergus first, to see if he knew anything about . . . the phone rang again.

I ran inside grabbed the receiver. "Hello."

"Mr. Zabarte, we're in luck."

"Fergus, I was just thinking about you."

"Good thoughts I hope."

"I guess. What do you want?"

"Do you remember that community relations conference I was going to attend? It now seems I am not required. If you and Florence are up to a very long trip, I'm driving north to Aberdeen tomorrow morning to pursue the lead on Gordon Tannahill. You're welcome to join me."

"How far is Aberdeen from here?"

"A long way, a little more than a hundred miles."

A hundred miles? I wanted to tell him that when I was in high school, living in Elko, Nevada, I'd drive damn near that far just to take my date to a first-run movie. But I figured the Scottish dude had more things on his mind than listening to stories of my life when I was a kid. I said, "We're game. What time do we leave?"

"See you at eight. Now, go ahead, Mr. Zabarte, it's your turn."

"We'll have plenty of time to talk about that during the long ride tomorrow, but I have one thing that's bugging the crap out of me. Ever since I got here, I've called you Fergus, not Mr. Murray. So cut the Mr. Zabarte, okay?"

"In Scotland, common courtesy demands we do not address someone by his nickname until we have known that person for many years."

"I'll make you a deal. All you have to do is count

each day we've known each other as five years. Okay?"

"As you wish, Mr. Za . . . Bear."

I hung up the phone and before I got my hand off the receiver, the damn thing rang again. I figured, shit, that's probably Fergus telling me that he just figured out it's against his religion to call me Bear. "Hello!"

"Bear! I've been trying to call you and your phone has been busy. Do not forget that you are here on my largess and as such I expect you to sit quietly and stay off the phone until I give you an important a task. Are we clear?"

What a pain in the ass! "Sure, Boss. Did Fergus call you about the drive to Aberdeen tomorrow morning?"

"Forget that. Get a hold of that woman of yours and come to my apartment at once."

"What's the problem?"

"Ice Conner just showed up in Carson City and he's gunning for you and Willow."

"No shit! I'll grab a couple of beers and we'll be there in a flash."

ELEVEN

Pinky Delmont-Pitlochry, Scotland

Five minutes and thirty-seven seconds passed
before Bear and Flo arrived at my doorstep. Willow
greeted them and I escorted everyone to the kitchen
where we sat around the brand-new white pine table.
Although we were thousands of miles from Carson
City, I detected a touch of fear concerning the
potential threat of Ice Conner in the eyes of Willow,
Flo, and even Bear.

Bear set three bottles of beer in front of him,
popped the top off one, and gulped down more than
he should have in polite company. "Okay, Boss,
what's the scoop?"

"First, a true gentleman would offer a beverage
to those close to him."

"Huh? Oh! Anybody else want a beer?"

I said, "It is too late to correct your faux pas so I
will move on. An hour ago, I received a phone call
from Thomas Hennessy. In case it has slipped your
mind, he's the lad to whom I turned over titular
control of my law practice while I am in Scotland."

"Boss, I forget. What does that titular thing
mean again?"

"My good man, simply stated, and in your case
anything beyond a simple statement would exceed
your mental capacity, and for the sake of all those

present, I will, once again, explain—"

Flo jumped up and nearly tipped over the kitchen table. "What the hell do you mean, for my sake? Pinky, I'll have you know that you are addressing the woman who was given the John Donne award for achieving the largest lexicon at my university."

Bear, his eyes locked on that woman's pair of attributes, said, "Wow, I never heard anyone call those baby's lexicons before. I thought lexicons were those little Irish people."

I said, "Enough tomfoolery. Titular means Hennessy has control without any real authority. Now, may I proceed?"

"Yup."

"Thomas informed me that he was accosted by a large man outside my office and the thug's description fit Ice Conner perfectly."

Flo said, "You called us over for this? Tell that shrimp shyster to call the cops. They'll arrest Ice and—"

"That was my first thought," I said. "However, I fear that action could force Conner back underground and I would rather know where he is than remain in the dark."

Bear said, "Hey, I can handle that dude when we get back home so forget him. Now, have I got a story for you. An hour ago an old fart pounded on our door and—"

Willow said, "Bear, we're not finished with Ice Conner. I should have listened to you when you expressed your concerns about him that night on the desert. Now, much too late, I understand why we should have pursued him and put the man behind bars."

Bear said, "Water under the bridge, Babe. Now, about that old dude who—"

I said, "My good man, I am in charge of this meeting! Back to Ice Conner. We need to come up with a possible modus operandi."

Bear drained the liquid from the last bottle and slammed the empty on the table. "Boss, what's an opera got to do with anything?"

I sighed. By now I should understand that one gets what one pays for. I made a mental note to begin the replacement process for an investigator with a higher IQ upon my return to Carson City. "My boy, modus operandi is not an opera. Now, my proposal concerning Ice Conner is to ignore him. The man does not know our present location and as long as he remains ignorant, he is not a problem. Do we all agree?"

Everyone nodded.

I said, "Go ahead, my boy. What about the elderly person who knocked on your door this morning?"

"After the Kid left for school, an old dude tried to bash our door down with a club."

Flo said, "There you go exaggerating again. He knocked on our door with his walking stick."

"Shit, that walking stick was bigger than a baseball bat. Anyway, the old coot's name was Henry Bramble."

Willow said, "Did he resemble a big gnome dressed in green and brown and was he riding a bike?"

Flo said, "He did have a bike. How did you know that?"

"I was jogging and saw him riding down the highway toward the Murray farm. What did he want?"

Flo said, "It's a long story. When you saw him were you close enough to see the right side of his face?"

"No. What about it?"

Bear said, "The poor bastard had an accident of some kind and I don't mind telling you, the right side of Henry's face looks like a plate of ground round cooked medium rare. But that's not the most important part about the dude. He's sure that the murder of Mary Patterson is just one of three girls who were murdered in Pitlochry over the last twelve years."

Willow sat up abruptly. "My God! Does the man have any proof?"

Flo said, "No, and worse than no proof, everybody in town, including Fiona and Fergus, knows Henry and they all think he's off his rocker."

I said, "Bear, you talked to him. What's your take?"

"Boss, I don't know. There were times when he didn't seem right. Like when he rambled on about the devil himself walking the streets of Pitlochry."

I had heard enough. "Team, it is time we move on. Tomorrow Fergus takes us to Aberdeen. Are we up for the trip?"

Willow said, "I'm not going. Fiona asked me to help her redecorate her kitchen. This may sound crazy to you all, but as a District Attorney I never find the time to work with my hands. My father was a cabinet maker and some of my fondest memories are helping him in his shop. I truly miss those days so the three of you go ahead and find the bad guy. I'm going to spend my day stripping off old paint from kitchen cabinets."

"Are you two going?"

Flo said, "I've never been to Aberdeen. I wouldn't miss the trip for anything."

"Me too," said Bear, "and the long drive will give me the chance to pump Fergus for more skinny about the Bramble dude."

"I agree. Now clear out of my apartment so Willow and I can have some peace and quiet before dinner."

TWELVE

Bear Zabarte-Pitlochry, Scotland

The alarm went off and Flo jumped out of bed. I rolled over and listened to the sound of rain bang against our bedroom window.

Flo said, "Get up. Rain or no rain, we're on semi-official police business now that we've become irreplaceable members of Fergus' investigative team."

I opened one eye and copped a peek of Flo pulling her sweat shirt over her head. A minute later, once my heart stopped pounding, I said, "Does this whole deal seem sort of weird to you? Gordon Tannahill's last known address was a hotel in Aberdeen and that was ten years ago."

"Weird? Hell yes. My advice, sit back and enjoy the ride. I know people who pay big bucks for a personalized tour of Scotland."

Once Flo put her bra on, I headed to the john for my morning freeze. "I guess you're right."

At eight on the dot, Fergus pulled up outside our door. Pinky sat in the front so me and Flo climbed in the back again.

Fergus cranked the heater up, and we drove into the rain for our all-expense paid, hundred mile tour of Scotland.

Fergus said, "Florence, Bear, what do you know

about the city of Aberdeen?"

Before Flo could open her mouth, I said, "Zilch."

"The area around Aberdeen was first settled about eight thousand years ago. Today, the population exceeds two hundred thousand and Aberdeen is Scotland's gateway to the massive, rich North Sea oil fields. Would you be interested in more information?"

"Nah. I'll just look at the scenery." That turned out to be a dumb move 'cause out my window the rain turned everything I could see into three colors of gray.

The car rolled through the countryside.

The beat of the windshield wipers damn near put me to sleep.

Thunk—thunk.

Fergus was concentrating on the weather and wet roads and I tried to figure out how to bring up Henry Bramble's serial killer story. I knew Fergus wouldn't want to hear what I had to say 'cause that would mean the Tayside Police force had screwed up, big time.

Thunk—thunk.

And if they missed two more murders, I wondered if Fergus was the Western Area Crime Officer assigned to all of them.

Thunk—thunk.

As we drove past the town of Blairgowrie, Fergus cleared his throat and said, "Fiona informed me you had a visit from Henry Bramble yesterday."

Flo said, "I'm glad you brought up Henry's visit. He's quite a character. What ever happened to his face?"

"He was a forester. One day he was up a tree

trying to clear a large branch above his head. Suddenly the branch broke loose, smashed the right side of his face, and the poor soul fell to the ground. I went out to the accident site and by my reckoning, the man fell at least thirty feet. But Henry's a tough old bird. He got up, found the severed part of his ear, dropped it in his coat pocket, and walked more than a mile into town. It was a miracle he wasn't killed."

Thunk—thunk.

I closed my eyes and thought about how tough that old coot was. Fall thirty feet— get up off the ground—find the hunk of his ear, and walk into Pitlochry.

I said, "How long ago did his accident happen?"

"'Bout five years ago. The poor man has never been right in the head since."

Pinky said, "By not right in the head, are you implying that the man's not reliable?"

"I'm sure he told you the story about Pitlochry's serial killer who's murdered three lasses over the past twelve years. I believe he ends the tale with, 'The devil walks the streets of Pitlochry looking for his next victim.'"

I watched Fergus' face in the rear view mirror. His jaw was tighter than a banker's wallet—like someone who wasn't happy with the way this conversation was going. Something was really bugging the dude.

Thunk—thunk.

I said, "Henry told me he saw you at the golf course the morning the skeleton of Mary Patterson was found."

"Aye, that doesn't surprise me. He spends most mornings walking the course looking for lost balls.

He finds them, cleans them up, and then he sells them to golfers for half a quid each. They're good balls. I buy them myself when I get the chance."

"He said he stops by the police station each day."

"Aye. In fact, I've always suspected that the uniformed officers at the station give him a cuppa to get first crack at the best balls."

Flo leaned forward and fired a volley into Fergus' ear. "Fergus, move off the golf ball stories and tells us what think about multiple murders in Pitlochry?"

"As I said, Henry's a good man. He's a beadle at the parish, but I'm afraid the accident left him a bit daft. I investigated his wild theories, and trust me, Henry makes a better beadle than a detective."

There was a couple of minutes of silence, and then I said, "What did you find out about the other two girls?"

Fergus glared at me through the rear view mirror. "Damn it, Bear, I told you that I investigated those cases. As far as we could find, both girls just took off. I thought we already agreed that Pitlochry's not New York or Paris. The fact that we've found Mary's remains doesn't change my conclusion concerning the other two! Changing the subject, if anyone's interested, we're entering Kirriemuir, the birthplace of Sir James Barrie. It was over ninety years ago that he wrote the play <u>Peter Pan</u>. They have a wonderful exhibit here that I'm sure Ettamae would enjoy visiting."

I stared at the buildings through the rain. "Thanks. I'll let her know when we get back to the cottage."

Thunk-thunk.

I closed my eyes and a picture of Henry popped up in my head. He's standing at the top of a tall, wobbly ladder sawing away at a big branch on a tree. Then this little Peter Pan dude, just like he looked in the movie, flies around Henry. The ladder wiggles, and a bunch of golf balls start falling out of a hole in Henry's coat pocket. Peter Pan flies down and scoops up one of the balls before it hits the ground, and says, "Excuse me, Henry, are your golf balls still half a quid each? . . . "

"Have you heard any more from that fellow, Ice Conner?"

My eyes snapped open and I was surprised to see I was in the backseat of Fergus' car next to Flo, not in the forest with Henry and Peter Pan. I said, "Conner? What do you know about Ice Conner?"

Pinky said, "Bear, I took the liberty of including Fergus in the question of what we should do concerning Ice Conner."

Fergus said, "Yes, Delmont felt I should be aware of all possible ramifications."

Flo said, "Pinky, by now nothing you do should surprise me, but precisely what ramifications are you talking about?"

Thunk-thunk.

The front seat of the car got as quiet as me and my cousin at Grandma Zabarte's funeral.

Thunk-thunk.

Then Fergus grunted, "Go on, Delmont. After all, they are in as much danger as Willow."

"After our initial meeting in my apartment, I received a second call from Thomas. He informed me that someone had broken into my office."

Flo said, "Probably Ice. I still don't understand. Why does that change anything?"

Pinky said, "Ice knows where we are. And not just Scotland. He's tracked us down to the Murray farm outside of Pitlochry."

I said, "How in the hell did he do that?"

"Conner discovered some paper work with my cell number and Fergus' address. He threatened to fly to Scotland and shoot Willow because she cost him his job on the police force. Bear, I am not sure what you did to the man, but you are second on his list of people to shoot. However, there is one small glimmer of hope."

Flo said, "I can hardly wait."

Pinky said, "I followed Fergus' advice and offered him one hundred thousand dollars. Along with the money, I promised to not prosecute him for breaking into my office."

Fergus said, "Aye. If the man is in this for money, your offer should slow him down a wee bit."

Pinky sighed.

Flo said, "Damn! Pinky, I've heard that sigh before. Go ahead, drop the second shoe."

Pinky said, "Fergus, this morning, before you picked me up, I called Thomas. It seems that after my phone conversation with Ice, the man broke into my office a second time and printed out all my bank records. With his latest knowledge, it is going to take a lot more than a hundred thousand to make Ice Conner disappear."

Fergus exhaled, "Delmont, you should have told me about that first thing this morning, before we left the farm."

"But—"

Fergus gripped the steering wheel so hard his knuckles turned white. "It's too late for that, but at least we know it's money that's motivating Mr. Conner. He has a pretty good idea how much money you have stashed away and he's betting you'll pay anything to keep Willow alive. The man's in for the big score. Have you talked this over with Willow?"

"No! She knows nothing about the original hundred thousand offer or the call this morning."

"Delmont, you could have made a grave mistake. My cousin is an exceptionally bright female and we might need her to resolve this situation. Now, back to the problem at hand. I've dealt with Conner's type before. The man's a blackmailer who is not afraid to kill, so he'll take you for everything you have, and I mean your last dollar. And once you've emptied your bank account, he'll show up in a year or so to bleed off what you've earned since his last visit. You're better off calling his bluff. Go back to the states and face him, man to man."

Pinky squeaked, "But that's out of the question!"

Fergus barked, "Delmont, is there more to this tale than you've told me?"

"No!"

Pinky's a wimp! He doesn't have the balls to face Conner man to man. I said, "Boss, if the meet's here in Scotland, or back in Carson City, I'll stand by you."

"My boy, Willow and I thank you."

A weird quiet filled the car as we drove into Aberdeen.

Thunk-thunk.

THIRTEEN

Pinky Delmont-Aberdeen, Scotland

Once the vehicle passed the city limits, Fergus said, "We're close now. The Stronvaar Hotel is on Maberly Street next to the railroad tracks."

While Fergus cruised through the streets of Aberdeen, I considered Conner's threat. In my opinion, the man would never kill Willow in cold blood. No, he would take his anger out on me and in the process, destroy my law practice. Overnight, all my years of hard work would vanish. The retirement funds I had tucked away could disappear. All that because Bear let an out-of-control thug escape. Fergus was right. Now that Conner had set his hook, he'd never let go. He would take each and every dollar I had. So a financial settlement was out of the question, but without a payoff, what could I do? For that matter, what could anyone do?

Fergus said, "We're here!" Then our dour Scot gave me an uncharacteristic smile. "Time to interrogate our prime suspect, Gordon Tannahill."

I glanced out the car window and my initial view of the building informed me that the establishment had seen better days. But even in its original state, I was positive The Stronvaar was not a hotel that I would enter, much less sleep in one of their beds. Three floors of rooms rose above a bank of windows. Through the hazy glass, I looked at a sparsely furnished lobby devoid of humanity.

The rain had moderated to a light mist and Fergus took advantage of his police status to park in the loading zone by the front door.

After the long drive it took me a few moments to get my legs under me while Bear and Fergus waited impatiently by the front door.

We entered and I immediately recoiled at the pervasive odor. The lobby smelled like the blackened bowl of a corn-cob pipe, an affectation of my Grandfather Delmont that I have striven to suppress since childhood. The lobby miasma was a mix of burnt tobacco and mold, on the brink of rancid, and the closer the four of us got to the front desk, the thicker the stench became.

I pulled a handkerchief from my jacket pocket, placed the layered cloth over my nose, and said, "Fergus, the air in this establishment is making me ill."

He spun around. "Delmont, we just drove many hours to pursue a murder case. I am not about to let a little stink stop me. My God, man, I grew up without indoor plumbing. This aroma is Chanel No.5 compared to that. If the air inside the lobby is too much for your delicate stomach then march back to the car and wait in the rain. And that goes for the rest of you. "

Flo said, "I'm fine."

Bear growled, "Me too."

Once again, unsupported by the two individuals that I had attempted to mold into my crack investigative team, I was forced to back down. "Fergus, I fear you overreacted to my remark. I am more than willing to accept a touch of physical discomfort to find the murderer of Mary Patterson. Let us move on."

Fergus walked to the front desk and pounded on the bell. A young man with spiked blue hair, milk-white skin, and three gold studs planted in his nose stuck his head out a door. "'Elp yu Gov?"

Fergus took out his Police ID and said, "We need to check your residency records back ten, eleven years."

The man's lip curled and he made a loud sucking sound as he pulled air past the decayed stumps of yellow-brown incisors. He mumbled something that sounded to me like 'fookin' coppers' under his breath and waved us through the door. The five of us entered a tiny office, no more than six by six, with a file cabinet and a pygmy desk. The clerk pointed at the bottom drawer and pushed his way out of the room while he continued to create that obscene sucking sound through the rotted remnants of his teeth.

Flo followed the clerk. "Too tight in here for all of us. I'll wait by the front desk."

I said, "I'm pleased to see that the management of The Stronvaar has diligently worked to hone the interpersonal skills of their employees."

Fergus frowned.

I said, "That was my attempt at American humor. A moment of levity."

Fergus forced a smile. "Aye." He pushed the single chair toward me. "You check out the desk drawers while Bear and I look through the books."

After about ten minutes of rummaging through drawers and flipping dusty pages, Fergus cried, "Aye.

I've found him."

> Name - GORDON TANNAHILL
> Checked in - June 4, 2002
> Checked out - 11-15-2002
>
> Address - 330 Frederick Street, Apartment 4
> City - Edinburgh EH2 2JR
> Storage Area - 17
> Country – Scotland
> Kin - Albert Tannahill, Brother
> Signature - Gordon Tannahill

Fergus called, "Hey lad, come in here."

The desk clerk stuck his head into the tiny cubicle and snapped, "Wa?"

"What's this mean, Storage Area—17?"

"We rent space to the blokes tha' go overseas ta work."

"How long is the rental for?"

"Five y'ars. If they don' return or don' send money fa' another five y'ars, we sell the lot."

Fergus pointed at the form. "The next line, Kin, indicates a brother, Albert Tannahill. Why is that here?"

"If tha' bloke leaves tha nam' of a relative, after five y'ars we call the relative ta see if tha' wan ta pack up the lot."

"We'll need to look at Storage Area 17."

"Oww! I don' 'ave time. I'm behind on me work."

"Damn it, I didn't ask, I told you to take us to number 17."

The clerk pulled out another book from the middle drawer of the desk, turned a few pages, and exclaimed, "Ah! Me records show seventeen is empty, 'as been for two y'ars. Tha' crap's long gone bay now."

Fergus growled, "Cut the bullshit, and lead the way."

The reluctant clerk walked us toward an ancient elevator. When the door slid opened, a brackish, salty stench of decayed sea life took up battle with the lobby's fetid odor. The elevator door closed, and as the elevator proceeded down one flight my stomach contents scrambled around looking for a quick escape through my esophagus.

When the elevator door opened, I trailed behind the group as I fought to control my gag reflex. We walked past an over-worked, hell-like furnace, and the powerful aroma of fuel oil momentarily replaced the brackish fetor. Eventually, once I reached a large open area with locked, wire mesh doors, I regained control of my gut and retained my alpha role as the head of the American investigative team.

We walked until we reached number seventeen. Fergus said, "Open it lad."

I said, "You heard him, get cracking."

"Oww! Yu fookin' coppers, yu ken see it's empty."

Fergus, who in my opinion, had showed more restraint with this foul-mouthed whippersnapper than I would have, grabbed him by his shirt collar, squeezed tightly and slowly lifted him into the air.

"Open the God damn lock, you worthless little bastard."

The clerk's cheeks rapidly turned from white, to cherry, then purple and I'm sure, had Fergus held him much longer, his face would have matched the blue of his spiked hair. He squeaked, "Righto, Gov!"

As the rusty hinges creaked, Fergus shoved the clerk ahead of us into the screened storage area.

I followed the miscreant and pulled a string hanging from an overhead bulb. A pale yellow light struggled to penetrate the twilight and barely illuminated the floor. There were identical storage areas on either side of us. In the gloomy light I could see they contained dusty trunks, suitcases and other items of the transient lifestyle. However, storage area number 17, formerly rented by Gordon Tannahill, as promised by the clerk's record book, was completely empty.

Fergus' gaze scanned the area, shook his head, and said, "Right lad, back upstairs."

It could have been the aroma from the clerk's rotting teeth, or the general basement stench, but for some reason my head started to spin. I fought back the urge to vomit, pulled out a handkerchief from my pocket, carefully turned and lowered my head to regain control. It was then, through the murky light, that my half-closed eyes spotted something in the corner on the floor. I steadied myself, waited for a moment when my stomach was calm, and said, "Just a moment, Fergus, there's something in the corner."

I shuffled over and fighting back the impetus to purge my morning repast, I picked up a piece of paper about the size of a playing card.

"Give that to me, Delmont," said Fergus.

"What'd you find, Boss?"

Flo pushed her oversized chest into my back and said, "Yes, Fergus. What did you just take from Pinky?"

Fergus moved under the single light bulb, scrutinized the paper scrap for a moment, smiled, then tucked the item into his jacket pocket.

Moving as fast as my feet would take me, I sprinted to the elevator and without waiting for the rest of the party, I closed the doors and returned upstairs to the cloying aroma of the lobby. A few steps later, and breakfast still intact, I cleared the lobby and breathed fresh, clean air again.

FOURTEEN

Pinky Delmont-Aberdeen, Scotland

After a few deep breaths, my digestive system settled, and my olfactory system returned to normal. As I reached Fergus' car, and although it was early afternoon, an ominous, pitch-black cloud transformed what had been a feeble daylight into an early dusk.

The rest of the team reached the car and once in, Fergus turned on the overhead map light and handed me the item he had stuffed in his pocket. Holding the artifact up to the light, I stared at a 4x6 photograph that had been torn across the middle. The captured moment showed two boys from the waist up. One looked to be around ten, the other a year or so younger. They both wore what appeared to be a school jackets with matching caps. When I turned the photo over, I could just make out the faint penciled words, Albert - 11, and Gor— The rest of the letters disappeared off the torn fragment.

"Delmont, good on you." said Fergus. "You were on top of your game in that basement. I'm embarrassed to admit that I was so pissed at that little shit that I missed this fragment."

"Exactly what you should expect from all members of my investigative team," I said. "We all contribute. In fact—"

Bear's woman interrupted, "I trust Fergus realizes that your investigative team includes the female sitting in the back seat?."

Fergus said, "I do, Florence, I do."

I turned my head, glared at her, and continued, "As I was saying, if that photo is what I think it is, then we know what Gordon Tannahill looked like when he was a boy. Obviously, that does not tell us what he would look like as a grown man, but in my opinion—"

Fergus said, "From the photo and the records we saw in the office, we know that Gordon has a brother named Albert. The names on the back of the photo would indicate that the slightly taller boy has to be the brother, Albert."

I said, "All this is very interesting but we remain approximately ten years behind our murderer."

Fergus said, "I disagree, Delmont. In fact, we are gaining on our man much quicker than you think. I'll give old Urquhart a call first thing in the morning. He should be able to supply me with a list of overseas contractors and soon we'll know where to look next. Our boy could be anywhere there's an oil well being drilled. At this very minute, Gordon Tannahill could be stacking pipe in Texas or pushing sand around Iran, while thinking he's gotten away with the murder of Mary Patterson."

I took another look at the boys in the photo. "And if you strike out with Urquhart?"

"We will find his brother and talk to him."

Our Scottish host was in a joyful mood as he gunned the engine, made a U-turn on Maberly Street, and deftly worked his vehicle through the busy city traffic to the M90 heading back to Pitlochry.

As I noted, our host was in a happy mood, but I was not. I had not left a lucrative law practice to meander about Scotland on a wild goose chase. The moment we returned to Fergus' farm I would discuss my concerns with Willow, and not in the bedroom, in a safe location such as the kitchen, where she would not be able to—

Flo cried from the back seat, "Oh my God, I haven't gone to the bathroom since we'd left the farm. Sorry, Fergus, but I have to pee."

Fergus' jaw clenched. "Florence, in the future, please inform me that you would like to visit the water closet."

"Why? Don't Scottish women have to pee?"

"I imagine they do, but in polite circles, those sort of bodily functions are not discussed so graphically in public conversation."

Flo said, "If I recall, you just informed us that you were pissed at that hotel clerk. I imagine that was just an exclamation of anger, not a description of bodily function on your part. Am I correct?"

The skin on the back of Fergus' neck matched his face. If the man had asked my opinion, I would have informed him that she was an impossible woman to deal with. However, there are those among us that are doomed to discover things the hard way.

The vehicle was as quiet as a tomb for a good thirty seconds before Flo broke the silence. "Fergus, I know I should have done something about this back at the hotel, but I would appreciate it if you could find me a gas station."

"Can't you hold it? We are no more that an hour

from the farm."

"No way. Find me a bathroom or a large bush. And after I take care of that problem, could you find a place to eat? I'm starving."

The car traveled in silence for a half a mile. Based on my experience with that woman, I was about to tell Fergus that he had better pull over at the next bush when Flo interrupted my thoughts.

"Fergus it's your choice—outside or on your back seat—it's all up to you."

Fergus snapped, "There's a place just around next bend called the Edzell Castle. Will that do?"

"As long as they have a bathroom, the castle will be fine!"

A moment later, we cleared the curve and an ancient walled castle came into view. Fergus pulled the car into the parking lot of The Garden Tearoom. "You go to the loo, and I'll see if I can find us a table," he called to Flo's back as she ran toward the entrance door.

The rest of us entered the tea room in a civilized manner. Fergus took a moment to speak to a waitress and the comely female guided us to a table by a window. Outside the glass was a stunning display of blue and white lobelias growing in the recesses of the castle wall.

I said, "Fergus, this is one of the most beautiful sights I have seen since my arrival in Scotland."

"Aye. The blue and white are the heraldic colors of Sir David Lindsay who created the gardens in 1604."

Bear said, "Did the Lindsay dude build the castle?"

"Nay. It's much older than that, built sometime

in the fifteenth century. By the way, I ordered us all a lamb pie and some tea."

That woman returned, pulled out a chair, and said, "I'm back. Did I hear you say you ordered me something to eat? What if I don't like what you ordered?"

Fergus gave her a long, cold stare, as if he were considering how to accomplish her immediate execution. "I don't know."

The waitress served our lunch. The moment the plate of lamb pie was set in front of me, the steam rising from the dish carried a pungent reek to my nose and brought back the gut wrenching memory of the Stronvaar basement. A touch of gorge rose up my throat.

I poked at my pie as Fergus said, "In 1562, Mary Queen of Scots held a council here before her army marched north to battle. A hundred years later, in 1651, Cromwell and his soldiers methodically butchered the local folk and used this castle as their garrison."

I noted genuine emotion in his voice as he recounted this history. It was obvious that even after four hundred years, the telling of Cromwell's atrocities could still bring a Highlander close to tears, but that did not slow down my stomach's reaction to the lamb pie. "Fergus, I am positive the meat in this pie is rancid."

Fergus took a sip of tea. "You have a problem?"

"Perhaps not rancid, but the filling is far beyond the pale for my standards."

"I fear some of our lamb is a touch stronger than what you're used to in America." Fergus picked up my plate and smelled the dark, greasy, brown gravy.

He laughed. "Delmont, the meat in your pie is not off, it's mutton, and it's from an old ram at that. Even I will admit that the meat from aged ram is an acquired taste."

Bear's woman said, "Pinky, I love my pie. If you're not going to eat yours, can I have what's left?"

I pushed the remains of the dish toward the witch as a brilliant shaft of sunlight spotlighted the wall of blue and white flowers. "Madam, the pie is thine."

"Boss, that's really nice of you, giving your food to Flo."

"My boy, there are times when my generosity surprises me. Fergus, I am going to the men's room. When I return, can we complete our journey?"

"Aye."

Moments later, as we cruised the M90, the bright sun's rays reflected off the still moist hills and I was beginning to see a different Scotland, with its thousand different shades of green. The pastoral beauty of the verdant countryside stood in stark contrast to the brooding, gray landscape present during most of my Scottish visit. Perhaps, I thought, there could be more to this land than incessant storms. It was a little after three when Fergus dropped me off at the apartment.

He smiled and said, "Delmont, in spite of the mutton pie, we made a good team today. I'll call you as soon as I get a lead on Gordon."

I waved goodbye and the moment I walked through the front door my cell phone buzzed. Perhaps this was the latest news from Thomas concerning Ice Conner.

"Pinky Delmont, this is your old buddy from the

desert, Detective Conner. Remember the night we met outside of Laughlin?"

My stomach, still a touch uneasy, did a full flip. The dark memory of that night on the desert flashed into my brain and shook me to my core. I had just turned over Brady Blackstone's murderer to Willow when Detective Conner, a man sworn to uphold the law, turned his weapon on me and threatened my very existence. All it would have taken was an involuntary twitch of his index finger and the life of Northern Nevada's premiere defense attorney would have been snuffed out.

Conner went on: "You think you're so damn smart but it only took me a few minutes to find your travel itinerary in the dumpster behind your office so I know where you are—on a farm outside of Pitlochry, Scotland! You thought you were so damn clever, but I was a homicide detective, and a damn good one, before you screwed up my life."

"What do you want from me?"

"I've been on the run since our little mishap in the desert. Part of me wants to put a bullet between your eyebrows, and do the same to that beautiful ex-wife of yours, Willow Stone, and I'll throw in Bear Zabarte to make it a three-for-the-price-of-one special."

For some reason he had neglected to include Flo, or he had a reason to leave her out of the equation. That seemed strange so I asked, "What about Flo?"

"She's safe. Any babe with a rack like that is a keeper."

A man with judgment that poor deserves to spend the rest of his life in jail. I said, "You told me that 'a part of you' wants to kill the three of us. What does the other part want to do?"

"Like I said, I've been on the lam for months and that costs major bucks. As much as I'd like to waste you and your crew, I might let you and your friends live for a large pile of money."

I made a mental note to include extortion on Conner's long list of criminal offenses the day I turned him over to the police. I said, "My good man, I have offered you the magnificent sum of one-hundred thousand dollars. What more could you expect?"

"I could get by with a million."

A million dollars! I fought to retain my composure as I contemplated the audacity of this scoundrel. "I am sorry. I cannot put my hands on that amount of cash."

"Pinky, can the bull shit. Remember? I have copies of your bank records. Hell, I could give you your latest checking account balance if you're interested."

Damn! In the future, I need to implement an office policy to shred all my financial documents before they are dumped. "Conner, the moment you hang up, I will contact my bank and—"

"Not so fast. I have one more demand. Remember the babe with the rack?"

"Bear's woman? Of course. How could anyone forget her? But—"

"No buts. She's part of the deal. I've been dreaming about her since that night on the desert. One million in cash, and the babe, or your office buddies are going to end up in your dumpster, sort of fresh meat for the maggots."

"My good man, I accept your financial demands

but handing over another human being to you, as if she were no more than my chattel, goes far beyond my authority as her employer."

"Not my problem. Now get your ass in gear."

"But I have no idea how she, or Bear for that matter, will react to your demands."

"Damn it, the time to talk is long gone. One million and the babe or I'll blow a couple of extra vent holes up the nose of your secretary and that little piss ant lawyer who clutters up your office. By the way, if you mention this phone call to the Scottish cops, or Interpol, I'll find you, pull out all of your finger nails with a pair of long-nose pliers, and then kill you."

This man was worse than a wild animal. "I understand."

"It's about time. You have twenty-four hours. If you don't call me back before that time ticks by, your secretary and junior lawyer will have super clear sinuses, but they won't be breathing."

I hit the End Call button and collapsed into a chair. The money was easy but convincing Flo to do anything, even for the good of the team, was . . . hold on, I should run this by Fergus. I hit his number and on the second ring he answered.

"Fergus here."

"This is Pinky and we need to—"

"Delmont, I'm on my way to an important meeting. Can't this wait?"

"No! I just received a call from Conner, my American friend, and he just gave me his monetary demand."

"Ah-ha. I guessed he would show his true colors soon."

"However, he wants more than money. He requires that Flo be included in the package."

"My God, I've never heard of such a demand. Money and a woman?"

"Now you understand why we need to talk."

"Agreed. I'll be at your place in less than an hour."

"Fergus, if Willow is with us, do not mention why we are talking."

"Why?"

"I do not want her to know that a madman is stalking her."

"Delmont, she'll find out sooner or later."

I sighed, "I know, and I'll bring her up to speed after we come up with a plan. Perhaps I will find the time tomorrow."

"I don't agree with your logic but it's your relationship. Open up a couple of Scottish Creams. I'll be there before you empty the first one."

As predicted, I had nearly completed my beer when Fergus knocked on the door. Without a hello, he marched to the kitchen table, lifted his beer, and emptied half the bottle in one swig.

"Delmont, you told me money and Florence. Let's take the money problem first. How much is he demanding?"

"One million cash."

"My God, that's an enormous sum. How will—"

"Fergus, that amount of money is not a stumbling block."

Fergus stared at me, as if my apparent wealth caused him to see me in a different light. "Excellent. Now, let's concentrate on Florence. I have an idea but to make it work we need to get your blackmailer onto Scottish soil."

"I cannot conceive how that will occur. Before he went rogue, Conner was a homicide detective so the man possesses a certain level of intelligence. Also—"

"Delmont, calm down, take a sip of beer and listen to me. Three years ago, my squad captured a kidnapper at a ransom drop not ten miles from here. That would be the perfect location to bait the trap."

"Fergus, now you are not listening to me. Conner will never come to Scotland. The man may be a hardened criminal, but he is not a fool."

"He'll come if that's the only way for him to collect the million dollars and the woman of his dreams. All we have to do is convince Florence to call Conner and tell him that she has been trying to come up with a way to leave Bear. I'll write out a short scenario for her so she'll be able to persuade that scoundrel of her undying devotion."

"If I know that woman, and I do know that woman, you will never get her to do that. However, I am positive that I could convince Conner that she has wanted to leave Bear for some time and is ready to make a move. Once Conner picks up his money, and his woman, he will know they are both in an extremely vulnerable situation. I will need a believable story to let him know they have an escape route and will be safe from prosecution."

Fergus snorted. "With a million dollars and the open borders of the European Union, a man and a woman could disappear just like all the other illegal immigrants do. Do you think you can persuade Conner that Europe will be a safer place to hide out in than the United States?"

"It is possible!" I lifted my beer bottle in

appreciation. "My Scottish friend, except for the possibility of resistance from Bear and that woman, I think we have come up with a viable plan."

FIFTEEN

Bear Zabarte-Pitlochry, Scotland

While I was shoving the last spoonful of that gooey oatmeal into my mouth, the phone rang. Flo picked it up. "It's Fiona and she wants to talk to you."

"Babe, whatever happened to the old days when you fixed me bacon and eggs? If you serve me one more bowl of this sticky crap, I'm going to—"

"You'll eat what I serve or you can fix your own breakfast. Now talk to Fiona, damn it."

I grabbed the phone. "Hi."

"Bear, Willow's helping me strip the old paint off the cabinets in our kitchen. If you have a spare moment, you and Flo are welcome to stop by and lend a hand."

How did the broads of this world keep coming up with endless, bullshit jobs like that? Can't they just let a dude sit down in a soft chair, with a cold beer in his hand, and watch a ballgame on TV?

"Thanks for the offer, but me and Flo have got some investigating to do."

"Oh? I thought Fergus told me that the investigation was done."

"Ah . . . we need to talk with that old coot again."

"Henry Bramble?"

"Yup. He's the coot."

"You're in luck. I have a meeting in Pitlochry today. If you want a ride to Henry Bramble's place, I could give you a lift. His cottage is only a mile north of my meeting. If that works for you, I could pick you up in an hour."

"Hold on a minute, Fiona." I wasn't sure what I should say. Yesterday, Fergus pretty much told us that because of Henry's accident, the old dude had lost a couple of bricks off his wall. And Fergus made sure that we understood that he and his department had done a great job investigating the Mary Patterson murder. Bottom line, Fergus told us to butt out, so what was my problem? If Fergus was right and Henry Bramble's stories were pure bullshit, then me and Flo would blow the day, but a wasted day talking to Henry Bramble was a hell of a lot better than helping Willow strip paint off old cabinets. And why did Fergus bite my head off when I brought up Henry's multi-murder idea? Three dead girls was too big a thing to let go. I had to know for sure that Henry was nuts. "Fiona, does Henry have a phone so we can let him know me and Flo are dropping by?"

"No, and he wouldn't answer it at this time of day if he did. Each morning, he walks the golf course. And don't worry about dropping in, if he's not home you can go with me to the board meeting and afterward you can take your lady friend to lunch."

My lady friend? What the hell is she talking about? Except for Flo, I don't have any lady friends.

"Sounds like fun," I lied. "See you when you get here."

The second I set the phone down, Flo was all

over my ass.

"Sounds like fun? An hour? Have you lost your mind? I'm wearing sweatpants and a sweatshirt. I'm not dressed for—"

"Cool it, babe. We're riding into Pitlochry with Fiona to get the straight skinny from Henry Bramble."

"I'm still not properly dressed, even for that crazy old forester with a wandering eyeball. Explain to me what we are going to ask him or I won't step one foot out of this place."

Jesus! There are times when she can be a pain. "We're going to nose around. Find out if Henry's accident turned him into a complete loony."

Flo nodded, like she agreed with me. That was a first!

She said, "Okay, but you need to make it quick. If it turns out that he's ready for the funny farm, we better have plenty of time left over so I can do some clothes shopping in town."

"Hey, you'll get time to shop as soon as I figure out where I can find a Red Sox game on this stupid TV."

"We're in Scotland. The Scots don't watch American baseball. They televise soccer, golf, and caber tossing."

"Caber what?"

"The caber is a long pole, around twenty feet, and it weighs more than a hundred pounds. I have seen men lift that giant pole off the ground and toss . . . Oh my God, look at the time. I have to change."

I grabbed the TV guide and was trying to find the game called Caber Toss when Flo yelled, "Let's go. Fiona's here."

Flo scrambled into the back seat and said, "Fiona, this will be my first trip to Pitlochry since the morning we met Fergus, Willow, and Pinky at the golf course."

Fiona looked up at the blue sky and smiled. "I promise this will be a better day. Just look at that sunshine and blue sky. Flo, you've got a day out of the box."

Twenty minutes later, just before we got to town, Fiona took a side road off the main highway. The street was right next to a really wide stream of water.

I said, "That looks bigger than a creek."

"It's a river called The Tummel. That building on the right we passed was the Festival Theater and what you see on the left is Loch Faskally."

Fiona slowed at a fork and turned onto a dirt road. She stopped by a small wooden sign. Me and Flo got out of her car, and I glanced around.

I said, "I don't see a house. Does the loony live in a cave?"

Fiona said, "Henry's not crazy. His cottage is down Clunie Path. You'll find the path at the wee sign and his place is located the other side of that large grove of birch trees. I'll wait here 'til you're sure he's home."

Flo carefully walked down the uneven path and I stuck right behind her. We went through a thick bunch of trees and I spotted a tiny stone building in a clearing under a giant pine.

I ran back to Fiona's car. "It looks like he's home. There's smoke coming from the chimney."

"Aye, he must be there. Henry would never burn wood and leave the place. He's too frugal to waste anything. I'll be back for you around one."

I waved and walked back down the path toward Henry's cottage. As I cleared the trees, I glanced around and Flo had vanished. All of a sudden there was a loud explosion that stopped me in my tracks. Thick black smoke floated out of the walls of a lean-to that was hanging on the side of the stone building.

I ran toward the smoke yelling, "Flo, where are you? Are you okay?"

Flo stuck her head around the corner of the lean-to and said, "Relax. I'm here with Henry."

I ran to her and there was Henry standing next to an old car. Once the old dude saw me he pulled a rag from his back pocket and wiped some grease from his hands. "Aye, Bear. She's fine."

I said, "What the hell happened? What was that explosion?

"I'm tryin' to start me car." He lifted the hood. "Come over an take a look-see."

I stuck my head under the hood of a little black car. I couldn't guess its age except it was old. "Cool car but that's a tiny engine. What kind is it?"

"'Tis a 1950 Austin FX3. I bought 'er after she spent a few years runnin' around the streets of London as a taxi. Ain't she a grand sight?"

Flo said, "From the look of her I'd guess she's been around longer than a few years. How many years was your car a taxi?"

Henry shrugged, "Dinna know 'xactly. Ten, maybe twenty years."

I said, "And when did you buy her?"

"Fifty years ago."

As I got closer I noticed the taxi sign on the roof. "Considering her age she looks pretty good, but do you get much call for a taxi in Pitlochry?"

He stared at his car, like he'd never thought about that, and shook his head. "Nay."

Flo said, "Regardless of its age, it's a cute car. Does it run?"

"Nay." Then Henry turned and said, "Come, I'll fix us a cuppa."

We entered through a rough wooden door into a single room joint, sort of like a studio apartment, and I could feel the heat coming off the cast-iron wood stove. The uneven floorboards groaned as me and Flo made our way to a couple of chairs next to a hand-made wooden table. Henry pulled out one of the chairs for Flo, then ran over to the kitchen area. He took a copper pot off an overhead hook, ladled some water from a ceramic crock sitting on a shelf, and stuck the pot on the wood stove. Then he opened up an old, metal container, grabbed a fistful of cookies, and threw them on a plate.

Flo said, "We don't want you to go to a lot of trouble, Henry. We had some questions—about your suspicions—concerning the missing girls."

He set the cookie plate in the center of the table, aimed his right eye in my direction and said, "Nay, they're not suspicions, I 'ave proof."

While Henry grabbed two cups off a small shelf, I checked out the room. To the left, about ten feet from the table, was a built-in bed, covered with a neat stack of gray, wool blankets. Behind Flo, the kitchen was decked out with had a wooden counter, a crock of water and two kerosene lamps. Above the counter were a couple of shelves with cans that looked like food, and two small sacks. One was labeled flour and I couldn't make out what was inside the other. To my right there was a bookshelf, a wooden rocking chair, and an old-time, hand-cranked record player. "Henry, does that old record player still work?"

He nodded and pointed to the bottom shelf of the bookcase. "Aye, it's me Gramophone an I 'ave an original recording of Caruso singin' <u>Nessun Dorma</u>. I'll play it for you."

A Caruso singing a what? I didn't have a clue what he was talking about but steam started to shoot out of the copper spout. Henry pulled the pot off the hot stove and set it down on the table.

"But first, you'll 'ave tea and cookies."

After he had placed hot cups of tea in front of us, Henry walked to the bookcase and found the promised record. He carefully cleaned the disk with a piece of blanket, stuck the record on the turntable, and cranked the handle on the side of the box. Pretty soon the noise of a dude's scratchy voice filled the room. At least I think it was a dude, or maybe it was the howl of a cat in heat. Two cups of tea, one stale cookie, and a couple of songs later, I said, "Henry, thanks for the tea and the music. Now, I want to see that proof."

"Aye." He jumped up, crossed the room to the bed, knelt down on one knee, and grabbed a small wooden box that was overflowing with all sorts of paper. He carried the box to the table and set it in front of me. The first thing I noticed was two or three old newspapers.

I was about ready to tell the old dude the only value of this crap was fuel for his wood stove when Flo jumped in. "Henry, that's a full box, and more than we expected. I don't think we have time today to get through all this. Can you give us an idea of what's in there?"

"Aye." He shuffled through the paper pile for a minute and pulled out a single sheet and handed it to me. It was a copy of a missing person report on Margaret Struan, 17 Larchwood Lane, Pitlochry. I scanned down the report and saw that Margaret, just as Henry had promised, she had disappeared a few days past her thirteenth birthday.

I set the Struan report down, and without a word, Henry handed me a copy of the missing person report for Kerry Claydon.

The date on this form showed that Kerry had also disappeared shortly before her thirteenth birthday. I noticed that she had lived on the same road as Margaret Struan, at 84 Larchwood Lane.

Then Henry handed me the missing person form for Mary Patterson. Before she disappeared, she had lived with her parents at 14 Bonnet Hill Lane.

I set Mary's report on the table and said, "I'll bet that Bonnet Hill Lane is close to the other girls."

Henry nodded his head solemnly. "Their 'ouses were no more than five 'undred feet apart."

Even an ignorant ex-bartender like me could see why Henry thought there was a connection with the disappearances of the three girls. They had grown up a few hundred feet from each other in a town of a couple of thousand people. They had all disappeared close to their thirteenth birthdays. I took a sip of tea and tried to ignore the fact that Fergus and the Tayside Police could have blown three murder investigations. But what really began to piss me off was that if that bulldozer had not uncovered Mary Patterson's bones, Fergus would still think she was a runaway teen. How could he miss the pattern? Was he hiding something? Or was he just another stupid cop?

I sat there and figured that Flo and Henry were waiting for me to say something. But all I could think of were more questions—like how come this old dude with the wonky eye knew more than the police? Or why did Fergus take us to Edinburgh? And why did he invite us to go with him to Aberdeen? For Willow's sake, I hoped that Fergus had blown the murder investigations of three young girls because he was just a bad detective. But what if Fergus wasn't dumb . . . hold on, you don't want to go there . . . wake up and smell the tea. It's too late, you've gone there whether you like it or not.

I said, "Henry, I agree there something weird with the three disappearances and I agree that the police didn't make the connection that we think they should have. In fact, me and you, and Flo seem to be the only people in Scotland who want to find out what really happened to those girls."

Flo jumped in. "And we can't tell Fergus that we don't agree with him."

Henry said, "Aye. I understand."

Flo said, "But that brings up another problem. The day we arrived in Scotland, Fergus told us that driving on the wrong side of the road was too dangerous for Americans, and without a lot of training he won't let us drive one of his cars. And we can't ask Fergus to drive us around the country to continue an investigation because he told us the investigation is over. But you could drive us in your car. How does that sound?"

"But I canna get 'er to start."

114

Flo said, "I'll ask Pinky to pay for what you need to get your car running and then we can find the serial killer."

The Henry's mouth opened and closed like he was trying to catch a fly.

I said, "Flo, I don't think the boss—"

Flo gave me her don't-go-there glare and said, "Give Henry the opportunity to respond to Pinky's generous offer."

Henry said, "You'll pay to fix me car!"

Flo nodded, "Yes, and Pinky'll pick up the tab for all the gas too."

"Babe, I still don't think—"

Flo said, "Do you want more?"

"Nay." Henry turned toward me and I saw a tear trickle down the scar. "I'll do it! It's more than enough. 'Tis a king's ransom."

Flo said, "Then we agree?"

"Aye."

Shit! Now what? Once Pinky found out that he was stuck to fix Henry's car, and pay for all the gas we'd use during our investigation, he'd kill me.

Flo glanced at her watch. "Fiona will be by to pick us up in a few minutes."

Henry stood there and didn't move, like he had something to say. Flo glanced at me. She seemed as confused as I was. Finally she said, "So it's agreed. You'll find a mechanic and get your car fixed?"

"Aye. I'll get a man workin' on the startin' problem right away, but somethin' else is bothering me."

Flo said, "And Henry, if we're going to be investigative partners, then we have to be honest with each other. What's wrong?"

115

Henry's right eye struggled to focus on my face. "Ah . . . Bear, Flo, 'xcuse me, but 'ave either of you ever done this sort of investigative work before?"

Jesus, the old coot was worried about driving around the Scottish countryside with a couple of greenhorns who didn't know the difference between a murderer and a fence post.

I said, "Henry, investigating murders is what me and Flo do for a living. Besides, we're the only two people within a hundred miles who don't think you're short the cheese in your cheese enchilada. Until we can convince Fergus, we're your only hope."

"I know some of the folk round 'ere think I'm a bit funny in me 'ead. I know I don't 'ear or see very well on the right side of me 'ead, but the rest of me is brilliant."

Flo said, "We know all about your accident and that's why we make the perfect trio. We'll take care of the seeing and hearing while you do the driving. Once we corner the killer, you and Bear can take him down."

I flashed Flo my nastiest stink-eye. "Babe, you've said more than enough for one day. We still have to talk to Pinky about—"

Flo said, "Sorry to eat and run, Henry, but we promised to meet Fiona by the highway at one o'clock."

He jumped up and ran to the door a lot faster that I thought a dude his age could move.

"'Old on, I'll walk with you to the road."

As we made our way down the dirt path, Henry said, "Flo, 'ow will I reach you when me car's fixed? I dinna 'ave a phone."

She said, "That's okay, we'll get you a cell

116

phone. We can keep in touch that way."

He stopped. "But I told you I dinna 'ave a phone."

The old fart didn't have a clue what Flo was talking about when she offered him a cell phone. I said, "Henry, a cell phone is a phone that works without wires. You can carry it in your pocket and make calls from anywhere."

His mouth dropped open.

I guess that shouldn't have surprised me 'cause I was talking to a dude who lived in a world of hand-crank record players, kerosene lamps, and an almost new 1950 Austin FX3.

Flo said, "Trust me, Henry. I'll show you how a cell phone works."

Fiona's car pulled up to the shoulder as we broke through the clearing.

She rolled her window down. "Hello, Henry, did you have a nice visit with Flo and Bear?"

"Aye."

We got in and Flo waved to Henry as the car pulled onto the highway.

"We're just in time for a bite of lunch and I know the perfect place." said Fiona.

While she drove into town, the broads rattled on about the Kid's school, but my mind was stuck on three Pitlochry teenagers and the question of why Fergus was so damn stubborn about the possibility there was a serial killer.

SIXTEEN

Pinky Delmont-Pitlochry, Scotland

During a quiet dinner, to protect her from angst, I avoided discussing my elaborate plan concerning Ice Conner with Willow. Later, after we went to bed, I kept one eye on the clock and with my twenty-four hour deadline slipping away, I quietly climbed out of bed, picked up my cell phone, and walked to the living room.

I hit the call-back button and on the third ring I heard, "It's about time! Okay, shoot. Hey, Pinky, I just made a joke. Shoot!"

"Conner, I agree to all your demands with one additional item."

He screamed, "I told you no changes. One million dollars and the babe or I ice your office buddies."

"My good man, I told you I agreed to the money and that woman, Florence. The only change is you will have to come to Scotland to complete the transaction."

"Do you take me for a complete fool?"

"On the contrary, I respect your intelligence. When we last talked, you informed me that you were a wanted man and had become weary of hiding out. I am offering you a new life in the European Union— from sunny Spain in the south, Finland in the north,

Bulgaria in the east, to Ireland in the west. I am talking about twenty-seven sovereign nations where all citizens cross borders without passport checks." I paused to give Conner the opportunity to absorb my last statement. One lesson I had learned early on was that clients would believe almost anything I said, as long as I gave them ample time to digest my facts. "Conner, that item alone should convince you. Today, illegal immigration in the European Union is a larger problem than what we face in the United States. My good man, as an American couple, you and Florence would have no difficulty blending in with the natives. Think of the possibilities; an apartment in downtown London. Or perhaps a condo on the beach of the French Riviera. All you have to do is fly to Scotland, pick up your money and your woman, and then disappear to live the good life. Do you have any questions?"

"Don't rush me. I don't know if you're feeding me a line of bull shit about illegal immigration or giving me the straight scoop. Shut up and sit tight. I'll call you back in a couple of minutes."

I had him! There was enough truth to my argument to make my statements concerning the immigration problems in the EU easily verifiable on the internet. I walked into the kitchen and just finished making myself a cup of tea when my cell buzzed.

"Pinky, according to what I read, the immigration in the EU is a hell of a mess. But I still have a problem. How do I know you're not setting me up?"

"My good man, are you unaware of the protocol called honor among thieves. I am gambling my life,

119

and the lives of my employees, that you will carry out your side of the bargain—you take my money and do what you must with Flo, thus sparing Willow, myself, and my office staff. As you can see, we are both taking risks. But in fact, I am taking the greater risk, my life and the lives of those I cherish. If I turn you over to the local police, all you are risking is a few years in jail. As I said, I am taking—"

"Shut up and let me think."

In court, whenever I concluded with my closing argument, I would monitor the eyes of the jury members to confirm that the salient points were penetrating their thick skulls. However, in this case I was limited to a change in Conner's vocal inflection, or a pause. After he hesitated for a good fifteen seconds, I knew I had him in my pocket.

"Okay, I'll come to Scotland."

"Do you have a passport?"

"I do."

"Excellent. I will contact my secretary and instruct her to give you two thousand dollars. That should cover your one-way travel costs. Take the next flight out of Reno to Glasgow, Scotland. Rent a car at the airport and get directions to the town of Pitlochry. I will contact my American bank and instruct them to make a wire transfer of one million dollars to the Royal Bank of Scotland, Pitlochry branch. They will convert the US dollars into British Pound Sterling. At today's exchange rate, that will give you six hundred and fifteen thousand, nine hundred pounds. I will have the cash and the woman ready to turn over to you in thirty-six hours. That should give you ample time to arrive in Pitlochry."

"Delmont, I figured you'd come around. Where do we meet?"

"I will scour the area for a safe meeting place and contact you. If you are not available because you are in flight, I will leave the meeting details on your voice mail. Now, it is the middle of the night in Scotland and I am exhausted. Good night!"

The next morning, the skies were blue, the sun was shining, and my life and death situation with Ex-Detective Conner had faded into the back reaches of my thoughts.

During breakfast, and to avoid discussing the Conner situation, I agreed to look over Willow's progress concerning her kitchen cabinet restoration project. For the life of me, I did not understand why a woman of her beauty, talent, and intellect would demean herself to partake in such a menial task.

As Willow had promised, the kitchen cabinet job was nearly complete. Three out of the four cabinets were covered with a pristine eggshell enamel and the last cabinet had been stripped of its old pigment in anticipation a new coat of paint.

I said, "Where is Fiona?"

"In town attending a meeting of the Women's Institute."

I rolled my eyes.

"Pinky Delmont, stop putting down something you know nothing about. By the way, before her meeting, she dropped Bear and Flo off at Henry Bramble's cottage."

"I have too many irons in the fire to concern myself with Bear and that woman." I grabbed her lovely hand. "How much longer are you going to damage your beautiful skin doing that sort of scut work?"

She said, "We will finish the job tomorrow. Now give me my hand back and tell me that you love the new paint job or you're going to spend some cold and lonely nights during the rest of our visit in Scotland. And while we're on the subject of nights in Scotland, how much longer do you think Fergus will need us?"

"Due to my stellar investigative work during the trip to Aberdeen, I have managed to steer your cousin in the proper direction. My guess is that he should be able to complete the task from this point on without our assistance."

"Does Bear agree with you?"

"I do not have the foggiest notion if Bear's limited mental capacity allows any thoughts beyond beer and baseball, much less the ability to formulate an educated guess concerning the progress of the investigation."

Willow shook her head. "My mother used to tell me, 'If you haven't got something nice to say about someone, then don't say anything at all.'"

"Due to your mother's untimely death, I never met her, but I am surprised that you turned out so well after being raised on that Pollyanna dreck."

"Don't forget cold and lonely." Willow jumped onto the first step of the ladder and draped a drop cloth around onell shoulder like a toga. "You have five seconds to tell me that you love my cabinets."

"I love your cabinets and you have far exceeded a craftsman's standards. Now what do I win?"

"Congratulations, you answered the question correctly and your prize is a wee dram of the water of life."

Willow stepped off the ladder, grabbed a glass

off the counter and poured in a couple inches of whiskey. "Do you want ice, or will you take your whiskey like a true Highlander?"

"Now I see why you wanted to do the cabinet work. Instead of coffee breaks, you and Fiona nip Scotch all day."

Willow poured herself a glass and we sat in silence for a moment while I contemplated the amber liquid in my glass.

She said, "You've been out of sorts since your return from Aberdeen. Is anything wrong?"

"I am not sure. Something about Fergus and the Mary Patterson murder remains out of focus. He is adamant that Henry Bramble is crazy, but what if that old man is right? What if a year from now a bulldozer turns up another set of bones on that golf course? Your cousin seems to be holding something back, and for the life of me, I can't figure out what or why."

"I agree. There's more to this story than we've been told, but why would he ask us to fly half-way around the world if he didn't want our help?"

"I do not know. Pour me a little more from that bottle and this time add a cube of ice. Now that I brought ice into our discussion, there is one trivial item I need to clear up."

She leaned forward. "Oh my God, are you talking about Ice Conner?"

My stomach tightened and I drained about three-quarters of the whiskey. "Yes, and I have to admit that I kept you out of the loop while I cleared up a few insignificant details."

"Who gave you permission to kept me out of the loop? Pinky Delmont, you tell me everything you know or you'll discover that there are things worse than a cold and lonely stay in Scotland."

I told Willow about Conner's threat to kill both of us along with my office staff. Then his million dollar ultimatum plus Bear's woman. Finally I told her about my call to Conner while she slept.

She said, "Let me get this straight. You're going to hand that crooked cop more than a million dollars and Flo?"

"To be accurate, at the latest exchange rate, six hundred and fifteen thousand, nine hundred pounds. By the time I convert my million, the exact amount could exceed a—"

"And you're willing to put up a million dollars to keep me safe?"

"Actually, I have no way to guarantee that he—"

"Pinky, shut up and listen to me. I thank you. Your secretary, and Thomas, thank you. Darling, no matter what my brain tells me to do, my heart says I still love you."

Before I could respond, my cell phone buzzed. "Hello?"

"Delmont, Fergus here. Have you followed through and talked with the American villain?"

"Yes. I called him a few hours ago and convinced him to come to Scotland. I informed him that I would have his money and that woman ready in thirty-six hours. Finally, I informed him I would find a safe meeting place."

"Brilliant. We'll use the same ransom drop area where we captured the kidnapper and recovered all the money."

"Fergus, are you positive this will work? I have more than a million dollars of my money at risk and—"

"Delmont, need I remind you that you'll have the powerful resources of the total Perthshire Constabulary at your back."

"Are we talking about the same group of police that has not yet solved the murder of Mary Patterson?"

There was a short pause, then each word that Fergus spoke hammered my ear like a series of staccato rim-shots. "I'll pick you up in a few minutes and we'll stop by my favorite pub in Pitlochry where you will buy me a pint to apologize for your remark concerning the lack of progress on the Patterson murder case. Assuming I accept your apology, I trust you will never again question the efforts of any member of the Tayside Constabulary! After your apology, we'll stop by the proposed drop location."

"Fine, now—"

"And if possible, we need to include Bear and Florence in our visit to the money drop. That woman is an integral part of the—"

Oh my God, I had not taken the time to contact Bear to inform him about his woman's pending encounter with Ice Conner. I said, "You are too late. According to Willow, Fiona took Bear and Flo to Henry Bramble's cottage about an hour ago."

"Damn. The ramblings of that old gentleman will just confuse those two. I'll pick you up in five minutes. You contact Bear and tell him we'll meet them at the Thistle Pub in Pitlochry."

"I will do that."

Fergus let out a long sigh. "Delmont, this opinion must be kept between the two of us. Frankly, I don't understand how you manage to work with that woman."

"Fergus, on that point we agree. She is impossible."

"Aye, she's a true bana-bhuidseach."

"A what?"

"In Gaelic, bana means female, and bhuidseach means wizard or witch. However, with that woman, it doesn't make any difference which language you speak, rather than resolve a situation, she exacerbates the condition. The worst sentence that your American villain could receive would be having to spend the rest of his life with that female."

SEVENTEEN

Bear Zabarte-Pitlochry, Scotland

When my cell buzzed, me and Flo were stuck in some weird chick joint that Fiona called a tearoom. I jumped up and said, "Excuse me ladies, but I've got to take this call in private."

I ran into the men's can. "Hello?"

"Are you aware that your little visit with that Bramble character has upset Fergus?"

"Hi, boss."

"Stop calling me boss."

"Okay. What's up?"

"Do not attempt to change the subject at hand!"

"You mean that part where Fergus is pissed off at me?"

"I believe that is obvious."

"Boss, the old dude with the wonky eye has a point. All three girls lived real close together and it looks to me like there's something in common about their—"

"Enough! As we speak my bank is transferring a million dollars of my personal funds into British Pounds. Very soon, Ice Conner will have traveled to Pitlochry where we will complete the money transfer."

"Are you sure that's a good idea? I don't trust that bastard to—"

"I did not make this call to solicit your opinion! Fergus feels that we are making the correct move and the decision has been made. Meet us at the Thistle Pub in ten minutes."

"We'll be there. This tearoom joint is driving me up the wall."

"What are you talking about?"

"Fiona took us to a tearoom for lunch. Boss, there are those frilly things on every table, just like my Grandma Zabarte had on the arms of her chairs. And there's no way anyone can call what they served me lunch. Just stupid little sandwiches filled with nothing but funny tasting lettuce. And tea, lots and lots of tea. Give me fish and chips anytime!"

"Have you finished venting?"

"I guess so. By the way, Flo told Henry you'd pick up the tab to fix his car so he can drive us around Scotland while we look for Patterson's murderer."

"She did what?"

"I told her you'd be pissed, but boss, she's right. Fergus won't drive us anymore, and if we're going to get to the bottom of this murder, it looks like Henry's our only bet."

For a couple of seconds, Pinky didn't say anything, yell at me, or call Flo a bad name. Then he said, "Five hundred dollars is the maximum I will contribute to this endeavor. Anything above that amount is yours. Now clear out of that tearoom and make your way to the Thistle Pub."

Pinky's a nasty little fart, but in his dumb way, he just told me that he wants to find the killer just as much as me, and Flo, and Henry. "Thanks, boss. Glad to see that you agree that the Patterson killer

128

is—"

"Do not utter another word. I am compelled by a solemn oath to cease pursuing that situation. And stop calling me boss."

"Okay, boss." I clicked my cell off and walked back to the table. "Flo, we've got to go and meet Pinky at the Thistle Pub."

Fiona said, "That place is just around the corner. You'll have plenty of time to finish your watercress sandwich."

"That's okay. I told Pinky I'd case the joint before he got there." I took five of those funny looking dollars out of my wallet and tossed them onto the table. "Fiona, will that cover lunch and a tip?"

"Twenty-five Pounds? That's more than generous. It was brilliant having lunch with you both. Do you know what's funny? I've never been able to convince Fergus to join me here. Bear, now that you've sampled the food you can give him a good report."

"Right! Flo, we've got to blow this joint."

Flo said, "I cannot imagine why you are in such a hurry. I, for one, would like to sit awhile and sip my tea."

"Babe, Pinky's coughing up five hundred to fix Henry's car. Now get your butt in gear!" I flashed her my stink eye.

She pushed her chair back from the frilly covered table and said, "Thank you, Fiona for the ride and taking us to this lovely tearoom. I know I enjoyed every minute and I'm sure Bear did too."

I said, "Right!" and dragged Flo out of that lacy joint.

The Thistle Pub was, just as Fiona promised,

around the block. We walked in and it took a few seconds for my eyes to get used to the dingy room. The walls were covered with a dark wood and there was a bar, tables, chairs, and a couple of dudes tossing those little pointy things at a target. The air smelled better than The Old Globe, but mostly the same cigarette smoke and stale beer.

Flo stopped, looked around, and said, "Pinky's not here so why the bum's rush?

"Babe, I had to get out of that joint. All that fancy stuff and tea was driving me up the wall."

"In your case it's not a drive, just a short putt."

"Huh?"

"Just a little golf joke. Now, tell me how you got Pinky to cover the cost of Henry's car repair."

"I told him we needed Henry to drive us so we could find the Patterson murderer. Then he said he'd pay for the first five hundred bucks. After than he said a bunch of crap about having to take an oath about something."

"Who covers the cost if the repair bill goes over—"

Pinky and Fergus walked in and saved me from having to answer Flo.

Fergus said, "Let's sit down at that table by the far wall." Once we all got there, Fergus called to the bartender, "Charlie, a pint of Scottish Cream for each of us, and my rich friend from America is picking up the tab."

Flo said, "I'd rather have a glass of red wine."

Fergus said, "Florence, in Scotland, we specialize in whiskey, haggis, oats, salmon, and beer. I do not recall hearing myself include red wine in that rather limited list. You drink wine when you are

130

in France. You're in Scotland now, so you'd better get used to drinking beer or whiskey."

Flo flashed me her nasty stare, like I should jump up and tell Fergus to go pound salt, but the dude was right. "Babe, the Scottish Cream is a great beer. Give it a try. Okay, Fergus, what's the latest idea on how we should handle this Ice Conner mess?"

"Finish your beer and then we'll drive to the money drop location. Once there, I'll explain what I have in mind."

I downed my beer and most of Flo's. Pinky paid the bartender, and that was weird. I'd never seen him pick up the tab without a big argument. There had to be something going on between him and Fergus.

Ten minutes later, Fergus pulled his car into an area that looked like a nice little park with big tables for family picnics. There was a lake, trees, and a couple of sets of swings for little kids.

Fergus said, "As I told you, I've used this recreation ground by Loch Faskally for a ransom drop. The forest and underbrush surrounding the parking area provide excellent cover for my men. There's just a single lane road under the railroad overpass that leads to the picnic benches. Once we block that exit, Conner's trapped. And if we set up the meeting late in the afternoon, after all the day visitors have gone, the whole area should be deserted."

I looked around. To the east was a railroad track running on top of a steep, thirty-foot high bank. A single lane road came through a tunnel under the raised track. To left of the tunnel, a bridge carried the railroad tracks across the lake. To the right, a high brick wall closed in the south side of the park and ran up to the train tracks. I said, "Why the brick wall?"

Fergus said, "It was placed there a few years ago to keep children from falling into the linn."

"Huh?"

"Linn is a word we use for a steep ravine. I think you Americans might call it a canyon."

"So once Conner comes through that tunnel, he has nowhere to go unless he swims across the lake."

Fergus smiled, "That's a good way to describe his situation."

I took a last glance around the area, "This setup looks pretty good to me except for one thing. Does that road to the dam go all the way across to the other side?"

Fergus said, "Nay, not a road. It's just a walkway, but I'll station a man on the other side to close off that potential escape route. Thanks for pointing that out."

I said, "Okay, now that we know where, the next question is when do we spring the trap?"

Fergus scratched his head. "Tomorrow, after I walk my squad through their paces."

He looked at me, Flo, and Pinky. "You three must understand there might be some personal risk. I'll be there with my men, but if this bloke pulls a knife or does something unexpected, there's no guarantee that anyone can react quickly enough to avoid—"

Pinky interrupted, "What are you saying?"

I said, "Boss, the cops face this kind of crap every day."

Pinky said, "How many times must I remind

you that I am not a member of the local police force! Fergus, I have put up a considerable sum of money to avoid personal risk. My God, man, it took me years to build up my law practice to this point, and I don't want to risk losing a million dollars because—"

"Cool it, boss. Me and Fergus, and all those other cops will protect your butt."

"And what about me?" said Flo. "Just because I didn't contribute a million bucks like old money bags here, shouldn't mean I'm not afforded the same protection."

I gave Flo's hand a squeeze. "Don't worry, Babe, you've got Fergus, all his men, and me! Hell, we've been around the block a couple of times and I've never let anyone hurt you. All we have to do is hand Conner the money and then let him walk. Right, Fergus?"

Pinky said, "Hold on. Fergus, you told me that he wasn't going to get away. Is there any possibility that man could escape with my funds?"

I growled, "Come on, Boss. That's the idea. Hand the dude the money and let him go before he does something stupid, like pull out a gun and shoot someone. Right, Fergus?"

Fergus said, "Listen to me. Once someone hands Conner the money, my men will come out from cover and arrest him. There'll be no danger as long as everyone remains in position—does his or her job as planned—and nothing unexpected happens."

The plan sounded good, but Fergus was blowing smoke if he figured that nothing weird could happen. Any time you set up a scam like this, something was bound to go wrong. To figure that everything will work was like telling me that you believe the tooth fairy will pass out a gold coin per tooth. Guessing that Fergus knew some shit was going to hit the fan, I said, "Should I pack heat for the drop?"

Fergus said, "Have you lost your mind? This is Scotland, not Dodge City. There's no way in the world I would allow you to carry a weapon. In fact, I don't see how you smuggled a weapon into the country. I demand you turn over all weapons to me until you leave Scotland."

Damn, now I'd put my foot into it. "Okay, I'll hand over my pistol as soon as we get back to your farm, but you have to give it back before we board the plane."

"We'll see about that. Now, are all of you comfortable with the plan?"

Pinky said, "One last question. Who is going to actually hand the money to that madman?"

Fergus said, "I thought that would be you. You're the one he's been negotiating with on the phone."

"Negotiation is one of those skills I have honed for the courtroom. However, actual personal contact is something that I avoid whenever possible."

Jesus, what a wimp! "Don't worry, boss, I'll take care of the money."

Fergus said, "All right then, we have the money exchange solved. All we have left on our plate is how we are going to turn Florence over to Conner. Now my take on—"

I yelled, "What did you just say?"

Flo screamed, "Turn me over to . . . have you lost your mind? What the hell are you two up to? Fergus, I demand you take us back to the cottage. We'll pack our clothes, pick up Ettamae from school, and hop on the first plane back home."

Pinky said, "I meant to talk to you about that, but I ran out of time, so calm down and listen to me. First, Conner is after the money, but he would not agree to the deal unless we included you in the bargain. Frankly, you should be flattered that the man is so besotted with—"

I grabbed the boss by his shirt and held my cocked, clenched fist about a foot short of his nose. The last time I put my fist that close to a dude, a brick wall got between a bastard's head and my fist. He ended up dead. I ended up in the slam staring at a murder two charge. That's when I met Pinky. Somehow, that shrimp lawyer got me off. I don't know how, and I don't care, he just did. Then, because I didn't have enough money to pay the bastard, he made me work for him, for free, to clear my debt. That's when Flo came along. She told Pinky that Abraham Lincoln freed the slaves a long time ago. From that day on, Pinky has paid me for my work and now I'm thinking about smashing his nose in with a single punch. I took a breath and growled, "You little shit, I don't know what besotted means, but where Flo goes or who she goes with has nothing to do with you. And if I ever hear you tell her she's besotted again, I'll—"

Fergus grabbed my arm. "Bear, calm down before you do something you'll regret. Now, back to the American villain. With Conner, we are dealing with a criminal, and as such, his actions tend to be predictable. I agreed with Delmont when he informed me about Conner's demand to include Florence in the ransom, but Delmont promised me that he'd talk to you both before now. On my honor,

135

there is no way that I would let that man escape from the drop area with Florence. Now, I'll walk my squad through their part in this caper tomorrow morning so we'll be ready to handle Conner as soon as he arrives. Delmont, can I at least count on you to give Conner directions to this location the next time you talk with him?"

I glanced at Flo. Her face looked like she found out her favorite aunt died. What the hell, she might fall for Pinky's line of crap, but I was damn sure if push came to shove, he'd throw her under the bus to save his damned money. I said, "Forget the directions for a minute. Fergus, what ever happens tomorrow, if that bastard lays a finger on Flo, I'll kill him where he stands."

Fergus said, "I can understand your desire to protect your woman, but—"

"No buts, one finger and he's dead meat."

Everybody stared at each other for a minute, and then Pinky said, "Fergus, give me your instructions."

"Once Conner arrives in Pitlochry, he needs to turn left off the main road onto Armoury Drive. Follow Armoury Drive under the train overpass to the picnic benches. That's where Bear, with Florence at his side, will be waiting with a suitcase full of money."

As Pinky finished his scribbling, Flo said, "I don't consider Conner a genius but he's not dumb. What happens if he doesn't fall for this scam?"

She sounds scared, I thought, but trying to act tough. "Don't worry, Babe, you clinched the deal. He'll be here."

That's when Pinky's cell buzzed. He glanced at

the screen and mouthed Conner's name. Then he said, "Hello . . . Yes, the money is here. A little over six hundred and sixteen thousand pounds is waiting your arrival."

Pinky listened to the receiver for a second and then he fed Conner the directions to the drop location. "Excellent! Everything will be in your hands in time for you and Flo to disappear into the night."

Pinky closed his cell and flashed the high sign to Fergus.

Fergus said, "Now, let's talk about the money for the drop. Delmont, first thing tomorrow, go to your bank and withdraw ten thousand pounds."

Pinky said, "But I told Conner—"

"Stop talking and listen for a change. I have access to thousands of counterfeit pound notes that we've used in decoy situations like this. Once you hand me the real ten thousand, within an hour my men will have a suitcase with your pound notes on top of each pile. Trust me, the Queen herself would accept as genuine."

Pinky smiled. "Only ten thousand? That will ease my mind a bit."

Flo snapped, "Fergus, if I know Pinky, and I do know Pinky, removing the possibility of him losing the other six hundred and forty thousand pounds will do a lot more than ease his mind a bit. Too bad you don't have access to a counterfeit Florence Sonderlund. That might ease my mind."

EIGHTEEN

Bear Zabarte, Pitlochry, Scotland

Damn it, not oatmeal again! I was about ready to grab the bowl and throw it in the trash when the Kid ran up and stuck a sheet of paper in my face.

"Bear, you've got to read this. Each year the school holds an historical pageant. My teacher, Mrs. Davies, asked me if I wanted to be a part of the school's dance group. There are only eight girl dancers. I'm the only foreigner and all eight get to wear an authentic Scottish costume. We'll learn how to dance and sing old fashioned Gaelic songs. According to Mrs. Davies, each costume will cost around twenty-five pounds, that's about forty bucks. I know that's a lot of dough, and I don't have any money, but maybe I can get a job baby sitting."

The Kid was stoked. I grabbed the release form, signed it, and said, "Hey, don't sweat the small stuff. We'll figure out a way to pay for the costume. Tell me, are the Murray boys part of the pageant too?"

"Yeah, but they only get to play stupid soldiers who wear plain brown pants, a brown shirt and carry a spear. They don't get to dance, or sing, or wear a fancy costume."

Before I could open my mouth the phone rang.

The Kid jumped up, "I'll get it." After a minute she said, "It's Uncle Fergus, and he wants to talk to you."

I ignored the phone for a second and said, "Flo, it's about time you made me a kick-ass breakfast, with bacon, eggs, and toast."

"It's oatmeal or nothing!"

I grabbed the phone, but between Flo's crappy oatmeal, and trying to figure out how I was going to tell Fergus that me, Flo, and Henry Bramble, his number-one pick for the village idiot, were going to wander around Scotland looking for Gordon Tannahill, I forgot to say hello. Before I opened my mouth,

Fergus saved my butt and said, "Bear, I found Gordon Tannahill, but I don't think you're going to like what I have to tell you."

"That's great news, I'm sure . . . hold on, what do you mean I'm not going to like it?"

"After Tannahill left Dundee, he worked for a couple of overseas contractors in Saudi Arabia. The last one was named NorConOil. I talked on the phone with their personnel director, the president of the company, and a couple of roustabouts who worked with Tannahill on a drilling rig."

"Come on, Fergus, cut to the chase."

"Two years ago, our murder suspect was stacking some drilling pipe next to a brand new well. The damn well blew up, and our boy Tannahill was killed in the explosion."

"Shit!" I sat back and thought for a second. "Fergus, before we talk about Tannahill, answer me one question. Do you Scots have to eat oatmeal every morning for breakfast?"

"In the winter, Fiona makes me a bowl every day. But in the summer I partake of eggs and bacon on occasion. Why?"

"Just wondering. Now, about that murdering bastard, Tannahill. I've an idea about him and I don't want you to get all pissed off. Okay?"

I heard him start to count.

"Fergus, what are you doing?"

"Attempting to control my temper. Go ahead. What's your idea?"

"Do you remember when we went to Edinburgh? That old babe made two copies of Tannahill's work record and you grabbed the extra copy before I could. Do you still have it?"

Fergus said, "Are all Americans as stubborn as you?"

Flo picked up my bowl of oatmeal and dropped it on my lap. She leaned over and whispered in my ear, "This time I made sure the bowl landed right side up. Next time, I won't be so careful and who knows, you could end up with hot oatmeal dumped on a part you don't want burned." She turned and walked away without saying good morning.

I said, "Fergus, except for Flo, I don't know about all Americans. Why?"

"Both you and Delmont are relentless, but at least in your case you've been blessed with a modicum of street smarts."

"I guess that's good. Now, back to that copy of Tannahill's—"

"The paper's in my office. I could stop by in a couple of minutes and you could ride with me to Perth."

"Before I say yes, tell me, is there a place in Perth where I could get myself a decent breakfast?"

"More than one. I'll be there in five minutes."

I set the phone down and said, "Babe, I've got to go to Perth with Fergus so I don't have time to finish this sticky stuff."

"Sorry, you're not going to escape that easily, I'll put the bowl in the refrigerator and nuke it in the microwave tomorrow morning. And before you ask, I can't go with you. I need to stay here and do a couple of loads of laundry."

That was all I needed to hear. I jumped up, scraped my fangs, and sprinted out the front door as Fergus' car pulled up.

I climbed in and Fergus said, "While we drive to Perth I request you listen to what I have to say and that you withhold all questions until I have finished."

What the hell was this all about? "Okay, shoot."

He merged into a space on the highway heading south and Willow's sour-puss cousin started to talk. "I wanted to become a policeman when I was a five year-old lad. After graduation from the University of St. Andrews, I ignored my father's advice, and became a member of the Perthshire Constabulary. Most of my fellow students at the university couldn't comprehend why a sane person would want to enter the profession of law enforcement."

When the car at his left started to nose into our lane, Fergus pounded his horn and yelled, "Go back to Glasgow where you belong." Then he shook his head. "I apologize. I sound as if I am prejudiced against all Weedgies."

"A what?"

"Sorry. Weedgies are what the rest of Scotland call the citizens of Glasgow. My personal feelings go back to my first year on the force when I found myself in a bit of a rammy with a gang from Glasgow."

"Slow down, Fergus. What the hell is a rammy?"

"Sorry again. A dust up. A fight. A gang of Weedgies were picking berries near Blairgowery and at the end of each day, they would take their wages into town and get drunk. After a few days, getting drunk was not enough fun so they decided to rammy with the local constable who happened to be me."

"Did you kick their ass?"

"I did, and they spent the night in Blairgowery's fine jail. Now, where was I? Oh yes, over the years, because of my college degree, hard work, and a little luck, I rapidly worked my way through the ranks in the Tayside force. Occasionally, I would question if my choice of profession was the right one for me, but after I was promoted to Western Area Crime Officer, I knew that I hadn't thrown away my education."

"Like you got to be a big cheese?" I really didn't have a clue what the dude was going on about but I jumped in so that he'd know I was listening.

"I guess you could call me that. My squad consisted of a dozen experienced detectives—good men who had worked years tracking down and arresting criminals. So there I was, the whiz kid with his college degree, but no managerial experience, and that lack of knowledge jumped up to bite me. During my first week as the Area Crime Officer, I turned over an important case, a suicide, possible murder, to a bloke named Malcolm Stewart. Malcolm had the reputation as the top detective in the shire."

He stopped talking for a minute while the traffic backed up. I still wasn't sure why Fergus wanted to spill his guts.

He cleared his throat and went on. "Pardon me, Bear, I misspoke with my last statement. Malcolm was the top investigator in Perthshire according to my predecessor. A couple of months after I gave Malcolm the suicide/murder case, I learned that his only real qualification for police work was that he and my predecessor were drinking mates."

He shook his head. "Early on, Malcolm decided that the bloke's wife had offed herself and closed the investigation. Months later, while checking out the personal records of my staff, I discovered that Malcolm regularly took off every Monday after payday. To an experienced manager, missing the Monday after a payday would have been a sure sign that the employee had some sort of abuse problem. But I was an inexperienced manager, so it took me almost a year to come to the realization that Malcolm Stewart, my brilliant detective, was a life long alcoholic. That's when I made my next mistake. I covered up his drinking problem and quickly arranged for his early retirement.

"But Malcolm's not the chief miscreant in my little story. No, that part belongs to Malcolm's old boss—my predecessor and my present boss—the Tayside Criminal Investigation Department Chief Superintendent!

"In the months after Malcolm left, I scrutinized all his past investigations—to make sure he had done a proper job, and one of those cases was the disappearance of Mary Patterson. No doubt, Malcolm preferred to down a pint with the present day Chief Superintendent rather then do a proper investigation into Mary's disappearance.

"Frankly, in my rush to cover up Malcolm's, and

my supervisor's drinking problems, I accepted, at face value, Malcolm's investigative notes concerning Mary Patterson so the final decision to close her case as a missing person was mine. That was the last time I thought of the wee lass until that morning when I was called to the golf course. The moment I spotted those bones lying in the mud by the green, I knew in my heart that they were the skeletal remains of Mary Patterson. The first day you and I met, and after I dropped you and Florence off at the cottage, I drove back to my office in Perth, pulled out all the old records and found to my shock that there were more lasses in the Pitlochry area that fit Mary's pattern."

I said, "Hey, Dude, you don't—"

"Bear, now you know why I couldn't continue Mary Patterson's investigation through normal channels. That's why I took the three of you to Edinburgh and Aberdeen. If anyone questioned what I was doing, I could tell them I was showing my American cousin, and her friends, my beautiful country.

"Then Henry Bramble, God bless him, knocked on your door and inside of five minutes you knew as much as I did. Believe me, once I contacted my cousin Willow in America, my only goal was finding Mary Patterson's murderer, not protecting my position.

"However, the moment I heard that Gordon Tannahill was dead, my fear that a serial killer could be running loose in Tayside was over. Also, the concern over my position, and my boss' drinking problem were gone.

"Now you inform me that you want to keep

digging into Gordon Tannahill's past work record. All I ask is that you investigate discreetly and keep me abreast of the results.

"Bear, from where you sit, my decisions were wrong, but at the time it seemed the best way to handle a bad situation. Remember that president of yours, Richard Nixon? The Watergate plumbers didn't bring the man down, it was the cover up that caused your disgraced president to resign. Two weeks hence, I have an appointment with the Chief Superintendent to discuss what I just told you. If I'm right, my boss will resign. If I'm wrong, I will resign. Now you know why I had to—"

I jumped in. "Fergus, I've never liked cops, but maybe the ones I didn't like were American cops. You've been damn straight with me. All me and Flo want to do is figure out who murdered that kid buried on the golf course?"

Fergus said, "That's easy, Gordon Tannahill."

"I know, but me and Flo promised Henry that we would investigate all three Pitlochry girl's disappearances. We owe him that much. I promise you that whatever we find, you'll be the only cop in Scotland to see what we come up with."

"Thank you, I appreciate that."

"Have you told Pinky about Tannahill getting vaporized?"

"Nay. Bear, between you and me, other than being my cousin's ex-husband, that wee lawyer doesn't seem to be of much use. It looks to me that you've figured out how to solve your cases in spite of him."

I laughed. "That's the boss, all right. But you'd better tell him about Tannahill or he'll get all pissed off and make my life miserable."

Fergus said, "I'll call him," but I could tell that Fergus thought he was wasting his time.

"Fergus, do you think the Red Sox are going to pull it off his year?"

"Bear, I don't have a clue what you are talking about."

I don't remember exactly if Fergus asked me to explain the game of baseball, but during the rest of the drive to Pitlochry and home, I explained the designated hitter in the American League and why the Red Sox DH was so much better than that damn Yankee DH, but I'm not sure how much got through his thick Scottish head.

He dropped me off at the cottage door. "Bear, I finally understand a batter gets four balls and only three strikes, but you lost me when you got to the designated hitter part. Before you return to America, we need to sit down with a pint at the Thistle Pub and give me the opportunity to explain rugby. Now there's a real man's sport."

He punched the gas and while I dodged a few hunks of flying gravel, I yelled, "Hey, what do you mean by a real man?"

Flo opened the door and gave me a big, juicy kiss with a little tongue, and walked me into the cottage. The tongue meant she was hot to trot, or she had found something really expensive she just had to buy.

She said, "You got some sort of guy thing going on between you and Fergus?"

"Nope. He's a cop and cops don't like to hear they've made mistakes, especially when they're talking about murder."

"Did he actually tell you he'd made a mistake concerning a murder?"

"Yeah! Well, sort of. Shit, I think so. What's important is that he's trying to fix the mistake."

I walked to the refrigerator and grabbed a bottle of Scottish Cream while Flo said, "What do you mean, he's trying to—"

"Fergus told me that the remains we found at the golf course are Mary Patterson's and he's positive that Gordon Tannahill killed her. Got anything for dinner?"

"Lamb stew. We'll eat as soon as Ettamae gets home. I still have to fix a salad."

After three, or four beers, the Kid walked in.

She said, "Hi, Bear. Have a good day?"

"Perfect. How about you?"

"School's tough, but fair, and my teacher's great."

Flo said, "Wash your hands. Dinner's on."

After the three of us polished off the whole pot of stew and a big salad, the Kid said, "Thanks for fixing dinner, Flo. I've got a ton of homework. Can I skip doing the dishes tonight?"

Flo said, "That's okay. It's Bear's turn to help with the dishes."

"It is?"

"Shut up and grab a clean towel. You're drying."

I was putting some silverware away when I remembered the rest of the day. "Babe, I almost forgot. Fergus dropped one more bomb. Now that Tannahill's dead, the Patterson case is closed."

Flo dropped her sponge into the sink. "Stop right there. What do you mean, Tannahill's dead?"

"Just what I said," I opened another beer. "The

147

bastard was vaporized in an oil rig explosion."

Then I handed her the copy Fergus gave to me.

"What's this?"

"It's the record of the jobs Miller and Urquhart gave to Gordon Tannahill before he went overseas. That's second copy Fergus grabbed so we wouldn't get a look."

She glanced at the paper. "But I thought you told me Tannahill was dead?"

"According to Fergus he is."

"What kind of an answer is that? Do you have any reason to doubt Fergus?"

"Nope."

"I don't understand. What do you expect to find off this paper that Fergus missed?"

I grabbed the sheet. "Babe, serial killers don't care about political boundaries, like State or county lines. In fact, the smart ones use those lines to their advantage. And the bad guys don't stack their victims' bodies in a neat pile in the center of town to make life easy for the cops." She looked at me in a way that told me she still didn't catch my drift. "Okay, here's an example. Do you remember reading about that truck driver who picked up and snuffed a half-a-dozen prostitutes in California, Oregon and Washington?"

She nodded. "Yes, the newspapers and TV were full of his trial. But what's that got to do with—"

"Hey, watch my lips. That's what I'm talking about. The murderer dumped six bodies along a thousand miles of Interstate 5. That road crossed a pot full of city limits, dozens of county lines, and three state borders. Think about it. Each time a body showed up, it was discovered hundreds of miles from the last one. Each body kicked off a different force of fuzz to start a new murder investigation. That's why it took so long for that truck driver to get caught. Each time the local cops found a body they chalked it up as a local murder."

Flo shook her head. "Okay, I'll give you that might have been the way it was in the old days, but with today's modern communication capability—"

"Come on, real life ain't like the movies where all the cops work together to grab the bad guy just before he cuts the throat of his next broad. I'm talking about the real world where the FBI, the state Highway Patrol, the Sheriff and city police hold onto every little piece of evidence like it's a piece of Christmas candy. Trust me, a cop doesn't get promoted unless he or she makes an arrest and nobody promotes a cop who helps an FBI agent."

Flo said, "But even if you're right, what does all that have to do with Gordon Tannahill?"

"Okay! Now let's move from the west coast of America to Scotland. Fergus is the Western Area Crime Officer for the Tayside cops. That's sort of the same as being the boss detective in the Washoe County Sheriff's department back home. With me so far?"

Flo nodded, but her eyes told me she wasn't sure where I was headed.

"Gordon Tannahill was a gypsy dozer dude, just like the truck driver who covered the west coast of the U. S., from Canada to Mexico and back. Tannahill worked all over Scotland. Babe, that bastard could be responsible for a lot more than three murders in Pitlochry. We need to check Tannahill's work assignments in Scotland against police records to see if any other girls turned up missing when he drove his dozer in their area."

Flo nodded. "You could be right, but I still don't understand why Fergus gave you Tannahill's work record?"

"Babe, we can do what he can't. Me, you, and Henry can drive all over Scotland and dig into stuff. If we come up empty handed, then we go back to America. But if we find something new, we turn it over to Fergus and he gets to close out another murder to Tannahill. Fergus is a hero, and he's still in line for Tayside's top cop job."

"Thanks for your explanation." Flo stretched and her boobs bounced around like two volleyballs wrapped in a gunnysack. "I'm tired. Are you coming to bed?"

"Not yet, I want to take a look at the crap that Fergus gave me."

She kissed me and rubbed her hand along the inside of my thigh. "Don't be too long. It's been awhile."

I said, "Now I get why there are so many kids in Scotland. Doing laundry must make the women horny."

"Hold on. Last night you tried to convince me that lamb stew was an aphrodisiac." She laughed, "See you soon."

I turned up the heater and set Tannahill's work record on the kitchen table. I checked the bookcase in the living room and found an old copy of <u>The Philip's Road Atlas of Great Britain</u>.

The only thing I knew for sure was that Gordon Tannahill, on assignment for that old fart at Miller and Urquhart, had murdered Mary Patterson and buried her body on the Pitlochry Golf Course. Now I had to figure out where else Miller and Urquhart had sent the murdering bastard.

The work sheet told me that in the year before Tannahill went overseas, he had worked at:

Edinburgh—February 21 through March 30—Harbor project.

Cupar—May 11 through June 2—Canal project.

Aberdeen—June 5 through November 14—Highway project.

I underlined the three towns and dates and stuffed the paper into my back pocket.

As soon as Henry got his car running, all we had to do was to head to those places, check through the police records, and find out if a girl went missing during the right time frame. Damn, this was going to be fun!

I turned out the light and crawled in next to Flo. Her naked body was pumping out heat like a furnace set on high. Maybe I could wake her up and show her the cool stuff I had found about Tannahill. Maybe she was still horny. But I knew she'd never fall for that line of bull. When my babe's hot to trot, a brick wall won't slow her down. But once Flo falls asleep, she wants to stay that way. Hey, maybe I'll get lucky in the morning!

NINETEEN

Pinky Delmont, Pitlochry, Scotland

Tannahill dead? Blown up in an explosion? I said, "Fergus, I cannot believe it. That seems too easy."

I pictured Willow's cousin sitting at his desk with an arched eyebrow and the identical expression he wore the last time I challenged his law enforcement skills. "Damn it, Delmont, I'm holding a copy of the man's death certificate in my hand." He hesitated and then, with a touch of sarcasm, added, "I'll make you a copy and drop it by if that would make you feel better."

Then I considered how Tannahill's incineration would be a convenient conclusion to the Patterson murder thus allowing my rapid return to Carson City and my floundering law practice. I said, "No need. So once you have incarcerated Conner for his crime of extortion, Willow and I are free to return to America."

"Delmont, are you inferring that your visit to Scotland was some sort of house arrest? You are free to do anything at anytime, and that includes buying a ticket on the first flight out of Glasgow."

"Calm down. Now, there is one item I would like to discuss, if it would not be too much trouble."

"What's that?"

"I understand that you gave Bear copy of the Miller and Urquhart work assignments for Gordon Tannahill."

"I did. Did you also require a copy?"

"I do. As Bear's superior, I feel the need to—"

"Delmont," the sound of exasperation in his voice was unmistakable. "I hate to keep repeating myself. I'm the Crimes Officer in charge of the investigation of the Mary Patterson murder. As the prime suspect, Gordon Tannahill is dead, in my professional opinion, the case is closed."

Now it was my turn to sound frustrated. "Fergus don't get mad at me. Remember, you were the one—"

A testy Fergus interrupted. "Delmont, no more than an hour ago, I concluded a phone conversation with Albert Tannahill, Gordon's only brother. He's a highly regarded professor of history at my old alma mater, the University of St. Andrews. And we agreed to—"

"I hope you informed him that his brother was a bastard who murdered a young girl and then buried her body with his bulldozer."

"No, I didn't," he sounded furious. "Damn it, Delmont, do all American lawyers come off like Clint Eastwood in an old Dirty Harry movie?"

I shouted back, "Don't call me Dirty Harry just because I find it hard to believe that Tannahill is dead."

The phone line was pregnant with silence. Then Fergus continued, but this time each word was punctuated with anger. "Dr. Tannahill and I have agreed to meet at the University tomorrow. God damn it, Delmont, the reason I called was to ask if

153

you wanted to go along."

Considering the thorn-in-his-side I'd been since my arrival in Scotland, I wasn't sure why he would voluntarily take me. "Fergus, I apologize for doubting you. Now, if I'm still invited to St. Andrews, I would love to join you." Before he could respond, I continued, "One last thought, and don not yell at me. I would like a copy of Gordon Tannahill's death certificate. I promise that I will not use the document to stir the pot."

Fergus said, "I'll give you a copy this afternoon."

"How far is St. Andrews from here?"

"Fifty to sixty miles. Why?"

"That should allow me plenty of time to authenticate the item."

"And just how do you plan on doing that?"

"I will have my cell phone with me. Fergus, I have contacts all over the world who are eager to work with me on a moment's notice."

"Delmont, I find that hard to believe."

I said, "As usual, talking with you has been a pleasure. We will continue this conversation tomorrow morning."

As I hung up the phone, Willow walked by and gave me a kiss. "What do you want for dinner tonight?" Before I could answer, she said, "How about Indian?" According to Fiona, there's an excellent Indian restaurant in Perth that makes an outstanding curry and chutney."

I said, "Excellent idea, and once we are there I can make a peace offering to Fergus."

Willow said, "What's been going on between you two that requires a peace offering?"

I said, "Nothing new. He and I just do not see

eye to eye on various items."

"If we're going out, I need to do something with my hair. Will you call Fiona and ask her if they can come? And we should include Bear and Flo. Call them and we'll make this a grand party."

Before I could say a word of protest concerning adding Bear and that woman to the list, Willow walked into the bathroom and closed the door.

I dialed Fiona.

"Pinky, that's brilliant. You'll love the food, but I should warn you that some of the curries, like the Vindaloo, are a wee bit hot. As long as you and Willow stick with the Madras you'll do fine."

"Fiona, you're talking to a man who eats Mexican food on a regular basis. If you think Vindaloo is hot, you should try nibbling a few Chipotle peppers."

Fiona said, "Do what you like, but don't say I didn't warn you. Have you called Flo?"

"Not yet."

"Fine. I'll call her, and assuming she and Bear haven't made other plans, I'll call the restaurant and book a table for nine people. One final point, I'm positive we can all squeeze into one car to save petrol. I'll call Fergus and ask him to meet us at the restaurant."

I pictured riding in her van packed with eight people. Granted three were not fully-grown, but the thought of being trapped between Bear and Flo for fifteen minutes was not a pretty thought. My silence informed Fiona, better than my words could have, that I was not pleased with the prospect.

"Pinky, it's only ten miles. All the strong men I know have endured a child sitting on their lap for fifteen minutes. So it's settled. We'll take one car to the restaurant."

That woman just manipulated me into dropping my argument and agreeing to her terms! For a brief moment I considered the hell that Fergus must go through on a daily basis. I hesitated, and then said, "After you call the restaurant for reservations, pick us up first. That way I will have my choice of seat."

Willow sat up front with Fiona while I was sandwiched in the second seat between Ettamae and Flo. As I refused to sit with the boys, Bear joined them on the third seat. Fiona was correct, I endured, but thank God the drive took less than fifteen minutes.

Eventually, we walked into the restaurant. Fergus was sitting at the bar working on a beer. When we approached, Fergus gave Fiona a kiss and a hug, Willow a peck on her cheek, and I heard a perfunctory grunt that sounded close to Delmont.

The hostess had set up a large round table, and I participated in my first Indian cuisine adventure that consisted of Dhal soup, rice, and three types of curry, one Vindaloo, and two Madras.

Everyone, excluding myself, seemed to have a great time during the exotic and festive dinner. Bear and Willow organized a contest for Ettamae and the Murray boys. They would take a bite of Vindaloo curry and then see who could hold out the longest before taking a drink of something cold to dampen the fire.

Fiona, usually surrounded with two boys and a husband, seemed to appreciate having some females around. She talked with Ettamae, Bear's woman, and Willow most of the evening. That left Fergus,

156

Bear, and myself, as the remaining conversational grouping and we spent most of our time avoiding direct eye contact.

After the waitress served up a large bowl of freshly peeled oranges, mangoes and bananas for dessert, Willow stood and hit her beer glass a couple of times with her fork. Once she had the attention of the table, she raised her glass and announced, "A toast to our Scottish kin, the Murrays."

I lifted my glass and smiled at Fergus, and ever so slowly, his frozen lips thawed into a small grin. Fergus stood and said, "Hear, hear." It seemed that in Scotland, a touch of kinship can make up for a lot of ill will.

The adults downed a gulp of beer, or red wine, while the kids worked on their lemonade. Fergus remained standing. "Now it's my turn. I'd like to make a toast to the Delmonts. We are bound by Murray blood for eternity. Ettamae, Bear, and Florence, with this toast, you are now honorary members of the Murray clan. "

I thought his toast was a kind gesture but a touch heavy on the eternal fealty to the bloodline. Everyone cheerfully clinked glasses and drank their liquid as the waitress laid the final check on the table. Willow grabbed it and handed the dinner check to me. With her nearly imperceptible nod, I accepted the check from her and handed it, along with my business credit card, to the waitress.

Except for a few complaints concerning the volume of food, everyone happily made their way toward the exit. Fergus stopped in the lobby and said, "Willow, you and the children ride back to the farm with Fiona. I need to talk over some important business with Delmont, Bear and Florence."

Willow flashed me her what-the-hell-is-going-on look and said, "Is that all right with you, Fiona?"

She nodded, "Anytime I can drive and don't have to sit in the back seat with those hooligan sons of mine, I'm a happy mother."

Fergus said, "Then we're off. First car back to the farm wins an ice cream treat."

Fiona gunned her engine and the car shot toward the road to Pitlochry.

I said, "Fergus, I thought we had everything settled?"

He looked at me, Bear and his woman, and said, "We have. Over the past few days I've talked with the three of you and I've decided to split the trio into two teams based on your unique talents. Delmont, you will accompany me to St. Andrews to interview Albert Tannahill, Gordon's brother. Bear, Florence, you are to ride with Henry to the last three locations where Gordon worked before he met his untimely death overseas. Does anyone have any questions concerning your assignments?"

I said, "None. And once we resolve the Conner situation, Willow and I will be on the first flight home."

That woman said, "I'm cool with that. Assuming our trips with Henry come up blank, we'll be ready to go home once Conner is behind bars."

"Babe," Bear said, "We can't go home before the Kid does her dance thing. Remember, I gave her five of those funny dollars so she could buy the material for her costume."

Flo nodded. "Right. And Pinky, I'll bet that Willow will want to stick around because that celebration is all about the Murray clan, her clan. Right, Fergus?"

"Aye. Her last name maybe Stone, but she is, and will always be, a Murray. Any further questions?"

That woman had no response to Fergus, so the four of us quietly rode back to the farm.

TWENTY

Bear Zabarte, Pitlochry Scotland

My day started out great 'cause Flo finally got the message and fixed me a kick-ass breakfast. Six slices of thick bacon, four eggs, sunny-side up, and a pile of toast made out of oatmeal bread was waiting for me when I sat down at the table. Just as I was sopping up the last bit of bright yellow egg yolk off the plate, some idiot fired off a shotgun outside the front door of the cottage.

Flo was putting away the dishes from last night and she jumped about a foot in the air dropping a cup. The damn thing hit the floor and shattered into a million pieces.

"Don't move, Babe." I said, "I'll figure out what's going on." I peeked out the window, and there was Henry standing next to his sixty-year-old taxi. Actually, the car was sort of hidden behind a cloud of black smoke that poured out of the tail pipe.

I said, "It's only Henry and his car."

Flo grabbed a broom and started to sweep the broken pieces of cup off the floor while I opened the door. "Hey, that was a quick fix."

He grinned from ear to half-ear.

"Aye."

Flo pushed me through the doorway and walked

around the car like a piss-filled dog checking out a fire hydrant. She said, "Henry, the car cleaned up real nice."

"Aye, she's a beauty all right."

Flo opened the door on the driver's side. "Would you mind if I sat behind the wheel?"

Henry shook his head.

Flo twisted the wheel and made noises like I used to do when I was six or seven and pretending to drive a race car. She looked at me and grinned. "Henry, could I take her for a short spin around the barn?"

"Aye."

She fired up the engine, and after a couple of sharp grinding noises, the car shot toward the barn.

I said, "Henry, did you remember the bill for fixing the car?"

"Aye." He pulled out a greasy wad of paper from his back pocket and shoved it toward me.

I opened the balled up bill and saw it came from the Pitlochry Automobile Works—Replace one burned piston. Tune, and lube. Total—£180. If I had this conversion crap down, it looked like Pinky's five hundred was going to cover the whole tab. Damn, I hoped Pinky remembers his promise. I stuffed the bill in my pocket and said, "I'll stop by the shop and take care of this the next time I get into Pitlochry. Will that be okay with the mechanic?"

"Aye."

Flo and the Austin zipped around the barn a third time and then skidded to a stop next to Henry. Flo winked at me and said, "Henry, if you get tired of driving while we cruise around the countryside, you can call on me."

Henry frowned. "We're not just cruising 'round you know. We 'ave important investigative work to do."

I said, "And we need to talk about that investigation. Flo, drag your butt out of that car and into the cottage. We've got stuff to talk about."

She jumped out of the car, glared at me, and gave me a snappy salute, the kind you see in one of those old John Wayne war movies.

"Yes sir, captain." She turned and marched into the cottage.

Henry's face went blank, like he wasn't used to Flo's normal pain-in-the-ass moves.

"Don't worry, Henry. That's her way of making a joke. Come inside, have a beer, and I'll show you what I've found out."

First thing, I told Henry that Tannahill's dead— got blown up someplace overseas.

"Are you sure? I 'ad a dream last night that told me 'e's alive."

"No accounting for dreams."

We sat down at the kitchen table. Flo popped the tops off two beers and set them in front of me and Henry.

Henry stuck his hand over his bottle and said, "Nay, but a cuppa would 'it the spot."

I said, "Great. I'll drink both." I showed Henry Gordon Tannahill's work record. "Henry, we're damn sure that Tannahill killed Mary Patterson, but now that he's dead, maybe we should drop the investigation."

Henry's wild right eye bounced up and down so bad that it looked like a ball in one of those Chinese ping-pong games I've seen on TV.

I said, "Or we can do what you want to do and check out the other spots that Tannahill worked—Cupar, Aberdeen and Edinburgh."

His eye stopped bouncing. "Aye. That way we can find out if there are any other murders that fit the dates of 'is work record. Bear, I won't rest 'til we finish the investigation. The parents of those lasses need to learn what 'appened to their kin." He picked up the sheet. "Cupar is close. We could do that today."

Flo said, "Excuse me, but is Cupar close to St. Andrews?"

"Aye. Do you like golf?"

Flo said, "I used to play a lot of golf. I'd feel as if I'd let some history slip through my fingers if I didn't see St. Andrews before we return home."

Henry said, "And you, Bear?"

"No golf for me. I'm a baseball man. Just want to watch the Red Sox kick the crap out of those damn Yankees."

Flo said, "For once in your life forget that stupid game. People have been playing golf at the Old Course in St. Andrews since the fifteenth century."

Henry scratched the scar on his cheek and asked, "Do you fancy playing eighteen on the Old Course?"

For a second Flo looked like a little girl who found her favorite doll. "I'd give anything to do that. I played golf on my college team. I never reached the top fifty female players in the NCAA, but I came real close. Henry, I've read that the Old Course is so crowded that there's no way I could get on with this short notice."

"I could phone me brother Cecil. 'E's the Caddie

Master at the Old Course. Did you bring your clubs?"

"No."

"No problem, me brother will set you up with a brilliant set."

Flo said, "Did you play golf, Henry?"

"Aye, but not since me accident. But before that tree branch 'it me I was the Pitlochry Club champion. I'll need to call me brother."

She said, "Hey, call him on my cell phone." Flo started to hand Henry her cell phone, but he backed off like a guy who thought the phone was a rattlesnake about to sink its fangs into his hand. "Go ahead, just push those buttons and talk to him like you would with a regular phone."

"Aye."

I said, "How far is the drive to Cupar?"

"'Bout forty miles. But St. Andrews is another eight, nine miles further."

"I'll call that an hour. Give us three hours. No, better make that four hours of investigating time. If we left here now, one hour plus four takes us to one o'clock. If Flo's going to play her silly-ass game, tell Cecil she won't be ready until two."

"Aye."

A couple of minutes later, Henry handed Flo her phone back. "Cecil dinna think you could get in a full eighteen starting at two. So he's set you up for ten o'clock."

Flo yelled, "Oh my God, I'm playing the Old Course in two hours!"

I said, "Hold on, I said two o'clock."

"Aye. But this way Flo can play golf while we do our investigating in Cupar. If we finish early, we'll be forced to go to a pub, drink beer, and watch a rugby match on the telly."

Good plan, I thought, the pub sounded great, but I didn't want to let Flo off that easily. "Henry, me and Flo are running on a tight budget. How much will it cost her to play eighteen holes?"

"She's playing with Cecil!"

I said, "What the hell does that mean?"

"It's free."

When he said free, Flo gave the good side of Henry's face a big kiss.

I pulled out my cell and called Fergus.

"Hello."

"Glad I caught you. Are you still home?"

"Aye."

"Me and Henry are driving to Cupar, the first town on my list. Could you come up with a letter telling everybody I'm a college professor, or something, doing research on missing teenage girls over the last thirty years. Say in the letter that I'm your cousin and really interested in the last ten years. Okay?"

Fergus said, "Aye. The letter will go like this: The bearer of this letter is a visiting relative from America. At present, he is working on his doctoral research concerning the differences between how American and Scottish police departments search for teen-agers who have gone missing. The scope of his research will be focused on the last decade. Will that work?"

"Perfect. Have you heard anything from Conner?"

"Nay. I have my contacts at the Glasgow airport car rental agencies on the look-out. He won't get into Scotland unnoticed."

"Good. Where are you and Pinky going?"

"The University of St. Andrews."

"Is that the same town where they have a place called the Old Course?"

"It is."

"We'll be there too. Henry's brother, Cecil, is the Caddie Master and he set up a round of golf with Flo. They start at ten this morning."

He chuckled. "I forgot all about Cecil. You never know what Henry's going to come up with."

A few minutes later, Fergus knocked. I let him in. "Here's your letter. Good luck and I hope you find something."

I yelled to Flo who was in the bathroom. "Finish up in there. We've got to get moving or you'll be late for your stupid golf game with Cecil."

TWENTY-ONE

Bear Zabarte, Pitlochry, Scotland

When Flo got in the car, she said, "When I woke up I knew this was going to be a great day."

"Babe, you never told me you played golf."

"That's just one of the many things you don't know about me."

"Many things?"

"Yes."

Shit, I hated it when she did that to me. We'd both been around the block more than once before we met in LA, but my stuff was just bar tending, a trumped-up murder charge, and a couple of dozen girl friends. Flo? She kept coming up with the weirdest crap, from more than one ex-husband —to being a computer wiz—to a pot full of shady business partners, and now she was a top college golfer? Does she make all this shit up, or what?

We only moved about a hundred yards, next to the bridge over Ordie Burn, when Flo told Henry to stop.

And that's another thing. Why in hell do these people call a little stream of water a burn when the stream should be called a creek?

Anyway, Flo told Henry to stop the car and he did.

Henry said, "Do you 've a problem?"

Flo shook her head. "It's just that I want to drive the car to St. Andrews."

I glanced at Henry. His wild eye bopped around, like he was trying to figure out a way to tell Flo to jump in the burn and swim back to the cottage. But after a couple of seconds, he got out and held the driver's door for her, like she was the queen, or something. Once she got in and settled, he said, "Don't push 'er too 'ard. She tends to bog down around thirty-five."

Fifteen minutes into our ride I handed Henry the letter Fergus gave me. "Read this. I think it might help us."

The letter looked real official—at the top, in fancy letters, it said Tayside Police.

Henry read out loud, "Bear Zabarte is an American scholar and he is working on a research project for his Doctorate in Police Science at the University of Nevada, Reno. Please allow him access to all records and information he requires to complete his research on missing persons."

Henry's good eye stared at the letter and then zeroed in on me. "A Doctorate in Police Science?"

"Yup. That's something you can get after you graduate from college."

"Aye, I know what 'tis."

"You think the doctor part is too much of a stretch?"

"Aye, and I don't see 'ow you ever graduated from college."

"You think the investigation would work better if you did most of the talking?"

"Aye."

Flo was doing a good job driving, but just like

Henry told her, every time the speedometer got close to thirty-five, the front end started to shimmy, and the smoke coming from the exhaust pipe in the rear changed from light gray to dark black. It looked to me like this car burned more oil than gas.

Henry said, "On the left is the city of Dundee, the Tayside County seat, and the office of the Chief Superintendent of Criminal Investigation Department."

Flo said, "Fergus' boss?"

"Aye." He pointed at a large brick building on a hill. "I think 'e's sitting there now, in the big corner office, behind a large desk."

Flo said, "Do you see Fergus in that office someday?"

"Nay. Fergus likes fishing with his boys too much. I fear being the leader of the Tayside police would wring the life out of the man."

We crossed the Tay Road Bridge, turned south toward St. Andrews and by nine me and Flo were following Henry's directions to his brother's office. Henry introduced us to Cecil. He had the same, fireplug build as Henry except he didn't have Henry's wonky eye.

Cecil pointed at a big, brown patch of land, and said, "That's the Old Course. The city of St. Andrews owns all the six golf courses on that spit of land between the town and the bay. All six are laid out on the sandy dunes. Unlike your courses in America, and in deference to the church, our courses are closed on Sunday. That patch becomes a gigantic park where families picnic next to the famous Swilken Burn."

There's that damn burn thing again. I jumped

in. "Cecil, do you know why a creek is called a burn?"

"Swilken Burn?"

"Yup."

Cecil stared at me for a second, then shook his head. "Nay. Florence, if we are to be on the first tee by nine, we need to hurry on to the practice putting green."

Flo said, "Aye. What time should they pick me up?"

Cecil looked at Henry. "Give us six hours. That's a grievous amount of time to play eighteen holes of golf, but the tourists get upset if we rush them."

Flo said, "Henry, Bear, see you at four. Cecil, how many strokes are you giving me a side?"

"Lass, I dinna know your game."

Flo said, "You can trust me. I'd say three strokes a side would be proper."

Cecil said, "Three strokes a side? Florence, I wouldn't give my 90 year-old grandmother three strokes a side. I should be playing you scratch, but to keep the peace between us, I will offer you one stroke."

"One stroke? No less than two a nine and that's my final offer."

Henry jabbed me in the side. "We should go. Once golfers start arguing over strokes, it's time for 'onest folks like us to leave."

I said, "Before we go, I know this is going to sound dumb, but your Old Course doesn't look like any golf course I've seen on TV. Where are the trees, lakes, and green grass? That's nothing out there but brown hills and sandy spots."

"Aye. Golf at the Old Course is the way golf should be played everywhere." He pointed at a deep hole filled with sand below us. "Do you know why that sand is there?"

"Nope."

Henry sighed, and dipped his head so he could focus his right eye. "Before golf was first played at St. Andrews, the dunes were used to graze sheep." He waved his hand south at the brown ground. "When the weather turned bad, the sheep would gather together and seek protection behind a small mound or 'illock against the wind and rain. Over the years, the wee feet of the sheep broke through the sod and down to the sand that lies 'neath the grass. The sheep created those sand bunkers. The links at the Old Course is true golf with wind, rain, real bunkers, prickly gorse, and brown grass."

He stared at me and I guess I still looked sort of stupid. Henry shook his head and said, "Bear, the game of golf is not supposed to be a friendly walk in a peaceful park. Golf is a battle with nature and life itself."

I patted his shoulder. "Henry, I've watched golf on TV and that was as exciting as watching two Sumo wrestlers bang into each other. Ready to head to Cupar?"

He sighed. "Aye. This way."

Cupar was crawling with people and the closest parking space Henry could find was about ten blocks away from the police station. We walked past a bunch of women with bags filled with stuff. Henry said, "'Tis a market day."

Finally we reached the police station. A uniformed dude sat behind a counter and he didn't see, or hear me 'cause he was working on a crossword puzzle.

I walked up and hit the counter with my fist. The dude jumped up, looked at me, and stuffed his puzzle out of sight. "Good morning, gentlemen. I'm Sergeant Thomas McCain. Can I 'elp you?"

"Hi. My name is Bear Zabarte and this dude is Henry Bramble. I'm from America and I'm sort of doing some research—"

Henry said, "This lad has come all the way from America to work on his doctoral dissertation concerning 'ow we 'andle missing persons cases in Scotland."

The cop cocked his head and stared at me. "Really? Any year in particular?"

"Aye. The year 2002."

I handed him Fergus' letter. "This was written by Western Area Crime Officer Fergus Murray of Tayside."

Henry added, "I believe the contents should clear up any questions you might 'ave."

We cooled our heels and watched the Sergeant's eyes scan the letter while his lips mouth each word.

He handed back the letter and said, "I'm 'appy to meet you Mr. Zabarte, and I'm pleased to see that Officer Murray endorses your pursuit of knowledge, but you must understand that this is a working police station in the small town of Cupar. I'm the only officer on duty 'til Angus, uh . . . Sergeant Methven, arrives. When 'e comes in, we'll see if 'e approves you 'aving a go at our records."

It was obvious that me and Henry's investigation had screwed up his perfect day.

Henry said, "Thank you, Sergeant McCain. Will Sergeant Methven arrive soon?"

"Aye." The dude sat down, grabbed his puzzle,

and went back to filling in the letters.

I glanced around. In front of the counter, the room was empty—not a chair or bench for anyone to sit on. It looked to me like people didn't drop into the Cupar station for a cup of tea like old Henry did in Pitlochry. I leaned up against the wall and watched the second hand of the clock go round and round. Henry seemed happy, but after two or three minutes, I started to feel like one of those fat broads waiting for somebody to ask them to dance at the high school prom.

After ten minutes ticked by, a uniformed dude with red hair and white sideburns walked through the door. His face was wrinkled and he was obviously older than McCain who sat behind the counter. The older cop stopped when he noticed me and Henry leaning against the wall. "Good morning, my name is Sergeant Methven. May I 'elp you?"

Sergeant McCain stowed his puzzle when the older dude walked in and said, "Angus, they 'ave a letter from Western Area Crime Officer Murray out of Tayside requesting our assistance reviewing some of our records. I told them they would 'ave to wait until you came on duty."

As I shook Sergeant Methven's hand, I noticed that he had four stripes on his sleeve. The cop behind the counter had only two, so the older dude outranked him.

Sergeant Methven said, "Good work, Thomas. I'm here now so you can escort these gentlemen to the record room." Methven and McCain traded places and we followed McCain down a hallway to a door.

The cop opened the door and took us inside the record room. I quickly scanned the room and thought, damn, it's Miller and Urquhart all over but a tenth the size. But at least there was a window, and only twenty file cabinets to go through instead of a couple hundred.

The dude pointed at the cabinet at the far wall. "I think you'll see all the information you're lookin' for is 'ere but it may be 'ard to find. Everything is filed by type of crime. The Mis-Per files are in the two file cabinets under the window. You said you were interested in 2002?"

Henry said, "That's correct, Sergeant."

He shook his head. "Many of our files are in a bit of a state. We 'ad so many drunkenness cases we had to move some into the Mis-Per cabinets so you'll need to check at least those eight cabinets to the left of the window. Also, I fear you will find many of the date tabs 'ave fallen off so finding the proper year might be difficult."

Henry nodded. "Thank you, Sergeant. We can manage."

Henry's words turned out to be really dumb. We spent damn near five hours digging through stacks of old folders as high as my shoulders. Also, the dude's guess of the number of files missing date tabs was off by about a thousand or so. And most of the folders were just lying in the file drawers, like stacks of old newspapers, not hanging there like that cool filing system Pinky uses in his office. But the worst part was the dust. Every time I picked up a file, another cloud of dust would hit my nose, and I'd sneeze. It took me fifty sneezes to figure out that the first cabinet was filled with really old cases. Thirty sneezes later, Henry finally found the right decade. I lifted out a four-foot stack of files, gave half to

Henry, and I took the rest. After awhile, Henry cried out, "'ere's one."

He handed me a folder stamped CLOSED in big red letters on the front. It was about a teenage girl named Verity McPher. She was sixteen when she disappeared on May 15, 1999, from a farm a mile north of Cupar. This was what we were looking for. "Good work. We know that Tannahill worked in the Cupar area from May 11 to June 2 so he was here."

I flipped to the back pages in the file. "Forget it. On the last page the cops say that Verity popped up in Edinburgh. She was arrested for prostitution and drugs on September 12, 1990. Damn, now we know why the case was marked closed."

We finished the rest of the files, and when I dropped them all into the third drawer, the last cloud of dust flew up my nose. Between my last two sneezes, I said, "Partner, looks like we struck out."

Henry frowned.

I said, "Struck out is an old baseball saying. What it really means is that we just wasted a bunch of hours and all we have to show for our time is . . ." I blew my nose. ". . . a million sneezes."

Henry sighed, "Aye, we struck out."

Like a couple of punch-drunk boxers, we walked back to the office. Sergeant Methven looked up from his newspaper and asked, "Did you find what you're looking for?"

Henry said, "Nay, but we want to thank you both for all your fine assistance."

After we returned to Henry's car, he said, "I was sure we'd find a couple of missin' lasses."

"Me too. Every investigation I've done I've come up with something. I'm not sure how many more afternoons I want to waste digging through dusty files, sneezing, and blowing my nose."

Henry grabbed my shirt. "But you promised we'd check out Cupar, Edinburgh, and Aberdeen. That means we still 'ave two towns to go."

Damn! With this dude, a promise was like getting married. "Slow down, I didn't say we're going to quit. You've got to remember the lesson that Ted Williams taught the rest of the world."

"Who's Ted Williams?"

"Ted, the Splendid Splinter! When the man was thirty-nine, he lead the American League with a .388 batting average." I glanced at Henry, and I could tell that batting .388 for a full season didn't convince him. "Ted Williams fought in two wars, and when he was almost forty, he was the top hitter in all of baseball. Just because he struck out once in a while, Ted didn't let his dauber droop and we shouldn't either. We'll figure out if Tannahill killed any more girls."

He shrugged his shoulders, started the engine, and in twenty minutes we picked up Flo at Cecil's office in St. Andrews.

We hardly left the parking lot when Flo started whining. "I'm still waiting for one of you ask me how I played? Or did you like the Old Course? Or did you clean out Cecil's wallet?"

"Babe, I was going to ask all that after I told you what we found at the Cupar police station."

Flo said, "Sorry, I forgot all about that. What did you find?"

I said, "Zilch. Other than a crappy filing system, we came up with nothing. In case you missed that, zero, nada. How about you? Did you play good? Did you like the Old Course? Is Cecil tapped out?"

"Yes to all questions. Henry, how'd you like to stop at the next restaurant we see and spend some of your brother's money on dinner?"

He knitted his brow, shook his head and said, "I dinna think so."

The Austin hit the top of a hill and I spotted a sign by the road that said: St. Michael's Inn. Rooms—Lunch—Dinner.

I tapped Henry's shoulder. "Hey, Cecil's money is buying dinner."

Once he figured out that somebody else was picking up the tab, Henry cranked the wheel real hard, and the Austin turned into the parking lot.

The minute I opened the door to the joint, the smell of food hit my nose and I figured out how hungry I was. But Henry? He stood at the front door, like he was confused or something. I pushed him in and the three of us passed a bar where a couple of dudes and one babe were downing brews. A really big guy with a giant gray beard met us outside the dining room and took us to a table next to a big fireplace. Once we sat down, he gave us menus, and said, "Your waitress will be 'ere in a jiffy."

As I checked out the list of food, I glanced at Henry. He was just sitting there and his menu lay in front of him.

Flo said, "Do you go out to dinner often, Henry?"

"Nay. In me whole life the only time I dinna eat at home, I was in the 'ospital after me accident."

I said, "How about I order some guy food for both of us?"

"Aye, you do that."

The waitress stopped by. She was about twenty,

had red hair, freckles, and a great pair of boobs.

Flo snapped, "Bear, pull your eyes back to the menu. The lady is waiting."

I ordered two pints of Scottish Cream, a glass of red wine, and told the redheaded babe that when she got back we'd be ready to order.

I said, "OK, Henry, there's some great stuff on the menu. Would you go for a steak, lamb stew, or fried trout?"

Henry's wonky eye jumped around. "Aye."

The waitress returned with our beer and Flo's wine.

Flo said, "I'll have the trout."

"Me and Henry will go for the lamb stew and a steak."

A couple of minutes later she served us a large basket of bread, a giant mound of bright yellow butter, and three bowls of a kick-ass green pea soup.

Henry polished off his soup, most of the bread and butter, belched a big one, and pushed his chair away from the table.

I said, "Hold on dude, there's more food coming."

His lips moved, like he was trying to say something. Then he blinked his broken eye, and pulled his chair back to the table.

The main courses arrived and I asked the waitress to set the steak and lamb stew in the center of the table. After she left, I said, "Henry, pick the one that looks and smells the best to you."

He grabbed the lamb stew and left the steak for me.

Thirty minutes later, and after Henry used the last piece of bread to mop up the last splotch of lamb gravy off his plate, he patted his bulging belly and sat back. "That was the best food I ever 'ad. Even better than the food at the 'ospital. I'll 'ave to try this restaurant idea again."

Flo giggled. "Now I understand how Dr. Frankenstein must have felt when he created his monster."

An hour later the car pulled up outside our cottage. The sky looked like a room with a ceiling painted gray and the wind was blowing hard. The cottage was dark and once the noise of Henry's little four-cylinder engine died down, Flo jumped out. "Thanks, Henry. I look forward to our next investigation."

She unlocked the door, took a long look, and turned. "Bear, get in here. Pinky and Fergus are inside waiting for us. Pinky received a call from Conner. It seems he landed at Heathrow, not Glasgow."

"No shit," I said. "Is he on his way to Pitlochry?"

"Nobody knows. Fergus is checking the car rental agencies at Heathrow."

"I tried to warn Fergus that we're dealing with a slippery bastard."

Henry said, "Is there a problem?"

Flo looked at me. I nodded and said, "Yup, I'm afraid there is. Come on in and join the fun."

After Henry met Pinky, and I polished off my first of three brews, Fergus told Henry the background story of Ice Conner.

Henry said, "Bear and I spent the whole day looking for a murderer and now this. Flo, do you 'ave an extra beer?"

Flo said, "You got it. Henry, we're partners in the Tannahill investigation, and now you know

179

everything about Conner. Maybe you can help us figure out what to do with a criminal who's come to Great Britain to pick up a million bucks and little old me."

TWENTY-TWO

Pinky Delmont-St. Andrews, Scotland

We arrived at St. Andrews. After we passed through an unusual combination of Medieval, Victorian, and Edwardian buildings, crowded with tourists bent on spending their hard-earned dollars on worthless trinkets, we reached the campus of the University of St. Andrews.

Fergus pulled into a parking spot with a sign that proclaimed Faculty Only, set the brake, and stared out the window for a moment. "Delmont, it's been many years since I graduated from these hallowed halls, and except for the model year of the vehicles parked on this street, nothing has changed." He pulled the key from the ignition. "Follow me to the faculty quarters."

The sun was surrounded by a cloudless, blue sky, but the air temperature was brisk with the scent of the sea in the breeze. After a few moments of vigorous walking, we stood before an imposing three-story Edwardian stone structure that looked as if it had been built before the state of Nevada had been admitted to the Union.

"This is the home of Professor Albert Tannahill." Fergus chuckled as we entered the building. "When I was a student, I would have considered my life a complete success if I could have lived in a building this grand."

He sprinted up a flight of stairs and I attempted to follow his example, but after a few steps I rapidly realized that my profession, unlike his, did not require that I maintain a high level of physical prowess. I took a few deep gasps, stopped and said, "Does your dream location include an elevator?"

"I'm sorry to report, no. Do you want me to slow down?"

"Not on my account!" I was not going to let Fergus get the upper hand! He turned and sprinted up the second flight and I followed his example to the landing. While my heart threatened to burst through my rib cage, Fergus checked the polished brass nameplates on the four doors that opened onto the alcove. He pointed at one and knocked gently. As my breathing returned to normal, the door opened. A man I guessed to be in his mid-forties opened the door. He smiled and said, "Please come in Officer Murray and . . . ?"

Before I could open my mouth Fergus answered, "This is Mr. Delmont."

We entered into a compact living area with floor to ceiling bookcases lining the walls to my left and right. A small fireplace took up most of the wall opposite the entry door and radiated heat from a bed of glowing coal. The floor space was filled with three overstuffed chairs placed in a conversational arrangement; two were covered in soft blue velvet and the remaining chair was upholstered in a brown leather. With a perfunctory hand gesture, Dr. Tannahill offered us the two blue chairs. "Would either of you care for a sherry?"

To me, ten in the morning could be considered a

touch early, and I had never developed an appreciation for sherry, but I was still struggling for my breath, and Fergus answered before I could respond. "Thank you, Dr. Tannahill. We both appreciate your hospitality."

The good professor walked to a teacart near the fireplace, poured three sherries, providing me the opportunity to study the man. He wore highly polished brown shoes. His tan wool slacks were graced with a razor sharp crease. Dr. Tannahill topped off his stylish splendor with a chocolate-brown cashmere sweater. When he handed me the glass of sherry, I had the occasion to study his face. My original estimate of his age seemed correct. His skin was smooth and chalk white, the sort of complexion one would expect from a man who lived this far north and spent all his daylight hours lecturing inside a building. He was clean-shaven and, as he turned to serve Fergus, I noticed a port-wine-stain birthmark, about the size of a quarter, behind his left ear.

"I hope you enjoy the sherry. Each summer, a Medieval History professor by the name of Archibald McManus makes an educational trek to Spain and he brings me back a full case. I've never been able to find this label in Scotland so Archie's largess is a true boon to me."

Tannahill sat down in the leather chair, took a sip, and said, "Now that everyone is warm and partaking in the harvest of Spain's golden sun, what can I do for you today?"

"We're investigating the murder of a girl in Pitlochry, and I fear the evidence points toward your brother, Gordon. I came today to get some background information from you concerning his childhood—stories only a brother would know. For example, what was it like growing up with Gordon? Did he exhibit any abnormal tendencies?"

"Ah yes, dear Gordon. I imagine the answer to your last question depends on who has written the definition of abnormal tendencies. But first, are you familiar with the study of eugenics?"

At this point, other than handing me a glass of Spanish sunshine, the good Doctor was acting as if Fergus was the only man in the room. Not used to being ignored, I leaned forward and forced my way into the conversation. "Eugenics is the science that deals with the improvement of the hereditary qualities of a race or breed. I believe the Nazis felt they had the inside track on using eugenics to develop the superior race."

Tannahill turned to face me, as if he were surprised to hear I was capable of expressing an opinion. "Ah, another voice is heard from and an American one at that. You are correct, Mr. Delmont, and I am amazed that one of your age is well versed concerning the history of World War Two."

I took a sip of sherry and was immediately reminded why I did not like the taste of oxidized wine. "Doctor Tannahill, as I recall, America was also a participant in that war. Now, if you can return your attention to the subject at hand, what does eugenics have to do with your brother?"

Doctor Tannahill shifted his posture and attention to me. For an instant, I detected a flush of anger in his eyes. Then he smiled, and said, "A colleague of mine here at the university, Professor Wilhelm Van Vorst, has made eugenics his life

184

study." Tannahill stood up and began to pace between his chair and the fireplace, as if he were beginning to lecture his students. "Van Vorst theorizes that due to the enormity of the human genome, there will always be a few genetic errors, the black sheep that occasionally pops-up in families. Van Vorst believes if any organized group, such as the Nazis, attempt to create the perfect race of people, they would have to weed out the genetic errors. My brother Gordon was a classic example of one of those genetic errors. Why do I say that? At this point in the discussion some family background is in order. Our parents were respected, well-educated people. Prior to getting married, my mother was a lady-in-waiting to the Queen. My father is a cousin of the Duke of Atholl. I was the first child and a year later my brother Gordon was born. I turned out to be a success and Gordon was a total failure. Mr. Delmont, do not forget, Gordon and I were both created from the identical, exemplary gene pool."

Tannahill hesitated, picked up the wine decanter, refilled our glasses, and continued, "Looking back now, I am positive my mother and father understood there was something different concerning Gordon from the day he was born, but I digress. My brother and I grew up and attended the same schools. I embraced learning. Gordon on the other hand hated school. I loved to read, but he abhorred books. I continued my education and received my Doctorate. Gordon dropped out of school at the first opportunity. Inspector, you asked specifically about abnormal tendencies? That's a good question. While I am not an expert in that field, I know that Gordon didn't fit in with the rest of my family. It was as if an ear of yellow corn had formed inside the green shell of a pea pod. Gordon was that ear of corn in my family of pea pods. After he left school, Gordon drifted around construction sites, and because he was bright, he quickly learned the craft of operating heavy equipment. The last time we talked, just before he went overseas, he was sitting in the same chair you are, Mr. Delmont, and he laughed at me. He scorned the brother who became the Master of the Scottish History Department at Scotland's premier university and do you know why?"

Fergus and I both shook our heads.

"My genetically flawed brother made twice the money driving a bulldozer as I received as a college professor. Now, I believe you stated earlier that evidence points to my brother concerning the murder of a girl in Pitlochry. I am afraid I know nothing about that, but I would, and could believe anything concerning the abnormal actions of my brother."

Fergus rubbed his nose, a nervous trait I had observed he employed when he was about to ask an important question. "Thank you, Professor. I appreciate your frankness. It's our understanding that Gordon was killed in an oil field explosion in Saudi Arabia."

"That is correct. Six months ago, I made the long trip to the far east to recover what I could of my brother's remains."

Fergus said, "Dr. Tannahill, to the best of your knowledge, had Gordon ever been arrested?"

"No, but I fear there were times when he should have been. My father spent a good part of his fortune covering up Gordon's transgressions during his school years, but to the best of my knowledge, he was

186

never arrested."

I said, "What exactly do you mean by Gordon's transgressions?"

He hesitated, as if momentarily embarrassed to speak. "I think we three know what I am talking about. My brother was infatuated with young girls. When I went to his living quarters in the oil fields to remove his personal effects, I found candid photos of naked girls in grotesque poses." He paused. "Officer Murray, Mr. Delmont, I'm not talking about professionally done pornography. The snapshots were poorly lit, and grainy, as if my brother had taken them himself."

The hair on the back of my neck stood up. Fergus leaned forward and said, "Do you still have the photos?"

"No. I destroyed the filthy things at once, and then brought my brother's remains back home to Scotland."

Fergus set his glass down and stood. "Thank you, Dr. Tannahill, for all your assistance."

I said, "Not so fast, Fergus." I had maintained silence throughout Tannahill's story but I could not control my anger any longer. "It seems to me that had your father let Gordon spend a few years in jail, it is just possible that a young girl from Pitlochry would be alive today."

Dr. Tannahill's expression reflected his pain. "Mr. Delmont, you're welcome to place my brother in jail if that simple act would fulfill your definition of American justice." Tannahill stood and walked across the small room to the fireplace. He reached for, and picked up an urn. I saw a startled look dart across Fergus' face and I am sure mine looked the same. A tear trickled down Tannahill's cheek. "Here, arrest him. This is all that remains of Gordon, my one and only brother."

Fergus said, "Doctor Tannahill, I don't believe taking the urn with your brother's ashes will be necessary. Now I'm afraid we have another appointment."

Tannahill cradled the urn in his arms and said, "I understand, Officer Murray. There is always more for the police to do to keep our streets safe."

We left the apartment and within a moment we were back on the sunny sidewalk. I said, "Are all the professors from your alma mater as strange as Dr. Tannahill?"

"I don't get you. What do you mean by strange?"

"For starters, this has been the warmest day in Scotland since we arrived and the good professor walks around his apartment wearing a wool sweater and builds a fire in the fireplace—or how about a couple of glasses of sherry at ten in the morning—or passing the urn that contains his murdering brother's ashes around the room like it was a plate of hors d'oeuvres?"

Fergus thought for a moment. "My guess is that Doctor Tannahill fits the mold of most the United Kingdom's academia. As I've pointed out before, you're not in America. In Scotland, we hold our university professors, particularly the Master of a Department, in high esteem. Doctor Tannahill does very little teaching, if any, and spends most of his time at the university doing research or writing about Scottish history. The university supplies the coal so it's my guess he lights a fire every morning out of habit. Finally, if my day consisted of reading dusty old history books, I fear I'd be nippin' a bit of sherry, if not a whisky or two, before lunch."

"What about that routine with his brother's remains?"

"He did carry on about his brother being a black sheep but it could be he still loves him. I can't say about your country, but in Scotland, blood is thicker than water."

"Fergus, I make my living defending criminals in court. A successful defense attorney must develop the ability to make quick decisions concerning potential jury members. Over time, I have—"

"Delmont, what has this got to do with Gordon Tannahill?"

"What I am saying is there's something about the good doctor that bothers me. I can not define what disturbs me, it is just an instinct I have. I know you want to close the Mary Patterson case, but I would feel more comfortable if you would run a background check on Doctor Tannahill."

He shook his head. "Delmont, I've got other cases that require my attention and . . ." He stopped and stared at me. I do not know what he saw in my expression but he must have sensed I wasn't joking. "All right. I'll run a quick check into our friend, Doctor Tannahill, and once that's completed I'll close out the Mary Patterson case as a probable murder by Gordon Tannahill, now deceased."

"But not before you have completed the background check on his older brother, correct?"

Fergus clenched his fists and his voice rose an octave. "Delmont, I've just about had it with—"

I glanced at my watch and said, "My good man, we have a little less than an hour before lunch. What

189

do you suggest we do next?"

Fergus stared at me for a moment, relaxed his hands, and said, "Let's go to the ruins of the St. Andrews Cathedral, a place that never ceases to calm me down."

We got in the car and headed a few blocks north towards the silhouette of a church spire. As he drove, Fergus said, "According to legend, St. Regulus carried the remains of the apostle Andrew to this spot, and he founded the church on this site in 1160. Before the Reformation, in the sixteenth century, St. Andrews Cathedral was the largest church in all of Scotland with thirty-one altars plus the shrine of St. Andrew."

Fergus pulled the car up close to the Cathedral ruins, into a 'no parking zone', and placed his police pass on the dashboard. We managed to make our way along the uneven ground until the stone remains of the main structure surrounded us.

"Delmont, you of all people need to experience the feeling of peace one receives standing inside the walls of the ruin."

I was not sure why he had singled me out, but the man was correct. The bustle of students at the University, the multitude of tourists that filled the streets, and the noise of the cars, all melted away once we became encircled by the delicate, nine-hundred-year-old ruin. Placed on the tip of a jut of land, and etched by centuries of exposure to unrelenting wind and rain, the worn sandstone walls and the crisp sea air made me feel as if I was standing alone in the center of a beautiful cathedral. I closed my eyes and let my mind reconstruct the rock walls, the vaulted ceiling, and the wooden altars.

We stood in silence for a few moments with the sounds of the sea, wind and birds our only companions. Slowly, the troubled concerns of Dr. Tannahill faded into the surrounding calm. After a moment I glanced at my watch. "We had better be going soon, or we will be late for lunch."

"Aye."

A few minutes later Fergus pulled into a parking lot. "Delmont, before we head to my favorite pub, the building on your right is the Royal and Ancient Golf Club House. In front of us is the first tee and eighteenth green of the world famous Old Course at St. Andrews."

My stomach growled. "Do they serve food at the Royal and Ancient Golf Club?"

"Nay. I stopped here so you could get a view of the world famous Old Course."

"Looks brown and dirty to me. However, I do not play golf so I may be missing some of the finer points. Now can we find a place to eat?"

"Aye."

Fergus drove us to a small pub on the outskirts of St. Andrews. We walked in and he said, "Let me do the ordering."

A waitress appeared and he told her, "Two fish and chips and two pints."

The beer was served in a few seconds and inside of ten minutes I was contemplating two massive pieces of batter-covered fried cod stacked on top of a huge mound of French fries.

"Delmont, in my opinion, this pub serves the best fish and chips in Scotland. How does your plate compare to what you get in America?"

"Difficult to answer as I have never consumed this dish before."

"You're pulling my leg!"

"My good man, I never jest. Now, how am I supposed to eat this steaming mound of food?"

"Sprinkle a bit of malt vinegar on the fish and be careful, the fish is hotter than the hubs of Hades."

I took my friend's advice and as I bit into my first French fry, my cell buzzed. "Hello."

"Pinky, it's your old buddy, Conner. Guess what? I just landed. Not exactly where you expected me to be, but here."

I tapped my index finger into the table and Fergus, lost in a giant piece of fish, glanced up.

I said, "Conner, what do you mean by here?"

"Like Heathrow here."

Damn! "What made you decide to land at Heathrow instead of Glasgow?" The instant I said, "Heathrow," Fergus pulled out his cell and keyed in some numbers.

Conner said, "I'm not a fool. You wanted me to fly to Glasgow, so I flew to Heathrow."

"I understand. Now, what is next?"

"Don't worry, Pinky. I'll get to your little Scottish town soon."

"I'm not worried." Fergus tapped my shoulder. "Conner, please hold for a moment, the waitress needs to pick up my plate."

"Take your time."

I held my hand over the cell and Fergus said, "I've called the London police. They'll have a couple of men check out the Heathrow car rental agencies. Keep him on line as long as possible."

I nodded. Into the phone I said, "My good man,

did you have a decent flight across the Atlantic?"

"Stop the bullshit. I'm not a fool. Look, we both know I've got to get out of this airport, so stop dancing around. Is the money ready?"

"Yes. The amount you requested is waiting for you inside a very nice suitcase and—"

"And Flo? What about Flo?"

"As I told you before, she has been looking for a way to escape the clutches of Bear for some time."

"Perfect. Now sit back and relax. I'll call you when I'm ready to pick up my cash and the broad."

TWENTY-THREE

Pinky Delmont-Pitlochry, Scotland

After a glance at the mountain of fish and fries, I knew that my delicate digestive system, already roiling from Conner's call, could not consume the food placed in front of me. I took a sip of beer and after the cooling liquid flowed into my stomach, I said, "Fergus, I have the uneasy feeling that Conner is two steps ahead of us."

"Calm down, Delmont. Let's review our situation. The man's at Heathrow, and unless he's a sophisticated traveler, he'll be wandering around in a mental fog for the next twelve hours."

"Fergus, I do not think any of us would classify Conner as sophisticated under any circumstances. However, I believe you would in fact agree that you have underestimated the man. I have reached the point where I feel it is time that Willow and I return to America. While you drive us home, I will call and make airline reservations for two on the next available flight out of Glasgow. Once you drop me off, and while I pack our bags, I want you to extract my ten thousand pounds from the suitcase, and—"

"So you're going to take a runner? Delmont, I figured you, as a lawyer, to be generally worthless, but to run from a common criminal does surprise me. Have you made your wishes known to Willow or

Bear?"

"Willow will understand my need to return to Carson City. During my absence, no one has represented the poor and downtrodden. They—"

"According to Florence, you rake in millions in legal fees defending some of your wealthy murderers. Does American English have a different definition of poor, or downtrodden?"

"Fergus, the retainers I charge my clients are none of your business. In fact, the amount of my fee is part of the attorney/client privilege, a sacrosanct principle that separates American Jurisprudence from—"

"Delmont, you've spent a good bit of time unsuccessfully defending your cowardliness, when we arrived at the farm. I'm going to stop by Bear's cottage and we'll have the opportunity to discuss this situation further."

"My good man, you have no right—"

The man ignored my entreaty. We left the pub, and drove in silence until Fergus stopped his car outside Bear's cottage. He jumped out and knocked on the door. That woman opened the door and said, "Fergus, what a nice surprise." She took a look over his shoulder and spotted me sitting in the car. "What's wrong with Pinky?"

There are times in a man's life when he has to take the bull by the horns, so to speak, and reestablish command of a bad situation. I jumped out of the car and said, "I believe Fergus misinterpreted the thrust of our previous discussion that might have left the impression that Willow and I are ready to return to Carson City. Fergus, did my last statement clear up any incorrect conclusions on your part?"

"Aye."

We entered the cottage and Fergus said, "Florence, Conner just arrived, but at Heathrow, not Glasgow. We need to put our heads together."

A short, stocky man who stood next to Bear said, "It looks to me that 'e's out foxed you."

I said, "Pardon me, but who are you?"

"Me name's 'Enry Bramble. You must be the wee attorney Florence told me about."

Flo snorted. "Aye, Henry, that's him all right and judging by what Fergus said, he's looking to put his tail between his legs and run back home. But that doesn't surprise me. Every case I've worked on with Pinky, he either doesn't have a clue of the danger he's in, or he's trying to figure out a way to take off and let Bear face his music for him."

I stood to my full height. "My good woman—"

"You little pip-squeak, I've never been your good woman, and never will be. Now that we have that straight, I'll heat some water for tea and dig out the whisky for those who want something stronger than Earl Gray. And folks, whatever we agree on, my butt is the only one at risk, so we'd better come up with a foolproof plan."

Fergus said, "Aye."

Bear slammed his fist on the table. "Hold on. This bastard wants to take my woman. Fergus, Pinky, I'm not going to allow that. What would you say if that dude wanted to take Fiona, or Willow, instead of Flo? Does that change things? Pinky, I don't give a shit about your money. Fergus, I don't care if the bastard doesn't spend a day in jail. Nobody gets out of this room until we agree on a plan where there's no way Conner ends up with my woman. Got it?"

It was obvious to me that I had fallen into a leaderless situation. I said, "I believe we all understand your concerns. Now, who will—"

Henry interrupted, "I'll keep a sharp eye out for strangers in Pitlochry. And once Mr. Delmont buys me a cell phone, I'll be able to contact Fergus the second I spot one."

I said, "Who told you I would purchase a cell phone and give the device to you?"

"Bear and Flo."

Bear said, "Look, boss, the old dude needs a cell to keep me and Flo up on what's going on. He doesn't have any extra bucks and neither do we. Hell, I gave the Kid twenty-five pounds for a costume and that just about tapped us out."

I shook my head. Clearly these people must think I was made out of money. "I will take your request under consid—"

Fergus said, "Henry, I could let you borrow one of the police mobiles."

Henry said, "That would be grand."

Fergus continued, "From my viewpoint, the original plan still works. The problem is that Conner didn't land in Glasgow, but don't worry, we still have the upper hand and—"

Bear said, "Dude, you sound like the guy who found a cockroach in his beef burrito, but finished it 'cause meat's meat. How far is Heathrow from here?"

"A wee bit less than five hundred miles."

Bear said, "Sixty miles an hour for eight hours is four hundred and eighty miles. That means the bastard could be knocking on my front door tomorrow morning."

Fergus said, "Aye, but no sane person in the UK would drive that far in one day."

Flo said, "Maybe no one in the UK, but I've known Nevada driver's who'd drive that far to find a better pizza. And I don't classify Conner as sane."

Fergus said, "Damn!"

I said, "Folks, we need to calm down and think rationally. The man just landed in a strange country. He must be experiencing some jet lag. I would guess we have twenty-four hours. That said, I move we close this session and go home. I don't know about the rest of you, but I need to resolve a bodily function that I would rather resolve of in the privacy of my home-away-from-home."

Flo said, "Let's get back together for breakfast at Pinky's place. All those in favor, signify by saying aye."

Before I could intervene, a chorus of aye's filled the room. I said, "I agree, tomorrow at my place at ten. But this will be a no-host breakfast so I suggest we all chip in a pound to cover the cost of—"

Bear said, "Ten's too late. Like I said before, if push comes to shove, I'll hand over Fiona or Willow to Conner. And boss, you're buying breakfast!"

Fergus said, "Right. Let's make it nine."

Henry said, "Fergus, before we meet for breakfast, I'll stop by the Pitlochry station and pick up me mobile with my morning cuppa."

Fergus said, "Brilliant! Let's go home."

Before I could demand a second vote, the rabble made a de facto decision to meet at my apartment—at nine—for breakfast—on my dime! So much for democratic rule.

TWENTY-FOUR

Bear Zabarte-Pitlochry, Scotland

Conner's call to Pinky had me wound up tighter than a bull's ass at fly time so I hardly noticed the Kid when she ran into the kitchen. She drained what was left of Flo's whisky into the sink, sniffed the glass, and said, "Yuck!" Then she glanced at the stove. "Flo, there's nothing cooking. What's for dinner?"

Damn, with everything else going on, Flo forgot all about fixing some food. I said, "I vote for pizza. I'll call Fergus and see if he'll drive us to Bankfoot while you and Flo set the table."

Flo shook her head. "I'm not comfortable staying here alone."

Until that minute, I figured that handling the Conner problem was just another messy deal, but the look on Flo's face told me something else. "Great. Fergus'll go."

I pulled out my cell and called Fergus. "It's been a busy day. How about you drive to Bankfoot to pick us up some pizza. "

"Brilliant! Fiona will call and place our order. What size and toppings do you want her to order?"

"Two large sausage and olive."

"Two large? That's a lot of pizza for two adults and a child."

"Right."

"Just sausage and olive?"

"Yup. Two large sausage and olive."

"Fine. I'll stop by in less than an hour."

"Thanks. With Conner running around Flo's not comfortable being here alone."

Fergus said, "I thought she was tougher than that."

Jesus, he could be a pain in the ass. I growled, "I don't give a shit what you think. Flo's the one taking the big risk, not Fiona, or Willow."

"I guess you're right. I'll be back with the pizza soon."

I dropped my cell back into my pocket as the Kid dumped a paper bag full of clothes on the table. I said, "What's that all about?"

She shook her head. "I told you already."

"I forgot. Tell me again."

The Kid giggled. "This is my costume for the school pageant at the Atholl Highlander's Parade." She held up a plaid skirt. "I can't wait to see if it fits. The Scots call it a kilt. My teacher told me it might be a little long because she put me with the older girls dance group. I'll have to try it on. Can I use your bedroom where there's a big mirror? Don't move! I'll model the costume for you and Flo in a minute."

A couple of minutes later, she called, "It's okay to come in now."

We walked in and like magic, the Kid had turned into a teenager. She wore a skirt and a white blouse with long sleeves. Dumped over her shoulder was a tartan of blue, black, red, and green that matched her skirt. The Kid turned slowly. "This is the tartan of the Murray of Atholl Clan. Isn't it beautiful? I love the way it crosses in the front and tucks into my belt. How do I look?"

I glanced at Flo and she was on the edge of blubbering. I said, "You look really cool, and as far as I can tell, that thing fits perfectly." Lucky for me, the Kid was checking herself in the mirror and didn't notice the tear fall out of my eye.

We followed her back to the living room. The Kid made a quick turn and the skirt flared out. "The teacher told me that I have to stitch the raw edge of the tartan. Bear, I know you don't sew, and I don't think Flo does either. Do you think Fiona will help me? I hope so because everything must be ready by Friday. That's when we dance and we're performing before an official dance judge."

Flo said, "When it comes to sewing, I'm a better winemaker, and I've never made wine."

The Kid looked at me, I shrugged my shoulders. "No hope here. Call Fiona and ask her."

"Okay. I'll check with her. I'll be out as soon as I take off the costume. I don't want to get it dirty."

I sat down by the wood stove and said, "Flo, the Kid's growing up."

"I know. Hey, after listening to Henry's old records of opera, I bought us a couple of used CDs. I'll put the one on while we wait."

"Which one?" I asked.

"Madame Butterfly."

"Is that the one where the Japanese babe falls in love with the American navy dude?"

"That's the one."

"Good. Most of those operas sound like screaming to me, but in the Japanese opera, that babe sings real sweet."

"The opera is Italian, not Japanese, and that babe, as you called her, is singing Un Bel Dei, a song of hope and love for her lover, an American naval officer."

The Kid ran into the kitchen looking like her old self wearing jeans and a tee shirt. I handed her three forks and said, "Kid, we've got a problem and you need to know what the hell is going on."

"Shoot."

"Me, Flo, and Pinky have a crazy ex-cop after our butts. He called a couple of hours ago to tell us he's in London."

"Is that close to Pitlochry?"

I nodded. "Sort of. He could drive here in eight hours."

"Is he dangerous, like that crazy woman who almost killed you at the winery?"

Flo said, "Yes, he is, but you need to know that—"

The kid waved a fork at me. "Bear, we've been through a lot in a short time and I trust you and Flo to do the best you can. Can't say the same for Pinky, but you knew that. Okay, the table's set, where's the pizza?"

Thirty minutes later, there was a knock on the front door. That could be Fergus, or it could be Conner. I moved to my right, peeked out the window as Fergus yelled, "Come on, Bear. By the time you get here the pizzas will be stone cold."

I opened the door and Fergus said, "Hand the pizza to Flo and step outside for a minute. We need to talk."

Shit I was hungry and the smell of hot sausage

was coming through the cardboard box. "Flo, help me here. Fergus wants to bend my ear for a minute."

She grabbed the two large pizzas and said, "Don't be too long or all of this will be gone."

I closed the door and Fergus said, "Tomorrow, after I run a quick check on Professor Tannahill, I'm closing the Mary Patterson case."

"So?"

"That means the investigative team of Zabarte and Bramble has finished its work. As the Mary Patterson case is nearly closed you need to return my letter of introduction."

"Hey, what the hell will I tell Henry?"

"You'll figure out a way to handle that little problem. By the way, Pinky and Willow are returning to America the morning following the festivities at Blair Atholl. You might want to book a couple of tickets before all the seats are taken."

Now I know how a broad feels after a guy dumps her. "Flo will talk to Willow about the airplane tickets."

"Bear, working with you has been interesting to say the least."

"Me too. Stay here. I'll be back in a flash with your letter. Fergus, could you make a copy and give it to me?"

"I can, but why should I?"

"Just want to show my old boss at the Old Globe Saloon that I was working on my PHD."

"But I made up the contents of that letter."

"I know you did, but my old boss won't know that."

TWENTY-FIVE

Bear Zabarte-Pitlochry, Scotland

At breakfast, we agreed to follow Fergus' original plan—meet Conner at the park drop area—give the crook the suitcase full of mostly fake money—arrest the bastard.

After we got back to the cottage, Flo made me help her pack, but Fergus saved my day when he called to give me Henry's new cell number.

"Babe, keep on working. I'm going to try Henry's new cell number to be sure it's working."

The damn thing rang and rang. Finally he answered. "Lo."

"Bear here. Why did it take you so long to answer?"

"Dinna know what button to push on the contraption."

And Flo thinks I'm dumb. "Dude, I forgot to tell you at breakfast, but I'm afraid our investigation is over. Last night Fergus took back our letter of introduction. Without that paper, we're out of business."

"But you promised and we still 'ave two towns to check."

I said, "Henry, it's over. We're beating a dead horse."

"'Uh?'"

"In America, when we say we're beating a dead horse, we means we're wasting our time."

"I know what the saying means, but 'ear me out. We 'ad an agreement that we'd try to track down missin' girls in Edinburgh and Aberdeen."

"But without Fergus' letter we can't con the cops into letting a couple of dudes off the street look at their records."

"Aye, but we can go to the library and check out the old newspapers."

"Damn it! That sounds like a giant pain in the ass to me. Hey, the odds were stacked against us from the get-go."

He didn't say anything and that told me he wasn't buying what I was selling. I said, "Partner, no one knows how many girls Tannahill grabbed, but I can tell you this, we don't have a snowballs chance in hell without the police records."

He didn't say a word and it looked like we were locked in some kind of a cell phone Mexican standoff.

But I can play the same game and after a minute went by Henry blinked first. "But Bear, you don't understand. The day we buried Mary Patterson, 'er dad stopped drinking."

"What?"

"After Mary vanished, the poor soul spent most of 'is day drunk. Since her funeral 'e's been sober—not a drop since that afternoon at the cemetery. I know this is a fact 'cause I'm a Beadle at the church and it's my job to know these things."

"Henry, one less drunk in the world is great, but what does that—"

"For every one of Tannahill's victims there's a parent, sometimes two, fightin' to get through each day inside a black nightmare. Some of them sit and cry. Some of them drown their sorrows with whiskey, like poor old James. They all do what they 'ave to do to escape from their pain. We may never know 'ow many Mary Patterson's are buried out there. Nor can we bring those lasses back to life. All we can do is to 'elp those parents give their daughters proper burials."

I liked Henry and figured out what he was trying to tell me, but without that letter I knew we'd be shoveling shit against the wind.

Thirty seconds passed. I was damn good at playing cell phone stand-off. Working for Pinky had made me one of the best, but this time I caved. "Damn it, I give up. But you have to pick between Aberdeen and Edinburgh. You only get one town 'cause I'm not going to spend two days going through stacks of dusty old newspapers."

"I'll ask the ladies who run the libraries to make sure the newspapers are dust-free."

Damn, working with Henry was as tough as working with Flo. "So which is it, Aberdeen or Edinburgh?"

No answer as the old dude was playing the stand-off game again.

I'd had enough of this crap! "Damn it, Henry, you have thirty seconds to make up your mind or I'll never talk to you again."

Other than hearing his breathing, not a peep out of the old dude.

"Fifteen seconds. After me and Flo watch the Kid do her thing with her dance group at Blair Castle, we pack up and fly back to America. If you're up to one last try, I'll do it, but only one town." I counted down, "Five, four, three, two—"

Henry jumped in. "Okay. It's Aberdeen."

My cell beeped with a call waiting and it had to be Pinky or Fergus. "Hold on. I have to pick up another call."

I hit the button and my stomach hit the floor when I heard Pinky say, "Conner's in Pitlochry. What are we going to do?"

"Didn't you tell me that we had a good twenty-four hours?"

"I was wrong. Bear, that criminal is loose and I fear for—"

"Calm down, Boss." I didn't feel calm but somebody had to keep Pinky from jumping off the bridge. "Have you talked to Fergus?"

"No."

Jesus, the little fart sounded like he was ready to cry. "Okay. Now, let's go over Conner's call. What'd he say first?"

"He is ready to pick up my money and Flo."

"You need to call Fergus and tell him that."

"Why?"

Jesus, what a dork! "Because he's got to get his men to the drop area. Remember, that little park by the lake."

"I forgot! I will call him at once."

"Good. Then call me back."

I clicked a button and said, "Henry, that crooked ex-cop is in Pitlochry. I told Pinky to call Fergus. Sit tight and I'll call you after Fergus calls me."

"Aye. I trust this affair will be resolved soon. Don't forget, we drive to Aberdeen to finish our investigation."

I said, "Henry, this deal with Conner is a hell of

a lot more important then our stupid trip to Aberdeen. As far as I'm concerned, the trip to Aberdeen is—"

I heard a click. Henry was gone and left me talking to myself.

TWENTY-SIX

Pinky Delmont-Pitlochry, Scotland

I called Fergus and told him Conner was in Pitlochry.

He said, "Bear was right. I continue to underestimate the man."

"He will be calling me back to discuss a location for the transfer of money and Bear's woman.

Fergus said, "It's a little after one. That's perfect. My men can be at the park inside the hour. Give the scoundrel the location and tell him to meet you there at four. Remember, Delmont, that four o'clock is the only time and the park by Lake Faskally is the only location."

"But what do I do if he doesn't accept my offer?"

"Delmont, what do you do if one of your clients doesn't follow your instructions?"

"I tell them it is my way or let me know into which arm they want the executioner to place the needle."

"See, I knew you had it in you. I'll pick you up along with Bear and Flo in forty-five minutes."

Before I could call Bear, my cell buzzed. "Okay, Delmont, where and when do we meet?"

"In Pitlochry there is a small park by Lake Faskally. Bear and I'll be there with the money, along with Flo of course, at four."

"I don't like the time. Move the meet up an hour."

"Damn it, do what I say or you can kiss your money, and that beautiful woman, goodbye. So far, I have agreed to all your demands, but now I draw the line. You will pick up your ill-gotten gains at the park by Lake Faskally at four this afternoon or you will leave Scotland empty-handed. Conner, you have thirty seconds. At the end of that time, I will hang up and call the local police. I will provide them with a complete description of you and tell them that you attempted to extort money from me!"

"I thought we agreed, no cops! Ours is just a simple business transaction between a couple of hard working entrepreneurs."

"My good man, I am happy to see that we are back on the same page."

Conner hesitated long enough to inform me that I had set the hook. "Okay. Four o'clock at the park by the lake."

"Conner, it has been a pleasure doing business with you." I clicked off the call before he had the opportunity to respond, downed two Ativan pills, and called Bear.

I said, "Bear, the drop will take place at the agreed location at four. Get ready, Fergus will pick us up in forty minutes."

"Right. I'll tell Flo so she'll have a couple of minutes to put her face on. Boss, by the time the Scottish law is finished with that bastard, he'll be a tired old man when he walks free."

"That is the plan, my boy, that is the plan. Now hang up. I need a few moments of solitude to allow the Ativan medication to clear away my disquietude."

"Huh?"

I clicked off and listened to Mozart while the medication calmed my nerves.

As promised, Fergus was on time. We picked up Bear, that woman, and the four of us headed toward Pitlochry.

Bear said, "Boss, did you come up with anything interesting when you visited with Gordon's brother—that St. Andrews college professor?"

"Let me see. He has Gordon's remains in an urn on his mantle. He is a distant cousin of the Duke of Atholl. He burns a coal fire during a sunny day. Oh yes, he serves sherry to guests."

Bear said, "And I thought my day in Cupar was a waste of time."

Suddenly Fergus turned left off the main highway to Pitlochry, crossed a bridge over the River Tummel, and passed the Fonab Caravan Park.

I said, "I thought we were going to Pitlochry?"

"We are, but first a slight detour." Fergus turned right at a sign directing drivers to the Pitlochry Festival Theater. He continued past the theater to a spot shaded by some trees and stopped the car.

"Bear, do you and Florence want to come?"

"Do you need us?"

"Nay."

"Me and Flo are fine

"Okay, we'll be back in a jiffy. Pinky, follow me."

After a short walk, I looked around, and said, "Fergus, I love the shade and the outstanding view of the Power Station Dam, but what are we doing on this side of the river?"

211

"I stopped under the trees so I can check out the drop area from here. This way we can't be seen from the picnic area."

I looked at the dam and my stomach tightened with a shot of trepidation. "Do you think Conner could be watching us."

"Nay, but we can't be too careful, can we? He knows what you look like so stay where you are and don't follow me."

He left me and walked toward the dam. I watched Fergus casually stroll half way across the dam. A few moments later, he returned. "I was concerned about Bear's question concerning a car using the walkway across the dam. There's a series of metal posts cemented into the walkway every twenty feet to discourage bicyclists. Walkers are fine, but there's no way a car could drive through that maze."

He glanced at his watch. "It's a touch past three. Are you ready?"

My insides churned with apprehension. "I think so. I have the suitcase with the money and that woman is waiting in the car."

"Fine. Let's go."

We arrived at the little park at three-twenty. Fergus waved toward a bushy area and two uniformed policemen suddenly emerged. They approached a woman pushing a child on a swing. They talked with her for a moment and the woman packed up her picnic, and her child, and immediately left the area.

Fergus said, "I have four men in plain clothes out of sight and those two uniformed men from the Pitlochry station. Their names are Sergeant

MacFarland and Sergeant Penman. They're both top-drawer. MacFarland will stay out of sight with me. Penman's task will be to drive a police car across the tunnel entrance to block the only exit once Conner comes through. Bear, all you have to do is hand Conner the suitcase with the money. As soon as he has the suitcase in his hand, MacFarland and I will arrest him and this sordid affair will be over. One final item, if anything goes wrong, if Conner starts to attack you, or do anything other than take the suitcase, duck for cover. MacFarland and I'll be over him like maggots on a dead grouse. Any questions?"

I heard another voice say, "Nay."

Fergus looked over his shoulder. "Henry, where did you come from?"

"I came across the walkway on the dam."

Fergus said, "Clear out, Henry. This is an official police action."

"Aye, I know that. I'm just 'ere to protect my investigative partners, Bear and Flo."

Bear said, "Cool it, Fergus. He won't cause a problem."

Fergus glared at Bear. "I decide who and what causes a problem. Henry, you stay close to me, or go back home."

"Aye"

I tuned out the ceaseless babble coming from the group and concentrated on the tunnel entrance under the railroad track. I glanced left and right. Fergus' man had done a good job. I could not spot any sign of him or his car. Satisfied we were ready, I handed Bear the suitcase full of money and ducked behind some bushes with Fergus. After a few moments of waiting, I found it difficult to draw a complete breath.

Twice, once at three-fifty-one and again at three fifty-six, I thought I heard the sound of an approaching car, but at four there was no mistake. However, what I detected was not the engine noise of an automobile, but the low rumble of a motorcycle. I peeked through the shrubbery at the tunnel beneath the railroad track and a man on a motorcycle stared back.

TWENTY-SEVEN

Bear Zabarte-Pitlochry, Scotland

While me and Flo waited by a picnic bench for Conner to show up, I felt like a ripe, red tomato waiting to be picked. I had the suitcase in my right hand and my left land held onto a leather belt I made Flo wear. She was pissed at me for making her wear the belt and kept complaining that it didn't work with the rest of her outfit, but I didn't give a shit about fashion, that bastard wasn't going to take my woman no matter what.

Flo said, "Did you hear that?"

Before I could say anything I heard a low rumble. It wasn't the noise made by a car, it was something else. "Babe, get ready for anything. That dude is not following the script."

A few seconds later a man on a motorcycle rolled through the tunnel under the railroad track. The cycle skidded to a stop and the man riding yelled, "Zabarte, I see you standing there with my babe. Do you have my money?"

Jesus. He was riding a Harley Fat Bob. I didn't know they made them over here. I waved the suitcase and yelled back, "Come and get it."

Conner straddled his ride and scanned the area. "The cash is in a leather suitcase? Nice touch. Before we go any further, open it up and let me see what's inside."

Flo whispered, "I just pray Fergus has a gag around Pinky's mouth."

"Me too."

Conner revved the engine and the bike rolled closer.

I said, "Does the Fat Bob ride good?"

"Is a pig's penis pork?"

"I thought all Harleys were made in America?"

"They are. This one was imported. Now, stop the bullshit and hand the suitcase to Flo. Flo, once you get the money from that Basque half-breed, walk toward me and climb on the back of my bike."

Flo said, "But I've never ridden on a motorcycle before. How do I know that it's safe?"

Conner said, "Hey, I'm your man now and from now on what I say goes. Just get on and you'll spend the rest of your life tanning those beautiful boobs on the French Riviera."

He wasn't close enough to jump him so I said, "How much did that Harley set you back?"

"A lot more than you can afford working for that cheap bastard, Delmont. give Flo the money."

"Sorry, but you'll have to move closer."

"Sure, and the Tooth Fairy will put a quarter under my pillow. Flo take the suitcase and hand it to me."

Flo whispered, "Give me the money. He doesn't trust you and he won't hurt me."

Conner laughed, "I heard her and she's right, I don't trust you. Now this is your last chance. Give Flo the suitcase and get out of my way."

The second Conner showed up sitting on a motorcycle instead of driving a car, I knew the shit

216

was going to hit the fan. I'd warned Fergus that some part of this stupid plan would go wrong but I had to admit that I never thought about Conner showing up this way. I had to do something and do it fast or Fergus and his keystone cops would pop out of the bushes and Conner might escape, meaning we'd have to go through all this again, and the next time, Conner wouldn't be so stupid. I said, "Okay, here's the money."

I popped the locks and held out the suitcase."

Maybe he thought Flo was going to give him a kiss, or maybe he thought that she was going to jump on the back of the bike, we'll never know what went through his pea brain. All I know was that the Fat Bob rolled a little closer.

I let go of the belt around Flo.

Conner started to get off the bike, then he stopped. "Flo, take the suitcase and hold it close so I can see the money."

She did.

His eyes scanned the stacks of pound notes. "Looks good. Now close the damn thing and climb on the back of my bike."

Flo said, "Conner, I can't do both. Here, you take the suitcase and I'll climb on the back."

Conner took the bait.

He was still too far away to grab and I didn't know what to next when Flo saved the day.

She wiggled her shoulders and her boobs jiggled like a bowl of grape jelly. Conner's eyes lit up and I'm pretty sure the dude wasn't thinking about money when Flo said, "Conner, I'm still not comfortable climbing up on the back of your motorcycle. Bear, I need some help. Come over here and lift me up."

After I took a couple of steps, Conner snapped out of it, revved up the engine, and yelled, "Stay where you are or I'm taking off."

That last step was all I needed. I jumped and grabbed hold of the back of the seat.

Conner snatched the suitcase out of Flo's hand and popped the clutch. The rear wheel of the bike spit up a wave of gravel and the rocks hit my face like they were being shot out of a hose. I held on while Conner drove toward the lake.

He gave me an elbow into my nose. "Get off my Fat Bob you ignorant bartender."

By his third elbow into my chops, I started to lose my grip on the seat. Just before we hit the lake, the bastard turned to his left.

That's when my fingers let go. As I hit the ground I heard Fergus yell, "Men, get him"

I remember hearing the motorcycle head toward the railroad tunnel and I guessed the cop had done his job 'cause the next thing I knew Conner had turned around and had aimed his bike at Flo. At least I thought he was aiming for Flo 'cause I forgot about the walkway over the dam behind me. Conner must have been going thirty when the cycle just missed me on its way to the walkway across the dam.

Flo ran over, helped me up, and said, "Are you okay?"

"I'm good. How about you?"

"I'm fine but you're a sight. You have all sorts of cuts on your face. What happened?"

"The rear tire on the cycle kicked up gravel. I guess some hit me."

"You guess? How about twenty pounds of gravel."

We both heard the motorcycle engine slow down, and then a chirp as Conner popped the clutch. The engine noise got further away and then a crash. Finally, after about ten seconds, something big hit the water with a loud splash.

TWENTY-EIGHT

Pinky Delmont-Pitlochry, Scotland

I tried to keep up with Fergus to assist in Conner's arrest, but my feet became tangled and I tumbled to the ground.

From my prone position, I watched the bike reach the tunnel entrance, but by this time, Sergeant Penman had done his job well and there was no escape in that direction.

The rumble of Conner's motorcycle slowed and I realized that the man had turned his motorcycle in my direction.

Fergus pulled out a gun, took dead aim at the man on the motorcycle, and yelled, "Give it up, Conner. There's no reason for anyone to get hurt. Get off that motorcycle, put the suitcase down, and raise your hands."

The policemen under Fergus' command started to close in on Conner. He screamed, "Pinky Delmont, you're a lying, double crossing bastard."

Then he gunned the engine, and as he shot toward the dam, the front wheel of the motorcycle brushed my left leg

Fergus yelled, "Conner, you can't go that way. It's not a road."

I was positive that Conner heard Fergus' warning over the roar of the motorcycle engine but he continued up the walkway. After the sounds of a crash, Fergus and I ran toward the walkway. Half way across the dam, Fergus found the Harley Davidson motorcycle smashed into a bent steel post, but no money, and no Conner.

The man riding the motorcycle had vanished along with my ten thousand dollars. Fergus leaned over the dam and stared into the water below. After a few seconds, he cried, "MacFarland, find a boat. I can see a body floating on the water near the second spillway but I don't think the man's still alive."

Excitement over, I limped back to the picnic area and spotted Bear sitting on the ground. That woman glanced at my leg and said. "Pinky, are you hurt?"

I looked down and the instant I saw the blood stain on my left pant leg, the image of all my bodily fluids leaking from my wound caused my knees to buckle.

She caught me and called, "Fergus, I need your help. Both Bear and Pinky are on the ground and bleeding."

Fergus rushed over, saw the blood stain on my leg. With the help of one of the uniformed officers, they carried me to the closest picnic table. After they laid me down on the cold surface, Fergus ran to his car and returned with a first-aid kit. He cut the clothing off my leg from my ankle to my hip. "Relax, Delmont, I need to check out your wound."

I stared at the sky and the sudden realization of my mortality made me feel very uneasy. I said, "Fergus, I can handle the pain, but the cradle I lie upon is as hard as a rock, a less than desirable way for a man of my means to draw his last breath."

That woman said, "Not surprising. The damn table's made out of concrete. Just shut up and lie quietly so Fergus can look at that wound."

I felt miserable, and held out faint hope for recovery, as visions of my successful trials scrolled through my mind.

Fergus stared at my leg for a moment and said, "There's a small incision on the back of your calf. I'll slap a plaster on it. Nothing to worry about."

I felt his hand push on the calf of my leg. "Ouch."

"Man-up, Delmont."

Feeling a touch foolish, I tried to make light of my situation to prove to Fergus how tough I was. "Fergus, now that you are finished, do you think I'll ever be able to play the violin again?"

Fergus gave me a look he saved for one of his sons after they've tracked mud onto the freshly mopped kitchen floor. A moment later, I noticed a large group of people had started to cluster around me. Once Fergus became aware of the growing throng, he yelled, "Sergeant Penman, this is a crime scene. Move those people back to the railroad bridge and cordon off the picnic area with tape."

I carefully placed both my feet on the ground and shifted nearly all my weight onto my good leg. I said, "Am I correct in my assumption that except for myself, no one else was injured?"

That woman said, "Are you blind? Bear's face is so chewed up that it looks as if he took a couple of spins inside a garbage disposal."

"Right. I had forgotten about him. What about the rest of the team?"

Fergus seemed to ignore my question and said,

"Has anyone seen Henry?"

I glanced around. "No." I collected myself for a moment and tried to take a step. My legs began to tremble so violently that I nearly fell. "Fergus, don't leave me. I can't walk."

He grabbed my arm. "Back up one step and sit down on the bench."

Not thinking clearly, I backed into the concrete bench with my injured leg and an involuntary scream escaped through my lips. I sat down hard. surprised to find that I was sweating and my hands were shaking, as if I had aged ten years in the last fifty seconds.

"Delmont, I can't fathom why, but you seem to have slipped into shock. You need to sit where you are for a couple of minutes. I'll look for Henry."

Fergus had accurately diagnosed my condition. By the time he returned, Henry was by his side, and I felt a hundred percent better.

Henry said, "Fergus told me you were worried 'bout me. I dinna mean to frighten you. I was looking for your money, but dinna find a farthing."

My money? Oh my God, was my money gone? "Fergus, you promised me that my ten thousand would be safe." I struggled to ignore the throbbing pain that radiated from my leg. "I thought I saw Conner drop the suitcase before he drove toward the damn."

Henry shook his head. "Nay, the suitcase was in 'is 'and when I lost sight of 'im. The money could be anywhere, on the path, in the lake, or in the river below the spillway. But I dinna think the suitcase popped open. If that 'ad 'appened, we'd be sittin' in a snowstorm of fifty pound notes."

Henry thought a moment. He looked at the growing crowd and said, "I could ask some of me mates to 'elp look for the suitcase."

Fergus' face lit up. "That's brilliant. Inform them that Delmont will pay a thousand pound reward to the person who finds and turns over an unopened suitcase."

I flinched. "Hold on! A thousand pound reward? You are talking ten percent and that is way too mu—"

Henry's wild eye circled madly. "But think of all the 'elp you'll get for that."

Before I could stop him, Henry turned toward the crowd, "Listen up men. What would you say if I told you 'ow to earn a thousand quid!"

The men yelled, "'Ear, 'ear." And while Henry explained, an occasional head would pop up and stare at me. A few minutes later, I watched the group split up. The largest bunch ran toward the dam. Others to the path. And a small group to the river. Like it or not, my thousand pound reward for the briefcase was now official.

Fergus said, "Delmont, do you feel stronger now?"

I nodded.

"Henry, help me with Delmont."

The two steadied me and I managed to stand. "Men, stick with me until I take a few steps."

Fergus said, "We're not going anywhere."

I put some weight onto my good leg, and took a tentative first step, then a second. I was a little shaky, but not too bad. "I will be fine, but stay close."

I heard a scraping sound coming from the lake and watched Sergeant MacFarland pull the boat onto the gravel shore. I watched silently as the uniformed policeman and Fergus lifted a body out of the skiff.

Henry said, "I think that's the rogue who tried to take your money."

While Fergus checked the body for identification, I glanced at the bloodied face and shuddered. "Fergus, that man is not Conner."

Fergus glanced at me. "What do you mean, that's not Conner." He got on his knees to get a closer look. "My God, Delmont's right. It's old Angus McMurtry. He lives, or I should say lived, in a cottage on the far side of the dam close to the theater. That walkway across the dam was the old boy's life line to Pitlochry. But if this isn't the American, where is he?" Fergus jumped up. "MacFarland, take few men, search the area, and don't come back until you find the American's body."

Henry leaned down and cried. "Angus was a fine man. A member of the church in good standing."

Fergus rolled the body over and we all could see where the front wheel of Conner's motorcycle had crushed McMurtry's chest—evidence that the upper torso of a human being was not engineered to collide with a high speed motorcycle. Fergus carefully avoided touching the bits of bone and other matter as his man took a photo of the mortal wound while I fought back the bile that rose in my throat.

Once the crime scene photos were completed, Fergus stood. "The poor bloke never felt a thing. He was dead an instant after the front wheel struck his face." Then Fergus glanced at the crowds walking the dam. "Henry, brilliant idea, convincing the town folk to look for Delmont's money."

Henry shook his head. "Once the word spread of

the thousand pound reward, my social standin' in Pitlochry jumped dramatically. I'm truly surprised every man, woman, and child in town isn't 'ere." Henry moved closer and looked at my face. "Pinky, you're as pale as a ghost."

I fought back another stomach churn. "Yes, I guess I'm not used to seeing the results of a horrific crash."

Fergus said, "And God help us if you ever do. Put your mind on something really brilliant, like a tumbler full of Scotland's finest single malt."

I recalled my favorite wine. "In my case, it is a Cabernet Sauvignon that's overflowing with currents and dark cherries, leather, and tobacco. From the first sip, the high note currents flood your palate, then the dark cherry opens up. And one cannot ignore the outstanding nose of leather and a warm, rich tobacco. Thank you, Fergus. Your suggestion did the trick."

Fergus said, "As soon as my men find Conner's body, between Bear, Flo and Willow, I'll have no trouble coming up with a positive identification."

"For my stomach's sake, please do not call on me. Any ideas how to find out where he was staying?"

"No, but as soon as I return to my office, I'll send out a bulletin to all hotels, motels, B&B's and inns. Sooner or later, one of those places will figure a guest skipped without paying his bill. Then we'll find out where his luggage is stashed."

I looked at Fergus. His ruddy face reflected the strain of the long day.

Henry said, "If I recall, Bear warned you that something could go wrong."

"Aye."

I said, "I hope you find Conner's body soon. We all need something positive to prove the bastard's dead."

Fergus hesitated, "Aye."

A moment later Fergus rejoined a uniformed officer standing by Mc Murtry's body.

My wounded leg was killing me.

Bear walked up and Henry said, "I'll keep an eye on the money search and call you with any news."

I said, "Bear, I hold you responsible for this mess. If you had just followed your instructions and handed Conner the money, that poor old man lying by the lake would be alive."

Henry said, "I dinna think that's a fair assessment, Delmont. My investigative partner did the best 'e could with the situation."

"Pinky," said Bear's woman. "I agree with Henry. In fact, I've had it up to here with your self-serving bullshit."

Henry moved closer to Bear's face. "You'll need some first aid on those cuts. We could put off the drive to Aberdeen and let your face heal."

Bear said, "That won't work. We're going home the day after tomorrow. Pinky, a word of advice. If you want to keep breathing, keep your trap shut around Flo until she cools down."

"You need to tell her to watch her mouth around me."

As Henry, Bear and Flo walked toward his old car, I called, "What about me?"

Henry said, "Delmont, you can catch a ride 'ome with Fergus."

I said, "Your actions insinuate that my leg wound is not worthy of a doctor's inspection. Is that what you are telling me?"

"You got it, Sparky," said that woman.

TWENTY-NINE

Bear Zabarte-Pitlochry, Scotland

The doc at the Pitlochry Med Center told me what I all ready knew. The scrapes and dings on my face were nothing to worry about.

As we walked back to the car, I said, "Babe, Henry, what do you say we hit that pub, grab a couple of brews and some fish and chips?"

Henry frowned, "I dinna think that's a good idea. There's a flock of men scouring the area for Delmont's suitcase. They might need me."

I said, "Do they have your cell number?"

"Aye, they do."

"If they need you, they'll call," said Flo.

I said, "Henry, cell phones can be great, but there might be a time when you want to get away, and you can't, 'cause people can call you and tell you to come home."

Flo said, "Bear Zabarte, are you talking about that time awhile ago when you were watching a baseball game in the bar at the Nugget, and the Red Sox won, so you got plastered?"

Henry said, "What's plastered mean?"

I said, "Drunk as a skunk. Babe, I don't get that way very often. That game was important, and the Sox won, and—"

Flo said, "Henry, Bear's right. Sometimes a cell

229

phone can be a pain in the—"

Henry's pocket started to buzz.

I said, "Henry, that's your cell phone."

He pulled it out, and after figuring out which end is up, he said, " 'Lo."

He listened, nodded and smiled. "Brilliant. I 'ave to drive some friends 'ome and then we'll meet back at the park. Bear, Flo, we'll have to skip the pub. They think they've found the suitcase."

Flo said, "Take us with you. We can catch a ride back to the farm with Fergus."

"Nay. Fergus and Delmont left long ago."

That's when I remembered my promise, and the long drive to Aberdeen. The day after tomorrow Henry would be pounding on my door at the crack of dawn. Damn it, six o'clock was too early to roll out of bed, head to Aberdeen and waste my day in an old library. I almost told Henry the trip was off. I mean what could the old fart do to me? Get pissed off? Forget it, I thought. You won't chicken-out on him. Nope, I told Henry I'd go and that's the end of it. "Henry, how about we take Flo with us to Aberdeen?"

He said, "I 'eard Ettamae was dancing with a group of girls that evening at Blair Castle. I'm sure Flo would rather stay 'ome with the child so she can work on her costume, or fix her hair, or do some of those things girls do."

Flo said, "Hey, I'm standing right here. If you have a question for me, just ask."

"Babe, what's your pleasure?"

"As long as Henry can guarantee that we'll be back in time to see Ettamae dance, I'll go with you. Fiona hemmed Ettamae's Tartan. She has her whole costume ready, and frankly, Ettamae spends more time with Fiona and the boys than she does with us. Count me in!"

Henry smacked me on my back. "Aye, we'll make a great team. I'll pick you up day after tomorrow at six."

Flo gave Henry a snappy salute. "Aye-aye captain. You can call us on your cell if you have further instructions?"

THIRTY

The buzzing of my cell phone woke me. Through fuzzy eyes I glanced at the clock and it showed twelve fifty-five am!

"Who is this?" I demanded.

"'Enry Bramble 'ere. Delmont, we found your suitcase and I was sure you'd want to receive the good news at once."

"Well, you are wrong. I am going to hang up now and—"

"Please don't do that. I'm standing on your doorstep. I'm wet, it's cold and I'd love a cuppa."

Willow rolled over. "What's going on?"

"Henry Bramble is at our front door. He has the suitcase full of money and he wants to drop in and have a cup of tea. I have never heard a more ridiculous demand in my —"

As she jumped out of bed, Willow said, "For heaven sakes, open the front door and invite the man in. He must have been working since Conner crashed and I'm sure he's cold."

I sighed into the phone, "Willow will open the front door and make you some tea. I will join you shortly."

Willow and Henry were sipping cups of tea when I entered the kitchen and asked, "Any news

232

concerning Conner's body?"

"Nay."

I looked around. "Where is the money you were in such a hurry to give me?"

He reached down and set the dripping suitcase onto the table. "As you can see, the case was still closed so the bloke who discovered the item should be in line for the thousand quid reward."

I said, "Not so fast. How do I know he didn't pocket a couple of fifties before he called you?"

"'Cause the lad told me so. In Scotland, a man's word is as good as, nay better, than a signed contract."

I said, "Henry. You just reminded me that I didn't sign a contract to pay anyone a thousand pound reward. In my country, the finder of this suitcase would have to—"

Willow slammed her cup on the table and a few drops of tea landed on the still wet suitcase. "Pinky, if you say one more word about not paying the reward, I'll never speak to you again. And I'm not kidding!"

"Willow, what I am trying to do is to point out the massive differences between our cultures. If you misinterpreted my words and feel I am attempting to back out of my agreement with Henry, then you are woefully mistaken."

I opened the suitcase and stared at soggy mounds of British money.

Henry said, "When you've dried out a thousand quid, give me a call." Henry stood and said, "Thank you, Mrs. Delmont for the cuppa. I can show myself out."

After I heard the front door close, and miffed at

the obdurate retired forester, I dumped the wet contents of the suitcase onto the kitchen table.

Somewhere in the soggy lumps lurked ten thousand pounds of my genuine money, and four hundred and ninety thousand pounds in counterfeit fifty-pound notes. My anger toward Henry ebbed at the sight of those wet blobs. I glanced out our window and noticed a light on at Fergus' farmhouse. I picked up the phone and dialed their number. Fiona answered.

"Fiona, this is Pinky. I trust I am not disturbing you."

"Nay. Fergus was snoring so loud I couldn't sleep. Why are you up so late?"

"Well—" Suddenly, for no reason, the madness of yesterday seemed very funny and for no discernible reason I began to chuckle!

Fiona said, "It's very early in the morning to phone me and tell a joke."

Unable to control my laughter, I handed the phone to Willow. She said, "Fiona, you have to come over and see what we have covering our kitchen table."

"I'll throw on a robe and be there in a jiffy."

When Fiona arrived, Willow walked her directly to the kitchen table. She took one look at the money and cried, "My God, I've never seen anything like it. Why is all that money wet?"

By now, Willow and I were laughing so hard that I had to sit down. I said, "You're looking at more than a half a million pounds on my kitchen table and all you want to know is why it's wet?"

Fiona's giggle increased. "Aye."

"Because your husband insisted on placing the

money inside a cheap, leaky suitcase. Of course he's not the only one at fault here. The suitcase did spend a few hours on the bottom of the River Tummel."

She burst into full-blown laughter. "And if Fergus had provided you with a waterproof suitcase, you wouldn't have this problem?"

Willow said, "Right. It's all Fergus' fault."

That did it. We all sat down and laughed for a solid minute. Finally, after the strain of the last twenty-four hours had dissipated in a moment of hysterical mirth, I said, "Any ideas how we can dry out this mess? It's too windy to hang them outside, and there's not enough room on the table."

Fiona said, "I have a few drying racks in the house that I use during bad weather. Give us a couple of hours and we'll have these ready for the bank."

In a few minutes, Fiona returned with two foldable wooden racks. We each grabbed a soggy stack and hung a single note onto the arms of the drying rack. Five and a-half hours later, using the racks, the table, the backs of the kitchen chairs, the counter top, the oven door, the couch, our bed, and every place in the apartment available to lay, or hang a bill, each waterlogged fifty pound note was nearly dry.

Willow said, "Fiona, I'd love to offer you a cup of tea while the money finishes drying, but I can't find a place to sit anywhere in the apartment. How about we go to your place?"

"Brilliant. I baked some shortbread cookies this, no yesterday morning, and I'll have the tea ready in a jiffy."

I had two cups of tea and more than my share of

Fiona's artery clogging shortbread cookies when Fergus walked into his kitchen. "What's going on?"

Fiona laughed, "Henry found Pinky's money and we spent the night hanging the bills out to dry."

"None of you slept last night?"

"Nay, but none of us have to go to work in an hour like you do. Want me to fix you some breakfast?"

"Aye."

Fiona said, "Willow, I didn't know that much money existed let alone that I would be hanging it up to dry."

Fergus said, "The majority of those notes are counterfeit. After you separate out Delmont's ten thousand pounds, arrange the counterfeit bills into stacks of two hundred and place a rubber band around each stack. Delmont, finding the genuine money from the thousands of bogus notes will be easier than you think. Take a genuine fifty pound note and lay it next to a counterfeit. Once they are side by side the real note is an obvious choice.

Willow said, "Now I'll need to find some rubber bands. "

"You're in luck, I save the ones that come each day wrapped around the newspaper. I've a jar full of them. Fergus, I heard that Pinky offered a reward to the man who found the suitcase. Do you know his name?"

Willow said, "Henry told us his name is Willie McGowan."

Fiona smiled. "Good for Willie. He's a fine young man, and a newlywed at that. I'm sure the young couple will find a good use for the money. Pinky, thank you for letting me come and play. It's not everyday a housewife in Scotland does much more than launder clothes, iron or fix her family dinner."

I said, "Fergus, I will have your counterfeit notes ready for you later today."

"Good. I'll stop by tonight and pick them up when—" His cell buzzed. "Murray here . . . Aye . . . Good bye." Fergus tucked his cell into his pocket and said, "I have a bit of news on Conner."

"Please inform me that you discovered his body."

"Delmont, I—"

"Do not tell me that he has escaped."

"My team brought in a dog. The hound picked up Conner's scent from the motorcycle and the dog's handler is positive the hound picked up Conner's trail about a mile downstream from the dam. That means the man could have fallen, or slipped down the face of the dam, into the river, and crawled out of the water a mile downstream."

"So he has escaped!"

"I'm not positive, but it's just possible he got away. I don't see how, but it's possible. Delmont, don't worry, he can't go far. Sooner or later, he'll—"

"He will what? Attempt to sneak into France and be captured by the border guards? I seem to recall a previous statement from you that Conner and Flo would disappear into the borderless European Community."

"Delmont, have you given Willie McGowan his thousand pound reward?"

"Do not change the subject. The fact that Conner walks freely through your jurisdiction causes me to fear for my life."

"What about Willow, Bear, and Florence? Don't

you have any concern for them?"

"Willow remains at my side. As to the others, they are not my responsibility. Now, what is your plan to find and incarcerate Conner?"

"I'm sure he'll turn up soon. He crashed his motorcycle. His accent identifies him as an American the moment he opens his mouth. The odds of him escaping beyond the borders of Perthshire are astronomical."

"That is what I was told before the man disappeared into the Nevada desert without food or water. A year later, Conner showed up at my office and threatens the lives of my staff. I need more assurance from you concerning my immediate safety.

"I will personally make sure that you, and my cousin, are safely on an airplane to America in two days. Now, back to my question concerning the town hero, Willie McGowan."

"Have I turned over his reward? No, we have not yet completed drying the money."

"Excellent. When I stop by your apartment later today, I will bring Willie, a reporter, and a photographer. You should be pleased. That reward will provide a boon for the whole town."

I said, "My mother would be proud to know that she raised a one-man economic incentive program. Fergus, unlike some who slept through the night, I am exhausted and in desperate need of rest. Goodbye!"

As we walked through the cool morning to the apartment, Willow said, "Pinky, why are you limping?"

"Willow, my love, my limp is caused by the leg wound I received during the altercation at the park."

"Wounded leg? You never mentioned a wounded leg. Pinky, what actually happened yesterday?"

"Come into the bedroom, my dear. I will give you the complete story and include all the gory details."

THIRTY-ONE

Bear Zabarte-Pitlochry, Scotland

"Bear."

I shivered as I stood by the shore of the lake. The sky was black and a cold rain dripped off my nose .

I couldn't see much because of the rain. Then the rain stopped, the clouds disappeared, and a full moon lit up the muddy shoreline.

"Bear."

A policeman stood next to me and said, "Sorry sir, but 'Enry tells me you can identify the body."

Why would Henry tell him that?

The policeman reached down. At his feet lay a wet, gray blanket that covered what looked to be a human figure. He grabbed the corner of the gray wool and slowly pulled. I saw a finger, then two . . .

"Bear, wake up, damn it."

My eyes popped open. Flo was shaking me.

"Wake up!"

I turned my head and my pillow was wet. "Hey, I'm awake, so stop already."

"But you were sweating like a pig, moaning and thrashing around. You must have had a bad dream. Frankly, the whole thing was eerie."

I laid my head back and stared at the ceiling. "I guess it was a dream, and you're right, it was bad."

"Do you want to tell me about it?"

I stretched my arms and rubbed my head. Everything had seemed so real. "I was standing on the shore of a lake."

"Like Lake Faskally?"

"I guess. The air was so thick I couldn't catch my breath. I heard a splash. I stared into the rain and there you were, swimming about a hundred feet off shore. Then you got caught up in some kind of a current and no matter how hard you tried, the current carried you away."

"That's ridiculous. Lakes don't have a currents. That's why they're called lakes."

"I know that, but this was a dream, and anything can happen in a dream. Are you going to clam up so I can tell you the rest?"

"Okay, I'll be good. Go on."

"I ran around looking for a boat and bumped into Henry who was just sort of standing there. I told him that you were swimming in the water and needed help. Henry nodded, like he understood what I said, but the old fart didn't move a muscle.

"I started to take off my shoes and jeans so I could swim out to rescue you when I saw a policeman push a small boat into the water. That's when Henry told me to stay out of the lake, that I'd freeze into an icicle before I got twenty feet and that the copper would rescue the swimmer."

Flo shook her head. "How can I swim in the same water that Henry says will freeze you before you get twenty feet?"

"It's my dream, damn it. Okay, the boat with the policeman finally gets to the spot where I'd last seen you and the policeman pulls something into the boat, but then it starts to rain, real hard, so I can't see if it was you. I yelled at the policeman to see that you're okay."

Flo said, "What did the cop say?"

"I guess he didn't hear me. I was shaking in the cold rain my teeth were rattling. I wanted to ask the cop why he didn't answer my questions but I couldn't get the words out of my mouth. Then, when the cop's boat reached the shore, I saw a mound covered by a gray blanket. He grabbed the blanket and lifted it up."

"Was it me under the blanket?"

"I don't know. That's when you woke me up."

I grabbed Flo and held her tight. Her skin was warm and soft. I whispered, "Do we have time to fool around?"

"Not really, but I could give you a rain check."

Not a great answer to a horny dude, but a whole lot better than a flat out no!

I got up and walked into our icebox bathroom, a morning visit guaranteed to get your feet moving real quick.

Ten minutes later, while the Kid set the table, she said, "I'm supposed to remind you that tomorrow afternoon we go to the Annual Parade of the Atholl Highlanders. After the parade, parents and good friends are invited to watch the authentic Scottish folk dancing. According to Fiona, there's an outdoor stage and seats for hundreds of people. "

"Don't worry, Kid, we'll be there, but we're going with Henry to Aberdeen first. We might miss part of the parade but me and Flo'll see you dance."

Ettamae flashed me a look that could turn a head of fresh cabbage into Cole Slaw. "You're not just shining me on?"

242

Flo said, "I'll be with Bear and Henry to make sure. You can count on me."

I said, "Hold on Kid. If we're in Aberdeen, how are you going to get to Blair castle?"

"Fiona will take me. Remember, the boys march in the parade dressed up as soldiers." She frowned. "Don't forget. The parade starts at five and my group is scheduled to dance on the outdoor stage around six to six-thirty. Fiona warned me that every seat will be filled so you'll have to be there before six."

"Sweetheart, we wouldn't miss seeing you dance for all the mouse ears in Disneyland," said Flo. "Is your costume ready?"

"I think so. Fiona will check the costume out." The Kid's eyes lit up. "Flo, you could come with me to Fiona's and we could turn this day into an all-girl party."

Flo shook her head. "Sorry. Henry's picking us up in a few minutes. Bear wants to check out the place where the cops think Conner crawled out of the river."

I said, "And you have to call Willow to check on our airplane tickets home."

The Kid frowned. "Tickets home? We're going back home? So soon?"

I said, "Come on, Kid, I figured you'd be ready to see your grandpa."

She said, "I kind of hoped that he could fly to Scotland . . . and we could live here . . . with Fiona and the boys."

Flo dropped her coffee cup. It hit the floor and made a hell of a mess.

The Kid grabbed a dish cloth and tried to sop up the coffee. "Flo, I'm grateful for everything you and

243

Bear have done for me and grandpa, but—"

I heard Henry's car pull up outside the front door. "Kid, we have to go. We'll talk about your crazy idea later."

Me and Flo crawled into the old Austin. He said, "Mornin', folks. After our stop by the river, what are we going to do next?"

Flo pulled out a tissue from somewhere and blew her nose. "While you drive, I'm going to call Willow and discuss our return flight."

"Babe, will you ask her for two or three tickets?"

She shook her head and blew her nose again. I don't know what it is about broads. They get teary-eyed at the drop of a hat. Hey, I like the Kid. And living with her hasn't cramped my lifestyle, but it was obvious to anyone with half a brain that a real family, like Fiona and the boys, would be a better fit for the Kid. And if we could figure out a way to get her grandpa over here, shit, that would be as good as doubling down when the dealer shows a five.

Flo sniffed a couple of times while she keyed in some numbers on her cell. "Willow? What's going on concerning our reservations back to Reno?"

As she listened to Willow talk her eyes got real wide. "Pinky told you what?" Flo frowned. "Look. Bear and I both work for that cheap bastard. He needed us in Scotland and paid for our flight. If he thinks we're going to get stuck for—"

She listened and said, "Good idea. I'll call his office and ask Kim to set up the return flight."

I said, "What scam is Pinky trying to pull?"

"No scam. Just part of his old screw-his-employees benefit plan."

Flo keyed in some numbers. "Kim, Flo here . . .

Florence Sonderlund, damn it. Yes, that Flo. Look, we need you to make three, no, make that two reservations for Bear and myself, Glasgow to Reno on Sunday or Monday. Got it?"

She listened for a second and then smiled. "Yes, book us on the same flight as Pinky and Willow. Are they flying first class or business? . . . I see. Make our reservations the same. Thank you, Kim. See you in a couple of days. No? Why not?"

She listened for a couple of seconds and started to laugh. "You don't have to convince me, Kim. I did your job for awhile and that bastard is impossible to work for. Trust me, you are doing the right thing. Keep in touch."

I said, "What's so funny?"

"After Kim books our business class reservations and makes sure they are charged to Pinky's office credit card, she's walking out the door."

"Wow! Is business class better than that tiny seat they crammed me into on the flight here?"

"You will be sitting in the lap of luxury."

"Great! Babe, I heard you tell Kim to make two reservations. Are you sure you'll be okay with that?"

"No, and don't ask me that question ever again." Flo dumped her cell into her purse and looked at me. Big tears were falling off her cheeks. "Bear, sometimes adults have to listen to their heads instead of their hearts. Living with a conventional family, like Fiona and the boys, will give Ettamae the best chance to live a normal life."

"I notice you didn't include Fergus with Fiona and the boys."

"Fergus is okay, but he's no different from all men—more concerned with baseball—or work—or football—or beer. I can't teach Ettamae how to sew, or cook, or—"

"Babe, you are great with the Kid. It's me, right?"

"No, the problem concerns men in general. Now let's change the subject."

"Sorry, but I have one more question about the Kid and her grandpa. We can't just dump her here and fly back to Carson City. I mean there must be some sort of law against that. And her grandpa's not Scottish. How will that work?"

"Don't worry. Remember my old friends at the State Department. I'm positive they can fast-track the paperwork needed to permanently move Ettamae and her grandpa to Scotland."

Just to make sure that the Kid problem was solved, I said, "Henry, do you trust Fergus?"

"Why?"

"The Kid wants to—"

Flo said, "Ettamae wants to stay and live with the Murray family."

"Aye. That family is part of the Murray clan like me. If you can't trust a member of your own clan, who can you trust?"

I didn't have an answer to that one so I sat back and let the Austin wobble its way to the river. Like Flo, I wanted to boot the Kid out of my brain for a minute, so I went back over everything I knew about the Mary Patterson murder and I had to admit that Fergus was right. Gordon Tannahill and this investigation was dead . . . Wait a minute, an hour ago the Kid said something about Blair Castle and the Atholl Highlanders Parade . . . Something was out of wack. Then I remembered that Pinky told me that Gordon's father was a distant cousin of the Duke of Atholl. I pulled out my cell and called Fiona.

"Morning, Fiona. I'm confused. What's the connection between Blair Castle and the Duke of Atholl?"

"Blair Castle is where the Duke of Atholl lives. Why?"

"I'm not sure. Is there more than one Duke of Atholl in Scotland."

"I don't think so. Perhaps Fergus can help you. He's a member of the Murray clan of Blair Atholl. Bear, excuse me, but I have to run. I have a church committee in thirty minutes. Bye."

The line went dead.

Flo said, "What's that all about?"

"Just something Pinky told me."

"Is it important?"

"Damn it, I don't know. Henry, what do you know about the Duke of Atholl?"

"The story begins in 1130 when Freskin was the Celtic chief in the province of Moray."

"Damn, you're talking about a thousand years ago."

"Aye"

"How long before we get to the spot by the river where the cops think Conner climbed out?"

"Could be ten minutes."

"Okay, fast forward your Duke of Atholl story a couple hundred years."

"Aye. In 1629, the Chief of Tullibardine was made the Earl of Atholl. In 1676, the Earl became a Marquise. Then in 1703, the Marquis of Atholl was confirmed as a Duke."

"Partner, that's a good story but more than I

needed to know."

"Bear," said Flo. "What's bugging you?"

"I don't know. I'll run it by Fergus after we get back home."

The stop by the river was a total waste of time. There was nothing but farm land and a farmhouse stuck here and there. According to Henry, the cops had combed the area and Conner was long gone.

Flo said, "So far, I'm sorry I didn't stay home and join the sewing party with Ettamae and Fiona."

I said, "Babe, cut me some slack. Henry, I give up. Let's head back to the cottage."

A minute later my cell buzzed. It was Fergus.

"Bear. Last night a man who fit Conner's description picked up his luggage at the Thistle Terrace, a B&B across from the North Inch Golf Course. He settled his bill and left on foot carrying a single suitcase."

"Is the North Inch Golf Course close?"

"No more than a mile from my office."

"Hey, we're only twenty minutes away. Meet me at the B & B and we can check out—"

"Bear, my men have done that and I have one more bit of bad news."

"Okay?"

"A Perth motorcycle shop rented a motorcycle to a man that fits —"

"I know, Conner. When did he rent the cycle?"

"Last night, just past nine according to the time-stamped rental contract."

"So that means he's got a fourteen hour jump on us. Let's see, fourteen hours at sixty miles an hour adds up to—"

Flo cried, "Eight hundred and forty miles."

Fergus said, "If he reached the continent, he could be anywhere in Europe by now."

"And for our sake I hope he stays there."

"Bear, don't get upset. By the way, the Innkeeper told me that Conner had her launder some of his dirty clothes and he left a few items."

"So?"

"I wonder if you have any idea what I should do with the lot?"

I guessed Fergus was an okay guy. I knew he was a cop, but there were times when I could get past that. And the dude was letting us stay at his cottage for free. But if Flo hadn't grabbed my cell phone, I would have told him exactly where, and just how far up, he could stick Conner's clean clothes.

She said, "I think it's best we say goodbye Fergus."

Ten minutes later, we were back at the cottage to start packing up.

Henry said, "I'll be by at eight tomorrow morning. We've got a lot of work to do if we're going to get to Blair Castle before the dancing commences."

Flo handed me my cell and said, "You've attended the dances in the past?"

"Aye. I've only missed one year, when that branch knocked me clean out of that tree."

I said, "Henry, keep your eyes peeled for Conner. Fergus thinks he's gone to France, or Italy, or somewhere. Me, I'm not sure. All I know is he'll do something unexpected. And don't forget, he'll be riding a motorcycle."

"Aye."

THIRTY-TWO

Pinky Delmont-Pitlochry, Scotland

I heard Willow's cell beep and feigned sleep to remain in the afterglow of our romantic rapture. However, when I heard Willow suggest that woman contact Kim to arrange their flight home, and to charge the flight to my business card, my euphoria vanished.

"Willow, you have no authority to give advice to that woman. Give me one reason why I should pay for their airfare."

"Off the top of my head I can think of many. For example, they both are employed by you. You paid for their flight to Scotland. And—"

I cried, "Cease. I asked for a single reason. Now, did one of them follow through concerning your advice and call my office?"

"Pinky, I have no idea what Bear or Flo did after I hung up. I suggested a course of action to her, but—"

I grabbed my cell off the night stand and punched the speed dial button.

"Hennessy and Delmont, how may I assist you?"

My original thought was to hang up. I was attempting to call my office and I expected a female voice to answer . . . hold on, Hennessy? "Thomas, is that you?"

"Pinky, thank God you called. This place is a mess. Kim just walked out the front door. The court clerk called. Judge Anderson demands you appear in his court at once or you'll face contempt charges. And—"

I calmed down as much as possible and said, "Did you answer my call to my office with the phrase, Hennessy and Delmont?"

"I did, but you need to take into account the massive amount of work I have done during your absence."

"Thomas, have you added at least a million dollars to the firm's coffers?"

"No."

"Then have you exculpated a dozen accused murders?"

"No. But—"

"No buts, and listen to me carefully. During my lifetime, neither you, nor anyone else, will ever place his or her name in front of mine concerning my legal practice. And, I might add, I am working on a codicil to my will that will prohibit you, or anyone else, from placing their name in front of mine concerning my legal practice even after my death. Do I make myself clear?"

His response took on the proper subservient tone. "Yes, Pinky."

"Now what did you say concerning Kim?"

"She packed up and walked out of here five minutes ago. Her final words, as her feet hit the sidewalk, were 'I quit.'"

"I will take care of that minor problem later. Next, I need you to check her desk and tell me what class of airline reservations she made for Bear and

251

that woman."

"I'm standing by her desk as we speak, and except for the phone and the Rolodex, the desktop is clean."

"Look through the drawers," I demanded.

"Pinky, in the right-hand top drawer there is a note addressed to you."

"Read it!"

"Dear Mr. Delmont, due to the abruptness of my departure, and for safe keeping, I took your business credit card with me. I do not trust . . . "

"Keep reading, damn it. Whom does she not trust?"

Thomas cleared his throat. "I do not trust Mr. Hennessy. I have written my home phone number below and as soon as you return from Scotland, call me and I will personally deliver your credit card to you." She signed the note, "Regretfully, Kimberly."

"Humph!"

"Pinky, I never gave that woman any reason to distrust me. In fact—"

"Thomas, cease babbling and listen to me. Check the Rolodex and give me the private phone number to Judge Anderson's chambers."

"How will the number be listed?"

He was no better than Kim. "It is listed after the letters, JAC. And Thomas, if I discover that you have copied that Rolodex, or written down any of the numbers, I will tell Bear to give you his version of a chiropractic spinal adjustment. The last patient who partook of Bear's adjustment expertise never walked again."

"Jesus."

"Now give me that number."

Inside of fifteen seconds, Thomas read me the seven numbers. "Pinky, do you need anything more?"

"You need to stay there until Kim's replacement comes in. I expect you to show her to her desk and once she is comfortable, you are to instruct her to cut you a check for five thousand dollars."

"Wow, is that a bonus?"

No. It is your final payment for services rendered."

"But I thought we—"

"Do not force me to discuss your lack of loyalty with Bear."

"But Pinky, I've been loyal, and—"

"Thomas, once you have your termination payment in hand, pack up your belongings and leave my office. In fact, I recommend you leave Carson City."

"But—"

"Goodbye."

I scanned through the phone list on my cell until I found the number for Rapid Replacement.

"Rapid Replacement. We supply top quality office help on demand. Louis Loomer, how can I help you?"

"I need to replace a secretary and I need her at once."

"Do I have the good fortune to be conversing with Mr. Delmont?"

"Louis, I need to replace that woman you sent me six months ago."

"And she replaced the woman I sent you a year ago, and she—"

"Louis, although you are the only clerical replacement firm in Carson City, need I remind you that Reno is a short thirty miles north and while I would rather do my business with a local firm, I will—"

"Mr. Delmont, do you need a temporary or a permanent replacement?"

"Louis, I require a permanent replacement. I appreciate that my legal practice makes certain demands on an employee, some of which they have never faced before. My needs are simple. The employee must show up on time and do what I ask of them. I seek someone as bright at Lu, the woman you sent me a year ago. Or one with more gumption then Kim, the loser you supplied who had less backbone then a jellyfish."

"Mr. Delmont, did you try to reason with Kim before she left?"

"How could I. At present I am calling you from Pitlochry, Scotland, and learned of Kim's departure via a phone call not fifteen minutes ago."

"My, my. The life of a lawyer is more glamorous then that of a simple businessman such as myself. The best I could afford last year was a week camping at Lake Tahoe with my wife. Are you familiar with the County campground near—"

"Louis, my cell's battery is running down. Find me a replacement. Next week, when I return, I will include a generous bonus along with your usual fee. In fact, if this replacement lasts a year, I will instruct her to send you a bonus of ten thousand dollars."

"Mr. Delmont. You are too generous. I will have a top notch replacement running your office in thirty minutes or my name isn't Louis Loomer."

I dropped the Loomer call and phoned Judge

Anderson's chambers.

"Pinky, I thought we had an understanding?"

"Your Honor, whatever you previously thought would be correct. But would you reiterate your view of our understanding?"

"No one from your office would ever again interrupt my lunch break."

"Yes, and no one should."

"But that exact occurrence happened yesterday."

Oh my god! "Not George Sterling again?"

"No. This time it was that new partner of yours, Thomas Hennessy. He approached me while I was eating my turkey and sprout wrap. The young man pleaded with me to transfer George Sterling, one of your pro bono clients to him. My anger at his interruption grew as I recalled the legal hours, and compassion you had exhibited toward Mr. Sterling as his attorney. I severely berated the young whippersnapper and sent him on his way with his tail between his legs."

"If you have a moment, your Honor, I can clear up the cardinal error concerning Mr. Hennessy."

"Go ahead, but make it quick. I meet my wife for lunch in ten minutes."

"And a lovely woman she is. How lucky you are, after all these years, to—"

"I said make it quick."

"And I will. You see, Mr. Hennessy took advantage of my absence to—"

"Then the rumor is true. You are vacationing in Scotland with your ex-wife, the District Attorney."

"Partially true, your Honor. You need to know that this is not a trip for my pleasure. I am in

Scotland because Willow pleaded with me to assist her cousin with a delicate family matter."

"I just checked the time and must leave in a minute."

"Your Honor, during my absence, Mr. Hennessy attempted to pull off a bloodless coup and steal my law practice. However, because of my friends, such as yourself, Hennessy failed. For that I thank you."

"Pinky, you've cleared that situation up to my satisfaction. Now, you have a few seconds left. What's your take on Scotland?"

"Your Honor, if you ever come to Scotland, I am positive you, and your lovely bride, would love every minute you spend in the country."

"I'll pass your positive review of Scotland on to my wife. Oh-oh, time's up. One final word on the subject of my free time. Talk with your office staff and inform them that if I am ever again interrupted during my lunch break, that person, or persons, and that includes you, counselor, will spend a weekend in the county jail for contempt of my court.

"Thank you, your Honor. My office will implement your suggestion immediately."

"Pinky, those were not suggestions. That was an ultimatum. Have I made myself perfectly clear?"

"You have, your Honor. My humble staff and I thank you for your forbearance concerning this delicate matter."

THIRTY-THREE

Bear Zabarte-Pitlochry, Scotland

Damn, doesn't it ever stop raining in this country? Big drops of water bashed against our bedroom window and woke me up ten minutes before the alarm went off. I rolled over and pulled the pillow over my head. I didn't want to ride all the way to Aberdeen. But what could I tell Henry? That we couldn't go because Flo had one of those women things? No, I couldn't flat-out lie to the old dude. Get up and drag your sorry butt down the hall to the can. Rain or shine, Henry'll be here in an hour.

When my bare feet hit the freezing floor in the bathroom, I yelled, "Shit!"

Flo called, "Hey, are you all right?"

"All I wanted to do was go to the can but I can't because my feet are too cold."

"Crawl back in bed with me. I'll warm you up."

"Babe, we don't have time for that. Henry'll be here in less than an hour."

"Hey, all I said was I'd warm you up."

"Oh."

Flo rolled out of bed and stretched. Damn, that broad had one fine body.

Flo said, "It sounds like rain."

"Yup."

"I don't want to drive that far in Henry's old

junker, in the rain. Call him up and see if you can weasel out of it."

I still had to take a pee, so I headed back to the can. I forced my teeth to stop chattering and said, "Can't do that. I told Henry me and you are going and a deal's a deal, so get moving. Rain or shine, we head for Aberdeen in forty minutes."

While I threw on an old pair of jeans, I thought about the day. If Henry took the same route, we should reach Aberdeen about nine . . . hold on . . . The last time we were riding in Fergus' car. Henry's old bucket of bolts can't go much faster than thirty-five, so we should get there around ten-thirty at the latest. By that time, the damn library should be open. Three hours better be enough time for us to look through a couple of years of dusty newspapers. With a break for lunch, we should be back by four-thirty, more than enough time to get to Blair Castle to see the Kid dance.

While me, Flo, and the Kid downed a bowl of cold cereal, I noticed that the rain was slowing down.

Flo carried our cups to the sink and looked out the window. "Hey, the sky's beautiful out there. The eastern horizon has taken on a deep, reddish glow as the sun breaks through the storm clouds. Ettamae, we'll see you at the castle."

The Kid said, "Thanks. Bear, you and Flo have a good day."

"Okay." About that time I heard Henry's car pull up and said, "Tell him I'll be out in a minute."

"What's the hold up?"

I said, "If you've got to know, I have to pee."

"I thought you did that awhile ago?"

"Babe, the plumbing doesn't work so good when

the pipes are frozen."

"Humph, I didn't have any problem."

"That's the difference between indoor and outdoor plumbing."

"I'll wait in the car."

Before I left the cottage, I grabbed a couple of extra sweaters. Riding in Henry's old Austin was almost fun on a good day, but a dude could wait a lifetime for a good day in Scotland. When I climbed in Henry handed me a newspaper.

"What's this for?"

"'Tis a long drive to Aberdeen."

I figured he was doing his best to make me feel good, but I wasn't buying it.

"Bear, I know you feel this trip is a waste of time, so sit back and enjoy a good read."

We hadn't gone a mile before another buckets of rain hit the windshield. Henry turned on the wipers and they bounced on the glass like a flat rock skips across a lake. I could barely see the white line that separated

the two lanes of traffic, or the bright red taillights on the car in front of us. I said, "Henry, can you see better than I can?"

"Nay."

"Slow down then."

"Aye."

After the Austin slowed, Henry said, "I thought you were in a 'urry so you could get back in time to watch the dancing?"

"We are in a hurry. It's your damned windshield wipers that are slowing us down."

Henry's wonky eye jumped around. "Do you think we should stop and see if someone can fix 'em?"

"Aye, 'Enry." Flo called from the back seat. "That beats the hell out of dying in a head-on collision."

He pulled off the highway at a place called Little Brechin, one of the dumber town names in Scotland, and found a small garage. For the next half hour, me and Flo sat close to a warm wood stove and sipped hot tea while a mechanic screwed around with Henry's old car. I tried to read the newspaper that Henry had given me, but all I could think about was something Grandma Zabarte told me—if you lie to someone, you'll pay for that lie somewhere down the road. As usual, Grandma was right. I hadn't told Henry that me and Flo didn't want to go to Aberdeen so the goofy windshield wipers were my payback. As I downed my second cup, Flo got up and looked out the window. "Hey, most of the clouds are gone and I can see the sun. Wipers or not, let's finish this epic trek to Aberdeen."

As he drove down the highway, Henry said, "Flo, did you like the newspaper article about the Scotsman who did the stunts for the Clint Eastwood movies?"

"Yes, that was an interesting article." She stopped and said, "How did you know I like Clint Eastwood?"

"Bear told me that Dirty 'Arry was your favorite movie."

"That's not true. My favorite movie is Sleepless in Seattle. Bear, why did you tell Henry that?"

"Babe. You told me that you loved Clint Eastwood movies."

"I do, but not Dirty Harry. The cop Clint played in that flick was a full blown psychopath and I've seen enough of those types to last me two lifetimes."

I hoped she was talking about Ice Conner. Flo stuck her face back into the newspaper and after awhile we reached Aberdeen. Henry drove around the town and finally found the library. Maybe my luck was changing 'cause without really trying we found a parking spot near the main entrance.

Henry talked to a wrinkled up old broad behind a counter and said, "Follow me to the viewing room."

We walked into another room and headed to another counter where there was another old broad, but this one didn't have as many wrinkles. This babe's face was too fat for wrinkles. I glanced at the clock on the wall and said, "Henry, we've got to get moving. Where are the old newspapers stored?"

The old broad said, "Sir, please exercise some control concerning the volume of your voice. I noticed your American accent and heaven knows our town needs all the tourists we can get, so I will ignore your initial transgression concerning proper library behavior."

"Huh?"

"Now that you understand the rules, a Scottish company transfers each daily newspaper in the region onto Microfiche. The Aberdeen library stores those films on the outside chance that someday, someone, even an American, will come in and want to view them. The desks to your left are set up with Microfiche readers. All you have to do is tell me the newspaper and the date. I will provide you with the film. It is up to you to scan through the film to find the item that interests you."

I said, "Thanks. Henry, give the lady the place and dates we're looking for."

While he talked to the broad behind the counter, me and Flo headed to a viewing table.

Flo said, "I've used these readers before. Once the librarian gives Henry the film, I'll show you both how everything works and you'll be on your own."

"Hey, where are you going?"

"Sorry. Watching all those printed words flash by on the screen makes me queasy. Trust me, you don't want to be in the car with me feeling like that."

Henry showed up holding a couple of small boxes. I said, "Henry, I'm sorry I was a grouch this morn—"

"That's all right, Bear. I know you don't think we 'ave a 'ope, but I couldn't rest without trying."

I smiled and stuck out my hand. He took it and just like that, we were buds again.

Flo said, "Now watch what I do." She sat down in front of a screen, sort of like a TV with knobs. Flo explained that you turned the knobs to control the speed of the pictures that moved across the screen.

She continued, "I was working for the government in D.C. when I figured out that viewing the films of old newspapers was not my favorite pastime. I once spent seventeen hours straight in front of a screen like this while searching the State Department archives for a . . . whoops . . . I'll bet those letters are still classified. Anyway, all I came up with was a stiff neck and a severe case of motion sickness. To keep from getting dizzy I suggest that you two follow this plan. Bear, you watch the screen for thirty minutes. Then Henry takes the next thirty minutes. While you're not viewing the screen, go outside, breathe some fresh air, and rest your eyes. If you need me, I'll be in the main section of the library reading a good book. Any questions?"

Me and Henry shook our heads. I said, "I'll take the first shift. See you in a half an hour, partner."

"Aye."

I took the first cartridge out of the box, dropped it into the reader, and watched the boring news of the Aberdeen area, day by day, page-by-page, float past my eyes. At eleven Henry took over and I walked outside to smell the salty North Sea. Before I knew it, Henry's thirty minutes was up and it was my turn to ride the word-filled merry-go-round again.

Our thirty-minute on-off job continued until two-thirty when Henry tapped my shoulder. "My turn. Bear, we're almost done. This cartridge will take us far past the date when Gordon was killed in that explosion."

I walked outside for a break, found a chair in the warm, afternoon sun, and closed my eyes. The next thing I knew Henry was shaking my arm. "Come quick, Bear. I found somethin'."

I struggled to wake up. "What?"

"I found a missin' lass in the paper."

He dragged me back to the viewing table.

"'Ere 'tis," he whispered. "'Ere's the story about 'er."

He pointed to a story on page three that told about a girl, Elizabeth Duncan, age thirteen, who had disappeared sometime after she'd performed as the lead dancer at the Aberdeen Scottish Dance Festival at the Marischal College Auditorium. The parents of Elizabeth pleaded for help to locate their daughter. The Aberdeen Police indicated they had no leads at that time.

For a second I felt really dumb. While I was out snoozing in the sun, good old Henry found the . . . wait a minute, that's when I noticed the date on the paper. What the hell? I turned and yelled, "Henry, that happened almost two years after Gordon went to Saudi Arabia and a year after he died in the explosion."

The old broad behind the counter said, "Sir, I warned you to control the unfettered volume of your voice. I shall have to ask you to immediately leave the library."

I jumped up. "Sorry, babe." What the hell, Henry's find was bullshit and I was going to leave anyway.

Henry said softly, "Aye, Bear, but keep reading. You need to see the name of the 'ead dance judge at the Festival."

My eyeballs returned to the screen, skimmed down the column to the last paragraph. I read out loud, "Albert Tannahill, Head of the Scottish Department of History at The University at St. Andrews, and one of Scotland's best known dance judges, told police that he saw Elizabeth leave after the final performance in a black or dark brown Vauxhall. He expressed sorrow to the girl's parents that he could not supply the police with a description of the driver due to the darkness of the evening."

My guts turned to water as I tried to figure out what I had just read. A teenage girl was missing in Aberdeen, but this time it was brother Albert, not Gordon who was involved. What were the odds that two brothers killed and buried little girls?

I sat back and stared at the screen. My brain was circling around like a dog chasing its tail. Albert

Tannahill, Gordon Tannahill, Albert, and Gordon! Slow down and think. Could Gordon still be alive? I jumped up. "Henry, we're idiots. Me and Flo gave up on our investigation because I thought that Gordon Tannahill was dead. But what if Gordon's still alive?"

Henry glanced at the broad behind the counter. "Bear, the librarian is staring at you and talking to someone on the phone. I think—"

Then the dog caught his tail! "That newspaper story you gave Flo this morning about Clint Eastwood's double. She read me that line, 'The double and Eastwood looked enough alike to be twins, or at least close brothers.'"

I thought back to the photo of the two Tannahill boys that Pinky found in the basement of the Stronvaar Hotel. Those boys were close enough to be twins. I grabbed Henry. "I saw a picture of the Tannahill boys and the only difference between them, besides a year of age, was that you could see a birth mark below the ear of the older brother, Albert. Pinky and Fergus talked to that dude a couple of days ago. I have to call Pinky and ask him a question."

He answered on the third ring. "Boss, when you were in St. Andrews did you happen to notice if Albert Tannahill had a birthmark under his left ear."

"Bear, I just called my office and discovered that you conned Kim into buying two business class tickets back home. Do you have any idea what that is going to cost me?

"Damn it, Boss, shut up and answer my question."

"Yes, I noticed the birthmark below, and behind Albert Tannahill's ear. It is commonly referred to as

265

a port wine stain. Now, back to your skullduggery. There is no way that you and that woman are going to set me back five thousand dollars for two—"

I dumped the call. Flo walked up and said, "What's happening in here. A couple of cops just came in and it looks like they're heading toward this room."

I said, "Read this."

Flo sat down and Henry pointed at the story of a missing girl.

Okay. In the photo, Albert had a birthmark and Gordon didn't. The man Pinky met in St. Andrews had a birthmark, so that dude had to be Albert, and Gordon must be dead.

The broad behind the counter pointed he cops in my direction. I leaned over Flo's shoulder, to tell her I was going to clear out, when I saw an ad near the bottom of the page.

TATTOOS!
Seaside Tattoo Parlor
Aberdeen's Only 24 Hour Parlor
1224 Regent Quay
651 842 599

Flo reached for the power switch to turn off the viewer. I said, "Don't touch that switch, Babe."

Two big cops grabbed me under my arms and lifted me off the floor. Everybody in Carson City calls me Bear 'cause that's my name, but also 'cause I'm almost as big as a Grizzly, so trust me, those Scottish fuzz were two strong dudes. As they dragged me out of the Viewing Room, I yelled to Flo, "Get a copy of that page. We're going to need that evidence when we talk to Fergus."

Henry rushed up to the cops. "Lads, the

American means well. I promise he will speak quietly from now on."

The cops, who were getting pooped from carting me around, set me down and the older one said, "We try to avoid placing tourists under arrest. It's bad for Aberdeen's image. You, Mr. Wobbly eye, will you vouch for the American?"

"Aye, I will."

They let me go and left the library.

Henry said, "Bear, please do not raise your voice again."

I promised him, and then whispered, "Henry, what if Gordon Tannahill had a birthmark tattooed under his left ear so he'd look like his brother? What if Gordon's not dead and is walking around as his brother, Albert?"

Henry's wild eye jerked around in shock and he said, "If that's true, Bear, your bairn is in grave danger."

"My what?"

"If you're right, Ettamae's in the 'ands of the devil 'cause Dr. Albert Tannahill is the 'ead dance judge for the festival at Blair Atholl."

I grabbed Flo and the three of us ran as fast as we could to Henry's Austin. While Flo climbed in, I pulled out my cell and keyed in Fergus' office number. I don't think it was my fault, or Henry's, but he started the engine and popped the clutch while I had one foot in the car, and the other on the curb. The car jumped and the cell squirted out of my hand like a watermelon seed pressed between your fingers. The phone hit once, then a second time. I heard the plastic crack on the first hit, and saw the glass screen shatter on the second. I picked up what was left of my cell and jumped into the car. The second I buckled my seat belt, Henry popped the clutch again and pulled a wild U-turn into a solid stream of traffic. Tires screeched and filled the Austin with smelly burned rubber.

I said, "Slow down, we can't help Ettamae if we're all killed in an accident."

He jerked his head around, like he was trying to focus his right eye on me. "Aye. I'll be careful."

While the little Austin cruised along on the A90 at its top speed of thirty-five, I said, "Flo, let me use your cell phone. We need to tell Fergus what we found."

She rummaged around the gunny sack she calls a purse and said, "Sorry, when you gave me the bum's rush this morning, I forgot to take my phone off the charger."

Henry said, "Bear, you can use mine."

I grabbed it and keyed in Fergus' office.

"Western Area Crime Officer Murray's line. This is Sergeant McCrae."

"This is Bear. Is he in?"

"Excuse me?"

"Bear Zabarte. We're the American's staying at Fergus' farm."

"I'm sorry, Mr. Bear, but Officer Murray left his office a few moments ago."

"Hey, I really need to ask him a question. Does he have a radio or a mobile phone?"

"Yes, he has a mobile phone."

"That's what I need. Give me the number."

"I'm sorry, but regulations do not allow me to give out Crime Officer Murray's mobile number."

I didn't have time for all of this crap. I yelled,

"Damn it, Sergeant, I have to get him a message. You can do that much can't you?"

"Yes, sir, I can relay a message to Officer Murray, but only in case of a dire emergency." He sounded pissed.

"Trust me, this is an emergency. Tell Fergus to call Bear at once."

"I'll read that back, Mr. Bear."

"Don't bother. Just get off your ass and pass that on to Fergus."

Flo barked at me. "Bear, you shouldn't talk like that to strangers. Apologize to the man."

I said into the phone, "I'm sorry I told you to get off your ass." But Sergeant McCrae was long gone.

We drove, and drove, but at thirty-five miles an hour, going more than a hundred miles takes a long time. I waited thirty minutes for Fergus to call. I tried Fiona's number again. No answer.

The high pitched whine of the Austin's tiny four cylinder engine nearly drowned out Henry's voice as he cried, "They must 'ave all gone to the festival."

I glanced at my watch. It was five after four. "Henry, how much longer?"

"Less than two 'ours to Blair castle."

Shit, try Fergus' office again. I keyed in his number and waited. On the fifth ring, a man answered, "Western Area Crime Officer Murray's line. This is Sergeant McCrae."

Not this dude again. "Sergeant, this is Bear again. Is Fergus available?"

"No sir. Would you care to leave a message?"

"I don't want to leave a message. Sergeant, we've danced to this song before. Fergus has a mobile phone. All I need is his number so I can talk to him."

269

"I understand, Mr. Bear, but the regulations state that I cannot give Crime Officer Murray's mobile number out to strangers. If this is an emergency, I can—"

I yelled, "If you won't give me Fergus' number, then call him and tell him to call Bear Zabarte on his cell phone."

"Mr. Bear, I gave your cell number to Officer Murray thirty minutes ago. If he has not returned your call, then I must assume he did not deem your call an emergency."

"Damn it man, my daughter's life's in danger."

McCrae said, "Mr. Bear, you should have told me that the first call. I'll relay that message and your mobile number to Officer Murray at once."

The line went dead. I gave Henry's cell back to him and said, "Henry, I'm going to . . . Son-of-a-bitch! Fergus can't call my cell. It's broken."

I grabbed Henry's cell back and hit the recall key.

"Western Area Crime Officer Murray's line. This is Sergeant McCrae."

"Sergeant, this is Bear again. I gave you the wrong call back number."

"Would you care to leave me the new number?"

"Yes, here it is—"

Henry's cell made a couple of beeps.

"Sergeant, did you get that? The new number?"

No answer. Shit! "Henry, when was the last time you charged your phone?"

"Charge it? I dinna know what you mean."

Flo leaned forward and rapped Henry on his shoulder. "Are you telling me that you've never recharged the battery in your phone?"

"Aye."

Flo said, "Can we go faster?"

"Nay. I could look for a telephone box."

Flo said, "You keep your eye on traffic, we'll look for a phone booth."

"Aye. They're bright red."

Flo said, "Bear, what else can we do?"

"Nothing. Just sit back and pray we get there in time."

I listened to the tires slap the cracks in the pavement as they disappeared underneath the car.

Flo leaned forward. "Take a look at your cell. That's better than just sitting here."

I pulled the broken box out of my pocket. I squeezed the sides together and the damn thing started to buzz. I hit a button and said, "Fergus?"

"Bear, Sergeant McCrae told me that Ettamae's life is in danger. What's going on?"

"Fergus, it's—" The right wheel banged into a chuckhole, I lost my grip on the cell and a hunk of the case fell into my lap. I stuck the piece back on and tried to hold it the magic way again. "Fergus? Can you hear me?" Nothing.

Henry said, "Do you think he got the message?"

"I don't know. How fast are we going?"

"'Bout thirty six."

"Crank her up to forty."

"But the front-end wobble will blow out the tires."

"Pinky'll buy you a new set."

"Aye."

The town of Pitlochry flashed by.

Flo said, "Can you go any faster?"

"Nay, we're going as fast as we can. I just 'ope

an pray the motor will 'old at this speed."

A long ten minutes dragged by when my broken phone buzzed.

"Fergus?"

"Aye."

"We found an old newspaper article in Aberdeen about a teenage girl who disappeared and—"

"Jesus Christ, Bear, I thought we agreed that the missing girl investigation was over."

"Damn it, Fergus, hear me out!"

"All right, you have sixty seconds."

"I know who killed Mary Patterson."

"So do I, it was Gordon Tannahill and he's dead. That was the big emergency?"

I screamed into my cell phone parts. "Gordon's alive! He's alive, damn it."

I didn't hear anything. For a second I wasn't sure if I was holding the parts right. Then Fergus said, "Say that again."

Thank God! "My cell is broken and I'm holding the damn thing together with my fingers. We found a newspaper article in Aberdeen about a teenage girl who disappeared long after Gordon Tannahill died in that explosion. You have that straight? A year after Gordon was killed. This teenager was a dancer at a Scottish festival in Aberdeen and the judge at the dance festival was your college Professor, Albert Tannahill."

"So what does . . ."

"I'd bet my ass that you'll find out that the three Pitlochry girls were dancers at the Blair Atholl Festival just before they turned up missing."

"But that doesn't mean that Professor Tannahill was involved."

272

"Fergus, this is the important part. Tannahill is a dance judge at the Blair Castle festival."

Even over the wobble noise and the howling engine, I heard Fergus say, "Son-of-a-bitch."

"Think about it. Gordon kills Albert and takes his identity. To frost the cake, he gets a birthmark tattooed under his ear."

"If you're right, one of those girls dancing tonight could be in danger."

"Hey, we're almost at Blair Atholl and we'll need police backup. Are you there yet?"

"Bear, I'm going to hang up now and contact Sergeant Proudfoot and Sergeant McKinlay. The Pitlochry station is a short drive from Blair Atholl. I'm in a barley field a few miles north of Perth and it will take me a couple of minutes to reach my car. With any luck, I'll be there soon after the uniformed officers. Now hang up and stay off your phone. I'll call you if there are any changes in my plans."

Occasionally, we'd catch up to a slower car in our lane and Henry would flash his lights, beep the horn, and pass the car. After one of those passes, the Austin's tires dropped onto the right shoulder. The car lurched and my cell phone flew off my lap.

"Sorry 'bout that, Bear. Are you okay?"

"I'm fine, but my cell phone is a goner. Now Fergus can't call me back."

"Try mine."

Nothing.

I said, "So you never used your charger?"

"My what?"

I was pissed, but not at Henry. I couldn't get mad at an old dude who didn't know he had to recharge his cell phone battery when he still used a

273

wind up thingamajig to listen to records. "Never mind, Flo'll explain later."

About that time, it started to rain. First the light mist barely covered the windshield, then the sky opened up and dumped big buckets of water and in a few seconds I could barely see through the windshield.

Flo said, "Henry, can you see?"

"Nay, but I'm used to the rain."

I said, "I don't think Flo was talking about the rain, she's thinking about the windshield."

"As long as I can see the car ahead of me, we'll be okay."

"Hold on, the Kid told me they're dancing on an outdoor stage. Maybe they'll cancel the dancing part because of the storm."

"Nay. I've lived 'ere all me life. The dance performance will move indoors, to the royal ballroom. We're almost there. Five minutes, tops."

Flo said, "Henry, now that we've almost reached Blair Castle, I'm not sure what we're going to do when we get there."

"The ballroom is where we'll find Ettamae and the other lasses. Once we get there, I'll take a left and drive us to the back entrance of the ballroom. I know exactly 'ow to find it."

When we neared the entrance to the festival gate, Henry gunned the engine and shot to the left. We went past at least twenty cars and twenty pissed off drivers before the Austin barreled through the entrance gate.

Then Henry hung a left and just missed a woman running through the rain behind a stroller with a big, round-eyed baby sitting inside. Once the

Austin cleared the woman and stroller, Henry cranked his wheel and drove alongside the castle's high white walls. That joint was something to see for a kid who grew up in Elko, Nevada.

"Henry," I groaned, "how will we ever find anybody in this place?"

He didn't answer, just tapped the brakes and pulled in behind a big truck with a sign on the back that said, <u>John Dewar and Sons, Whiskey</u>. We followed the truck until it stopped. Two men jumped out and began unloading cases of booze.

Henry said, "They're delivering whiskey to the restaurant. The ballroom lies just around that corner. Bear, trust me, that's where we'll find Tannahill."

He stopped the car behind a white wall with one closed door in the middle. Henry jumped out. He ran to the door and pounded frantically. The door opened and a young girl, dressed in a costume like the Kid's, came out. While I scrambled out of the Austin, I kept one eye on the girl. Before I reached her, she disappeared back inside. Henry grabbed my arm and said, "The lass told me that Ettamae's dance group is up next. We must 'urry."

I stood at the door and glanced back. Flo was checking out her face in a small mirror she carried in her purse. "Forget that, Babe. Get inside!"

The three of us ran through the door into a dark backstage area filled with giggling teenage girls. I spotted the Kid and two other girls about to dance onto the stage to the wail of the bagpipes.

I was so happy to see we got there in time that I damn near cried. I glanced around the dark backstage. "Henry, I don't see Tannahill. You guard this exit. Flo, go out into the audience and keep an eye on things. I'll try to find Fergus, or Tannahill or both."

Henry nodded, and took up guard duty by the door.

Flo whispered, "Be careful."

"Hey, I'm always careful."

"Like last year? At that winery in California? Listen to me, be careful. If you find Tannahill before Fergus does, don't do anything stupid."

"Right."

THIRTY-FOUR

Pinky Delmont-Pitlochry, Scotland

My cell buzzed.

"Pinky," said Fiona. "Are you ready to go to the Blair Castle festival?"

Earlier, Willow had attempted to convince me to attend the 'small town' affair and I had voted no. Willow still had not made up her mind when the phone forced her hand.

I called to the bedroom, "Fiona wants to know if you are ready to go to the festival."

Willow walked into the living room. "I can skip it."

"Sorry, Fiona, we have decided to pass."

"You mean you're not going?"

"That is correct."

"But Pinky, the Blair Castle festival is an occasion not to be missed. People come from all over the Highlands to partake in the festivities. You do know that Ettamae was chosen to dance with a group of girls from Pitlochry. That is a real honor for the lass and you wouldn't want to miss that would you?"

I was about to say yes I would, when Willow took the phone from me.

"Fiona, we have a lot of packing to finish. Do you honestly feel a couple of jaded Americans would enjoy the festival?"

Willow listened for a moment, and then she said, "I see. . . an opportunity to exchange cultural values . . . excellent. Pick us up in five minutes. Bye."

I said, "Who anointed you to make a unilateral decision concerning when, where, and with whom, I exchange cultural values?"

"Can it, Pinky. We're going home tomorrow and this will be our last chance to see Scotland as it was and is today. Fiona told me that it will be raining soon so dress accordingly."

"I refuse to go if it means I will sit in the rain while children prance about an outdoor stage."

"Won't work. Fiona told me that in anticipation of the storm, the dancing part of the festival has been moved into the grand ballroom. Isn't that exciting?"

"I think I would rather watch the frost melt off the ground, a pastime I have taken up more than once during our sun-filled visit to your cousin's homeland."

"Be quiet and act excited. Fiona just knocked on our front door."

Fifteen minutes later we watched the conclusion of the piper's parade. Frankly, the Founder's Celebration at Virginia City surpassed this festival ten fold. Willow and Fiona seemed to enjoy everything, oblivious to the storm. At least they pretended to be unaware of the cold wind and rain, while I was more than ready for a sheltered venue. I said, "Fiona, I am freezing. Take me back to the farm or find me some cover from this incessant weather."

"Brilliant! Follow me and be quick about it or all the seats will be taken."

Inside of five minutes I stood in a dry, and impressive hall. Fiona said. "Pinky, I'll bet you're glad you came now. This is the Duke of Atholl's grand ballroom. Once each year, in the depths of winter, the Duke invites everyone to a resplendent ball. Fergus and I have attended most years. And see how the Duke's staff has set out row upon row of folding chairs, transforming the ballroom into an emergency auditorium for the dance festival."

I glanced around and saw we were in a large room supported by heavy wooden beams that crossed the ceiling. The walls were covered with beautiful wooden panels that took my eyes to a multitude of mounted deer antlers.

Fiona said, "Pinky, you and Willow take the two vacant chairs to your right. I'll sit down here and save the seat on my left for Fergus. Now, relax and enjoy the show."

The house lights dimmed and the curtain opened. I immediately spotted the child with the bright red hair. I leaned toward Willow and whispered, "Is the girl on the far left . . . What is her name?"

Willow whispered back. "Ettamae. Why is her name so difficult for you to remember?"

At that moment the music started. The six girls began their dance, and that was when I spotted Dr. Albert Tannahill. He wore his dress kilt and stood on the left side of the stage, in the shadows behind four pipers and a drummer.

THIRTY-FIVE

Bear Zabarte-Blair Castle, Scotland

It was real dark backstage so I felt my way along the left wall until I bumped into a doorknob. I opened the door a crack and peeked out. Not twenty feet away, near the aisle, sat Willow and Pinky.

"Psssst! Willow. It's Bear. Over here." She spotted me and ran over.

"Bear, where've you been?"

"Aberdeen."

Willow looked behind her and said, "I think all the seats are filled. Where's Flo? And Henry?"

"Flo's backstage somewhere and Henry's guarding the back door."

"Why's he guarding the door?"

"Follow me. I'll bring you up to date."

Once me and Willow got backstage, I told her what we'd found in Aberdeen.

Willow shook her head. "I can't believe it. Have you informed Fergus?"

"Yup. He said he'd be here with some uniformed cops. Hey, take a look, the Kid's doing her dance."

While the Kid danced, I opened the door to the auditorium and checked the room looking for Fergus, or his promised uniformed officers.

Willow whispered in my ear, "Do you have any idea what's delaying Fergus?"

That's when I noticed the dude standing behind the pipers. He looked around forty and wore one of those Scottish skirts for men. I said, "You got any idea what Professor Tannahill looks like?"

"No, but Pinky and Fergus do. I'll get Pinky."

A couple of seconds later, Pinky waltzed up and said, "I should have known it was you. I was finally beginning to enjoy the dances and now—"

I kept my eyes on the dude standing behind the band and said, "What's Professor Tannahill look like?"

"You can see for yourself. He is standing behind the pipe band. That is Dr. Albert Tannahill. He's the man Fergus and I interviewed in St. Andrews."

"Boss, we don't have much time so just go with me on this. That bastard isn't Albert Tannahill, he's the murdering brother, Gordon. He goes by the name of Albert, but he's actually Gordon Tannahill, the bastard that murdered Mary Patterson. Henry and I are positive that he's responsible for at least one more murder in Aberdeen and God knows how many others. Fergus might find some of the bodies now that he knows where to look."

Pinky said, "Have you lost your mind? According to Fiona, Dr. Tannahill is a renowned dance judge. He's judging all the dance groups tonight to determine which group wins the award." Then Pinky stopped flapping his mouth for a minute and said, "Bear, did you just tell me that he's the—"

"That's why Henry's backstage guarding the door. After the show is over, Fergus and his men will arrest Tannahill. Then this screwed up murder investigation will be over and we can go back to Carson City."

Pinky's cell buzzed. He listened for a second and said, "Hold on. Bear, it's Fergus and he wants to talk to you."

I grabbed Pinky's cell and said, "It's me. Shoot."

"Bear, I reached Sergeant McKinlay and Proudfoot's out. He's on patrol in the west Highlands and he won't be available so McKinlay's coming alone. In fact, he should be there by now. I had a flat tire just south of Bankfoot. I'm back on the road and will arrive at Blair Castle in a few minutes."

"Hold on." I peeked out the door and said, "Fergus, a big cop just walked into the auditorium and he's standing by the main exit."

"That's McKinlay. Bear, we have everything under control. Don't do anything stupid. Tannahill's a killer. He wouldn't think twice about adding an American investigator to his tally."

The curtain closed and out of the corner of my eye, I saw the Kid walk over to Tannahill. They talked for a second, then he took her hand, and they moved to the shadows.

"Fergus the bastard is holding Ettamae's hand. I'm going to grab him now and do what I have to bring him down. Pinky, let's get him."

I grabbed Pinky's arm and pulled him across the stage. The bagpipes started up, and for a second, me and Pinky were in the middle of six girls wearing plaid skirts. I pushed Pinky through the dancers, and as we passed the pipe band, I saw Tannahill and the Kid head toward the side exit.

Me and Pinky ran and got to the exit as Tannahill and the Kid disappeared behind a fancy screen. I got to the screen, kicked it away, and I was staring at a solid wall.

Pinky said, "Obviously, a secret passage way. These old castles are riddled with them." He started to tap on the wall. "There has to be an opening somewhere."

I rubbed my hand on the wall and felt a low spot. I pushed on it and bingo, a door opened. Me and Pinky stepped in. The secret door closed and we were standing in a black space. I felt to my left and found a wall. On the right I could feel another wall. I said, "Follow me, boss." I ran about four steps and crashed into something solid. I staggered back and bumped into Pinky. My nose felt broken and I spit out a couple of chips from my teeth.

"What is going on, Bear? Why did you stop? Why are we not pursuing the young damsel?"

Staggering around like a beat-up boxer in the tenth round, I heard the Kid yell, "Help! Help me, Bear."

"I hit something hard. Pinky, stay behind me. We're going to have to take this slow but move as fast as we can. We've got to find her before it's too late."

Nose leaking blood, or snot, or both, I stuck both arms in front of me so I wouldn't crash again and moved forward.

THIRTY-SIX

Pinky Delmont-Blair Castle, Scotland

To say I was surprised when Bear dragged me across the stage would be a classic understatement. I demanded, "Unhand me. Why are we on stage? Do you not understand that these girls are in a competition?"

Bear said, "I know that, but Tannahill's getting away."

The curtain closed. Suddenly Bear was pushing me in front of him, this time toward the stage right exit. "My good man, where are we going now?"

He stopped at a blank wall and said, "Shut up, Boss. Tannahill and the Kid were here a second ago and now they're gone."

I gave him a short dissertation concerning how old castles are riddled with secret passageways. While Bear pounded on wall, a female voice came over the sound system and asked for Dr. Tannahill to come back stage to tally up the results of the competition.

Suddenly, Bear pulled me and the next thing I knew we both stood in pitch blackness. "Bear, do you have any idea what is going on?"

"Boss, follow me."

I heard Bear run a few steps and then hit something very solid.

"My boy, I think I should go back to the lobby and get help."

"No. Follow me and walk slow. We've got to find the Kid before it's too late."

"My good man, I fear I cannot bring myself to continue in the dark. I have a rare eye affliction that causes vision problems in total darkness. You go ahead. I will return to the lobby for help . . . Bear? . . . Where are you?"

He was gone. I turned and after a few attempts, my hand discovered the passageway escape button. I pressed it and the bright lights and noise of the exiting throng flooded my senses. I stepped into the light, took a few steps and immediately bumped into a police officer. "Good evening. My name is Pinky Delmont and at present, I am lodging at the farm of Fergus Murray, the—"

"Aye, Mr. Delmont. Officer Murray tol' may ta find ya."

"Why would Fergus do that?"

"I dinna know."

"Did you see a large man and myself run across the stage a moment ago?"

"Aye."

"That man is my investigator. Officer, there is something very suspicious going on here tonight. I would appreciate it if you would check the ballroom and find a woman who goes by the name of Willow Stone."

"Sorry sir. Inspector Murray tol' may to watch the exit for Professor Tannahill."

"Officer, at present, Professor Tannahill has kidnapped one of the dancers and he is, as we speak, making his way down a dark, secret passageway!"

"Sorry sir, but I must follow ma orders."

About that time Willow appeared at my side and said, "Pinky, what's going on?"

I pointed in the direction of the secret passageway. "Tannahill, the child, and Bear are on the other side of that wall, making there way down a secret passageway. You and I are waiting here until Fergus arrives. At that time I will instruct him how to open the passageway so he, and his men, can pursue Tannahill."

"But what about the girl, and Bear?"

"Willow, Tannahill has killed before and the prudent path is to wait until Fergus arrives."

"Pinky Delmont, you are a craven coward. If you won't go and find that child, at least show me the way inside."

"My dear, you have the audacity to brand me a coward?"

"I do, and on top of that, I'm sorry I ever married you."

"My dear, you leave me no choice but to throw caution to the winds and plunge into the abyss to rescue the child. Officer, do not leave your post and when Fergus arrives, tell him that Pinky and Willow are following the murderer through the black void."

"Aye."

THIRTY-SEVEN

Bear Zabarte-Blair Castle, Scotland

I yelled, "Hang in there, Kid. I'm right behind you."

I know she heard me 'cause she yelled, "Help me, Bear!"

I heard a slamming noise in front of me and I slowed down until my hands hit solid wood. I pounded the wall and yelled, "Let her go, you bastard."

I nearly jumped out of my skin when a voice beside me said, "I understand your problem lad, Use the door on your right and then turn left and left again. That will take you to the other side of the wooden wall."

"Who is that?"

"You dina know me. I live down 'ere. Now 'urry, 'e's getting away."

"Thanks who ever you are." I opened the door, turned left, then left again and charged ahead. "Ettamae, can you hear me?"

She didn't answer. All I heard was the sound of dripping water. I couldn't have lost her. But what if I had missed a door or turned the wrong way? I stopped and felt my way along a rough rock wall. After a few steps, my right hand banged against something hard. It was a round, metal ring. I pulled on the ring. A door creaked open and I was in another passageway and at the far end I spotted a sliver of light.

I called, "Ettamae, are you out there?"

Her voice came back, "Help me."

I ran and spotted a door on the left. I tried the handle—it felt like it was locked. Had I made a mistake? I kicked the door with my shoe and it gave a little. The second time the door popped open and I walked into a large square room. The walls were covered with old pistols and swords, but the room was empty. I called, "Ettamae."

"Bear, he's hurting my arm."

I ran to a door on the other side of the room and opened it a crack. Tannahill and the Kid stood in another room. Until that second, I hadn't thought about what I was going to do when I caught up with them. Tannahill was pulling on a door that led to a garden, but I could see that it was locked with a chain. I took one step inside, then two, and now stood about ten feet from the Kid. I said, "Hey! Are you having a little trouble with your escape?"

He turned and faced me. He wasn't big. Shit, I could take him down with one hand tied behind my back. I said, "That really sucks, Tannahill. Did someone go and chain your door?"

His eyes were red and almost glowed.

"Tannahill, you can't get away. Police are guarding every exit. The grounds are surrounded. It's over, let go of the Kid and give up."

As I talked, she tried to pull away, but Tannahill tightened his grip. She screamed, "Let go of me!"

For a minute, Tannahill held her tight. Then, he

turned her around and pushed the Kid into me. Her head hit my broken nose. We both fell and I cracked my head on the hard floor.

I don't think I blacked out, but my bell got rung, long and hard.

Stunned, I laid there for a second and watched Tannahill take a giant sword off a wall filled with all sorts of swords, spears, and shit. He held the steel blade over his head and said, "I've never handled a broadsword before. Perhaps I should try it out first."

He turned, lifted the damn thing up and dropped the blade onto an oak table. The blade sliced the two-inch wooden slab in half as easy as a sharp knife cuts through a ripe watermelon.

He chuckled, "I'm sure this weapon will accomplish the task."

The Kid helped me stand up. I put her behind me and we slowly backed toward the door—away from Tannahill and that giant can opener. Sweat dripped off my nose. I tried to say something, but my tongue got so dry that it stuck to the roof of my mouth. I coughed. "Tannahill, you could use that sword to break through the chain and get away before the cops get here."

While he glanced at the chain, I whispered to the Kid, "Don't worry, Fergus is coming." I really didn't think that Fergus would show up, but I was about to piss in my pants and I didn't know what else to say.

Tannahill turned and dragged the tip of the heavy blade across the hardwood floor.

I said, "Hey, you're screwing up the Duke's floor there. Pick that damn thing up."

Suddenly, like a cat toys with a mouse before

the kill, Tannahill jabbed the pointy end into my leg.

I looked down at my calf and blood was spurting out. "Shit, Tannahill, that hurt."

He said, "Don't listen to him, Ettamae. I'm not a killer. I'm your dance judge. All I want to do is to take a few pictures so I can keep you in my scrapbook."

Tannahill lifted the blade over his head, like he was taking aim at my neck. Somehow I got enough spit in my mouth to say, "Before you kill me, you owe me a couple of answers. I thought you died in Saudi Arabia. How come you're still alive?"

Tannahill glanced around the room. Figuring that his only audience would be dead pretty soon, he said, "I'm alive because my older brother came to visit me in Saudi Arabia. One day, while I was at work, he snooped around my apartment and discovered a box of photos that I had taken of my favorite female dancers." His eyes looked at the Kid. "You're familiar with the type of photos I'm talking about. Unusual poses of young girls, that sort of thing. That afternoon, my favorite brother—come to think of it, Albert was my only brother—just happened to die in an unfortunate explosion." Tannahill smiled, like a dude who was thinking about a great Thanksgiving dinner. "It was a painless way to die, I'm sure. Were you aware that the TNT did such an efficient job that I had a difficult time finding enough bits and pieces of Albert large enough to cremate? But I persevered and today, dear Albert, or what's left of him, resides in an urn on my marble mantle in St. Andrews."

The way this dude talked told me that he loved to hear the sound of his voice. If I could just keep him going, Fergus was bound to show up someday.

I said, "I can see why you left Scotland. I mean this country's colder than a well digger's ass, but Saudi Arabia? That's almost as bad as Utah."

"Another excellent question!" Sweat started to drip off Tannahill's forehead. "The weather in Aberdeen is abominable, and I had a very difficult time . . . ah . . . disposing of my last . . . let me just say that I felt it was time for Gordon Tannahill to move on." His focus moved back to the Kid who hid behind me. I could hear her crying softly.

Tannahill shook his head. "There are so many young Scottish lasses who want to believe that, with a little assistance, they could become professional dancers. I tell them that I can help them reach their goal. All they have to do is participate in a little photo session. Isn't that right, Ettamae?"

The Kid's quiet sobs grew to a full-blown blubber. My left leg was bleeding and hurt like hell. A loud voice screamed inside my head, 'Fergus, where are you?' My lower lip trembled as I said, "One final question. Didn't anyone at the university notice that you had replaced your brother?"

He lowered the flat of the blade onto his shoulder and chuckled. "I must admit that I was a bit worried at first. But with the birthmark tattoo and all, I discovered that if you plied the good professors with enough sherry, they would believe most anything."

I backed the Kid a little closer to the door as Tannahill said, "Did I tell you that my loving parents, may they burn in hell, did not share their wealth with both of their sons? It seems that they disinherited me and left my brother Albert

291

everything. Today that works out to be a very comfortable income of twenty thousand pounds a year. So you see, my life as Albert was secure, and safe, but I feel compelled to add, very, very boring. After awhile, my. . . ahhh . . . fondness for young dancers overwhelmed my need for safety and comfort. Now, the past moments have been a pleasure, but I think we've talked enough."

He lifted the blade again, dipped his head in a mock bow, and said, "It's time for me to take my leave."

I lifted my arm, but after seeing what happened to that oak table, I knew I was wasting my time. I whispered to the Kid, "As soon as the sword starts down, run as fast as you can through that door and no matter what happens, don't look back."

Down to defending myself with my arms, I waited for the end. After what seemed like the longest seconds of my life, I heard another voice cut through the silence. "Gordon Tannahill, you are under arrest for the murder of Mary Patterson. Now put the broadsword down or I will be forced to shoot."

I opened one eye and saw Tannahill's face freeze. I also noticed that the muscles in his arms were beginning to twitch from the weight of the steel blade he held above my neck.

Slowly, I looked to my right and there, just inside the door stood Fergus. He held a really old, powerful-looking gun in both hands. As far as I could tell, the weapon was aimed at the center of Gordon Tannahill's head.

Fergus took several steps forward. "Tannahill, this weapon will blow your head clean off, or it might misfire. Go ahead, ask yourself, do I feel lucky? Well do you?"

Did Fergus just quote Clint Eastwood's famous Dirty Harry line? I held my breath while Tannahill tried to decide what he should do—face a murder trial—or swing away. If he took the first choice, he would spend the rest of his life in prison. On the other hand, if he chopped off my head, he would add a Basque bartender to his list, and get a well-deserved bullet to his brain.

Finally I reached the point where I didn't give a damn either way. I cried, "God damn it, Tannahill, shit or get off the pot."

Gordon lowered his arms, and the sword crashed to the floor. Sergeant McKinlay appeared out of nowhere, slapped a pair of cuffs on the bastard, and whisked him out the door.

That was when my legs, both the good one and the bleeding one, let go. Fergus grabbed me just before I hit the floor. The Kid took my hand and whispered, "Thanks, Bear."

I took a deep breath. "You're welcome."

Pinky and Willow ran into the room and Pinky said, "I see I have arrived in time to save the young girl and my investigator from certain death."

Fergus said, "In time, or five minutes late, it doesn't matter as Tannahill's going to jail for the rest of his life. Bear, your nose is bleeding."

I nodded. "I crashed into something while I was running through the dark tunnel."

Willow said, "And your leg! You're bleeding all over the floor."

"I know. He stuck me good with that damn sword. Fergus, I've never been so glad to see anyone in all my life—but what's with the gun? I thought you told me this was Scotland where no one packs a gun?"

Fergus took my hand, lifted me off the floor as a little smile zipped across his mouth. "Aye. That's true, this is Scotland where we toss cabers, not shoot pistols. You see, I had a bit of difficulty finding this room and on my way I grabbed this old pistol off the wall."

It took me a couple of seconds to figure out what he said. "Are you telling me that pistol is an antique?"

"Aye."

"Jesus, if you had pulled the trigger you could have been hurt. I read in Popular Mechanics that old pistols like that can explode."

"Nay, I didn't have a thing to worry about, Bear. The old thing isn't loaded!"

About then an old dude wearing a plaid skirt waltzed in. Pinky said, "Bear, I'd like you to meet the Duke of Atholl."

"You mean the dude in the skirt?"

"That is correct. The Duke owns Blair Castle and his kilt is made from the Murray Tartan."

"Sorry about bleeding all over your floor, Mr. Duke."

The guy smiled and patted my shoulder. "The floor is of no concern. I am pleased as punch to discover that except for your leg wound and the broken nose, you came through this arduous ordeal unscathed."

"Me too. Hey Duke, could you pass on a thank you for me?"

"I would be delighted."

"When I was running through that dark tunnel,

the one that starts at the ballroom, I got lost and a guy told me which way to go so I could keep up with Tannahill. Tell that guy thanks. If it wasn't for him, Tannahill would have gotten away, with Ettamae."

"My boy, are you describing the passageway between the ballroom and the main castle?"

"I guess so."

"To the best of my knowledge, that passageway has been unused since World War One."

"But I don't understand."

The Duke said, "Bear, in Scotland, not everything is black and white as it is in your country."

"Huh?"

Fergus said, "Now, the Duke has an announcement to make."

The dude in the skirt said, "To honor the capture of the heinous murderer, Gordon Tannahill, I will place one hundred thousand pounds into a trust fund. The fund will go toward the construction and maintenance of a Children's Park in Pitlochry. Fergus Murray will chair the trust fund board and he has suggested a local man, Henry Bramble, as the person responsible for the construction and ongoing maintenance of the park."

I think Pinky said something after the Duke, but I didn't give a damn 'cause I laid down on the floor and closed my eyes.

THIRTY-EIGHT

Bear Zabarte-Carson City, Nevada

A couple of days after Fergus clamped the cuffs on Tannahill, we went home, but before we left Scotland, a couple of really cool things happened.

The first thing? After Fergus bandaged up my leg, he drove us back to the cottage where me and Flo talked about Ettamae.

Then we talked to Ettamae.

Then we talked with Fergus and Fiona.

I was about talked out when Fiona wrapped her arms around Ettamae. "Child, with your red hair and freckles, I knew you belonged in the Murray home from the moment I laid my eyes on you."

Fergus gave Ettamae a hug. "Aye, and we've both longed for a daughter."

So Ettamae stayed in Scotland to live with the Murray family outside of Pitlochry. Flo's old buds at the State Department worked everything out, and in a couple of days, Grandpa Ollie flew to Scotland to join the family in Pitlochry.

The second thing? Pinky's brand new secretary turned out to be an old one. Mabel, the old broad with the cat named Fluffy or Puffy, just happened to waltz into the Rapid Replacement office looking for a job about the time the owner was going to throw in the towel. It seems that by now, every secretary in

Northern Nevada knew what an impossible bastard Pinky was—except Mabel figured she knew how to work around Pinky's chicken shit ways—so Loomer signed her up!

I figured that Mabel must have been so broke that working for Pinky was better than mopping the men's can at the Old Globe. But Flo thinks Mabel's got something on Pinky and the old broad knows exactly what she's doing.

By the end of the week, things were almost back to normal. Flo lounged around our pool soaking up some rays. I got a little work from Pinky, enough to keep me busy but not enough to make me miss a Red Sox game on TV.

In fact, Scotland was gone out of my head when Flo walked out of her office (Flo needs an office to feel official, so Flo has an office in what was our old back porch) and she handed me a piece of paper.

"What's this?" I asked.

"It's addressed to you. Read it."

From bramble@scot.net (Henry Bramble)
To: BearandFlo@nevd.com (Bear and Flo)
Dear Bear:

I said, "Hey," I said, "it's a letter from Henry to me."

"It's an email to both of us but who's keeping track. Go ahead, read it."

I pray you get this letterrrrrr. There it goes again. Ettamae told me I had to be careful about holding down each keyyyy too long.
At Fergus' suggestion, and because the

trust fund pays me a handsome sum to supervise the construction of the new children's park, I asked the power company to wire electricity to my cottage. Bear, living on the wire is grand. Today, Fergus drove Ettamae and myself to Perth where they helped me to purchase a computer. The two just left after helping me set up this confounded machine. It's a thin looking thing and it's called a MacBook Air. Ettamae tells me it's the lightest Macintosh made! Macintosh, now there's a proper Scottish name for a computer! She told me that everything is connected and according to her, all I have to do now is type my letter to you, and then click on a button that says send. You will be pleased to learn that the park will be named The Mary Patterson Memorial Park. So far, construction is progressing ahead of schedule. As soon as the park is completed, I will inform you. Perhaps you and Flo can return to Pitlochry next summer to see the new park in action. Thanks to your bravery, and The Duke of Atoll's generosity, the wee ones living in Scotland's Highlands will have a safe place of their own to playyyyyyy.

There, it happened again.

Last week, with the help of Ettamae, I purchased a new music box called a CD player. Whilst none of my old, big records will fit the new machine, the new ones, wee, shiny round things, fit perfectly and the music sounds much better. I think the CD player is a good thing, but just in case something goes wrong,

Ettamae tells me I should keep my old records and call them my music backup. I do not understand all the lingo in this computer world.

Flo said, "Hurry up. The next paragraph tells how Ollie is getting along."

"Clam up. I'm reading as fast as I can."

Ettamae's grandfather, Ollie, is happy. He joined the Pitlochry Senior's Club and plays the records at the Friday night socials. As you know, Ollie's blind, and he can't see which record he's putting on, so the senior dance has become the most exciting weekly event in Pitlochry.
Ettamae says hello and asked me to tell Flo she'll be sending her weekly email a bit late because of heavy school work.

I said, "What weekly email? Babe, what's Henry talking about?"

"Nothing that concerns you. I'm just maintaining a line of communication between us girls."

"Oh."

"Bear, I have work to finish. Read on."

"Work? I thought it was time for your hour by the pool."

"Read, damn it!"

Yesterday, during my daily walk through the golf course, I found six excellent golf balls, and took them to the police station. Over a cup of tea, I talked with Sergeant McKinlay. He told me that after checking through all the Mis-Per records in Scotland, the police discovered a total of ten missing lasses that fit the dance festival pattern—our three here in Pitlochry, two in Aberdeen, one in Cupar, and four in Edinburgh. Each of the poor lasses had the misfortune to participate in a festival where that devil incarnate, Gordon Tannahill, was the dance judge.

As I write you this letter, of the three missing girls in Pitlochry, the only remains that we've discovered were Mary Paterson's. So far that murdering bastard, Tannahill, has not been forthcoming with information concerning the final resting places of the other unfortunates. According to McKinlay, the antiquated police procedures used in the past for Mis-Per investigations are being changed from paper to computer data bases. The Tayside Criminal Investigation Chief Superintendent took an early retirement due to, as Scottish newspapers called it, <u>The Mary Patterson Murder—A Bollixed Mess</u>, Willow's cousin, Fergus Murray, has become the most famous policeman in the country with the arrest of Gordon Tannahill that night at Blair Castle. Fergus' picture has appeared in all the newspapers and I hear he's even been on the telly. According to Fiona, Fergus was offered the position of Chief Superintendent in charge of Criminal Investigation's for Tayside, but he turned down the promotion because he did not want to move his family off the Murray farm and into the big city of Dundee.

I think you should know that Sergeant McKinlay gave me a copy of a file concerning an unsolved murder in Pitlochry. Perhaps during your return trip to Scotland next summer to visit Ettamae and the park, we will find time to investigate the case.

Remember, I still have my Austin and I will be ready to drive you and Flo wherever we need to travel.

Please give my love to Flo.

Cordially,

Your investigative partner,

Henry Bramble

By the way, yesterday, over a cup of tea, Sergeant McKinlay attempted to give me a second unsolved murder, but I refused to accept the case. With all of your other investigative responsibilities in Carson City, I was positive that we could only handle one case at a time.

On a serious note, Bear, please avoid passing my final thoughts on to Flo, concerning . . .

I said, "Whoops. You weren't suppose to hear that last part."

Flo grabbed for the paper. "Too late. I've already read the email."

"Oh. But I thought—"

"Bear, your computer literacy is zilch, so I'll be gentle. I printed that email off the one that's on my computer screen. Do you understand? I don't need that paper to find out what Henry tells you."

"Okay."

. . . I am positive that Flo, not the money, was the true motivation behind Conner's actions. According to the latest report from Interpol, Conner's motorcycle was found in a dumpster at the Zagreb Airport. Fergus tells me that is not good news. Zagreb lies between Budapest to the east, Vienna to the north, and Venice to the west. From that location the man could go anywhere. Fergus says not to worry, but I don't agree. Whilst you place your head on your pillow each night, keep one eye open for that scoundrel. He could show up anytime, anywhere, and I fear the man won't be as gullible the next time you meet.

P.S. Please email me back. Ettamae tells me that I need to receive an email from someone so I can be sure this contraption works.

THIRTY-NINE

Pinky Delmont-Carson City, Nevada

The aroma of Lemon Pledge tickled my nostrils the moment I entered my office.

Then I noticed the picture of her cat, Fluffy, or Puffy.

Finally I heard her say, "Hi, Pinky. Remember me?"

It was Mabel, the plump, matronly female who defied me while I was in Quebec City solving the Brady Blackstone murder. She sat behind her desk as if her insurrection, quitting, and firing, had never happened.

"I fail to see how I could forget. What, pray tell, brings you back to my office?"

"Mr. Loomis told me you were desperate."

"At that moment he was correct."

"Pinky, please hear me out."

I paused for a good fifteen seconds—to allow time for the woman to stew in her juices. "You have one minute."

Mabel said, "Pinky, I was wrong. I know I exceeded my authority and I understand why you had to fire me."

I gave the woman a cold stare. "But you quit before I could inform you that you were no longer my employee."

303

"As usual, you are correct, I did quit. But if you can find the forgiveness in your heart, I want to come back."

"You have twenty seconds left to plead your case."

"Please!"

"Are you finished?"

"Yes."

"Mabel, your exact words to me were, 'I will not allow you to make that kind of mistake.' Previous to that statement, no employee of mine had the effrontery to challenge my authority. That is why your plea falls on—"

"Please, I'll never make that mistake again."

The phone rang. Before I could tell her to leave, Mabel grabbed the receiver and said, "Law Office of J. Pincus Delmont. One moment please. Willow is holding on line one."

"Mabel, under the circumstances, I will retain you for this day. As for the future, at the end of each day, I will make a decision concerning the next day. If I inform you your services are no longer required, I expect you to quietly, and immediately leave the premises. Otherwise, you will continue with your present duties. Assuming there are no further questions, I will pick up Willow's phone call in my office."

I entered my private office, sat down and picked up the phone. "Hello, my love. Above and beyond my undying adoration, what can I offer you?"

"Put a cap on it. I arrived at my office this morning to discover we have a fresh murderer in jail."

"How fortunate. What is his name?"

"He is a she and her name is—"

Mabel opened my door and said, "Pinky, a lady is waiting outside. She wants to talk to you about defending her sister."

"Willow, I have an office emergency. I will have to call you back."

Willow said, "So much for your undying adoration."

"Goodbye." I snapped. After I set the phone down, I said, "Mabel, show the lady in."

A stunning redhead walked into my office. Mabel closed the door as the redhead asked, "Are you the famous attorney I was told about?"

I jumped up. "I am."

"A mutual friend, Lucinda Blackstone, recommended you."

"Ah, Lucinda. Her name brings back fond memories. And your name is?"

"Miranda Reed. My sister, Vanessa, is accused of killing her husband. My sister would not swat a fly. Mr. Delmont, according to Lucinda, you are the only attorney in the state who can figure out how to arrange for my sister's immediate release."

To say that Miranda was comely would be a gross understatement. From her bright-green eyes to her attractive ankles, the woman was an incredible specimen of femininity. "Ms. Reed, please sit down and in the future address me as Pinky." As she sat, I caught a flash of a sculpted thigh. "Would you care for something to drink? Coffee, tea, or?"

"Pinky, please call me Miranda. Now I know it's very early, but the past few days have been a living hell. Do you have any brandy?"

Ah ha! A woman who understands the finer

things in life. My response to her inquiry was interrupted when my phone buzzed.

Mabel said, "Pinky, Willow's holding on line one."

"I do not want to be disturbed."

"But what should I tell her?"

"My good woman, this will be the first of many tests. You will come up with a plausible explanation that satisfies the caller and myself or you can pack up and make your final exit."

Miranda stood. "I apologize. If that is an important call I can—"

"Please sit down. When it comes to my clients, nothing is more important." I turned, opened my credenza, and scanned my liquor supply. "Ah, here is my Martell Cordon Bleu and trust me my dear, it is never too early to imbibe a fine Cognac." I poured an inch of the amber liquid into two snifters and set one down in front of the distraught woman.

She sat down and presented me with an extended view of her shapely thigh. A single view of a woman's thigh could be an accident, but twice, I think not! "Miranda, start at the beginning and do not concern yourself with time. If we reach the cocktail hour before you finish, you are in luck because I buy all my new clients dinner."

Miranda smiled. "Lucinda told me that you were more than a lawyer to her. Pinky, I'm looking forward to watching you clear my sister from this trumped-up murder charge, and actively articipate in all of your fringe benefits."

I chuckled. "My dear, it has been sometime since Lucinda was my client. Can I trust you will remind me of all the benefits she mentioned?"

Her sensuous lips lingered on the edge of the crystal snifter for a moment. Then Miranda took a sip of brandy, smiled, and crossed her legs for a third time. "Pinky, there is no way on this earth that I would ever forget to do that!